the Archie DIGEST LIBRARY

Betty AND Veronica

– in –

Color Blind

Spotlight

visit us at
www.abdopublishing.com

Exclusive Spotlight library bound edition published in 2007 by Spotlight, a division of ABDO Publishing Group, Edina, Minnesota. Spotlight produces high quality reinforced library bound editions for schools and libraries. Published by agreement with Archie Comic Publications, Inc.

Library of Congress Cataloging-in-Publication Data

Betty and Veronica in Color blind / edited by Nelson Ribeiro & Victor Gorelick.
    p. cm. -- (The Archie digest library)
    Revision of issue no. 119 (April 2001) of Betty and Veronica digest magazine.
    ISBN-13: 978-1-59961-265-2
    ISBN-10: 1-59961-265-8
    1. Comic books, strips, etc. I. Ribeiro, Nelson. II. Gorelick, Victor. III. Betty and Veronica digest magazine. 119. IV. Title: Color blind.

PN6728.A72B48 2007
741.5'973--dc22

                           2006049178

All Spotlight books are reinforced library binding
and manufactured in the United States of America.

Contents

Betty and Veronica®

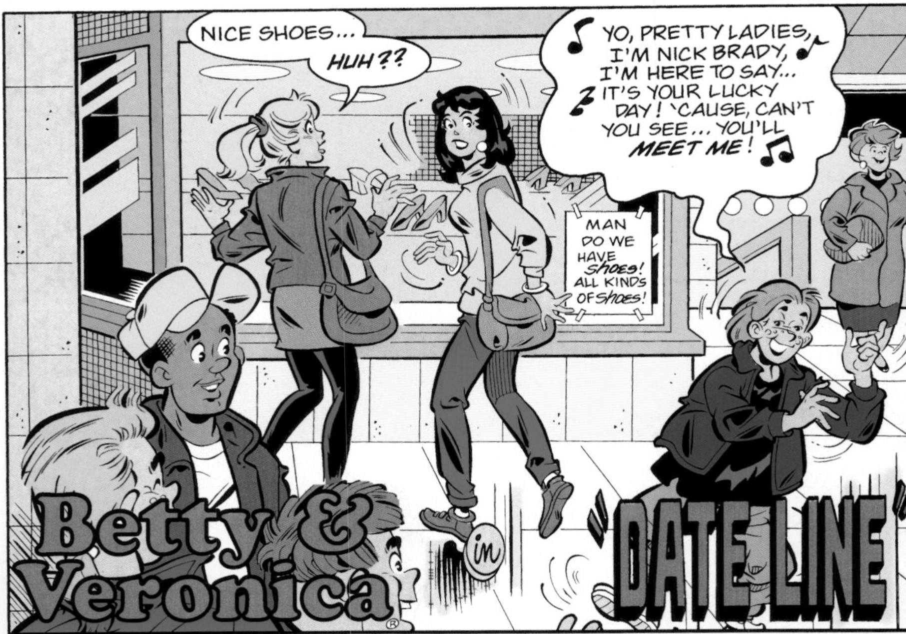

NICE SHOES... HUH??
YO, PRETTY LADIES, I'M NICK BRADY, I'M HERE TO SAY... IT'S YOUR LUCKY DAY! 'CAUSE, CAN'T YOU SEE... YOU'LL MEET ME!
MAN DO WE HAVE SHOES! ALL KINDS OF SHOES!
Betty & Veronica® in "DATE LINE"

SCRIPT: MIKE PELLOWSKI PENCILS: TIM KENNEDY INKS: KEN SELIG
COLORS: BARRY GROSSMAN LETTERS: VICKIE WILLIAMS
EDITORS: NELSON RIBEIRO & VICTOR GORELICK EDITOR-IN-CHIEF: RICHARD GOLDWATER

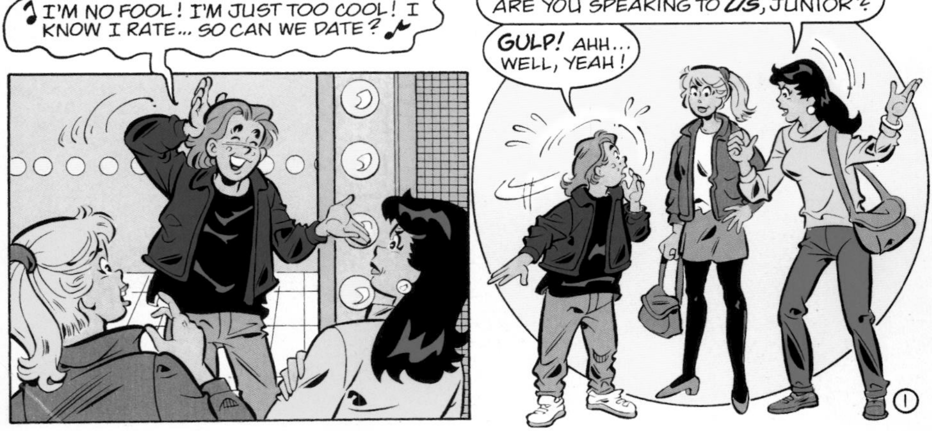

I'M NO FOOL! I'M JUST TOO COOL! I KNOW I RATE... SO CAN WE DATE?
ARE YOU SPEAKING TO US, JUNIOR?
GULP! AHH... WELL, YEAH!

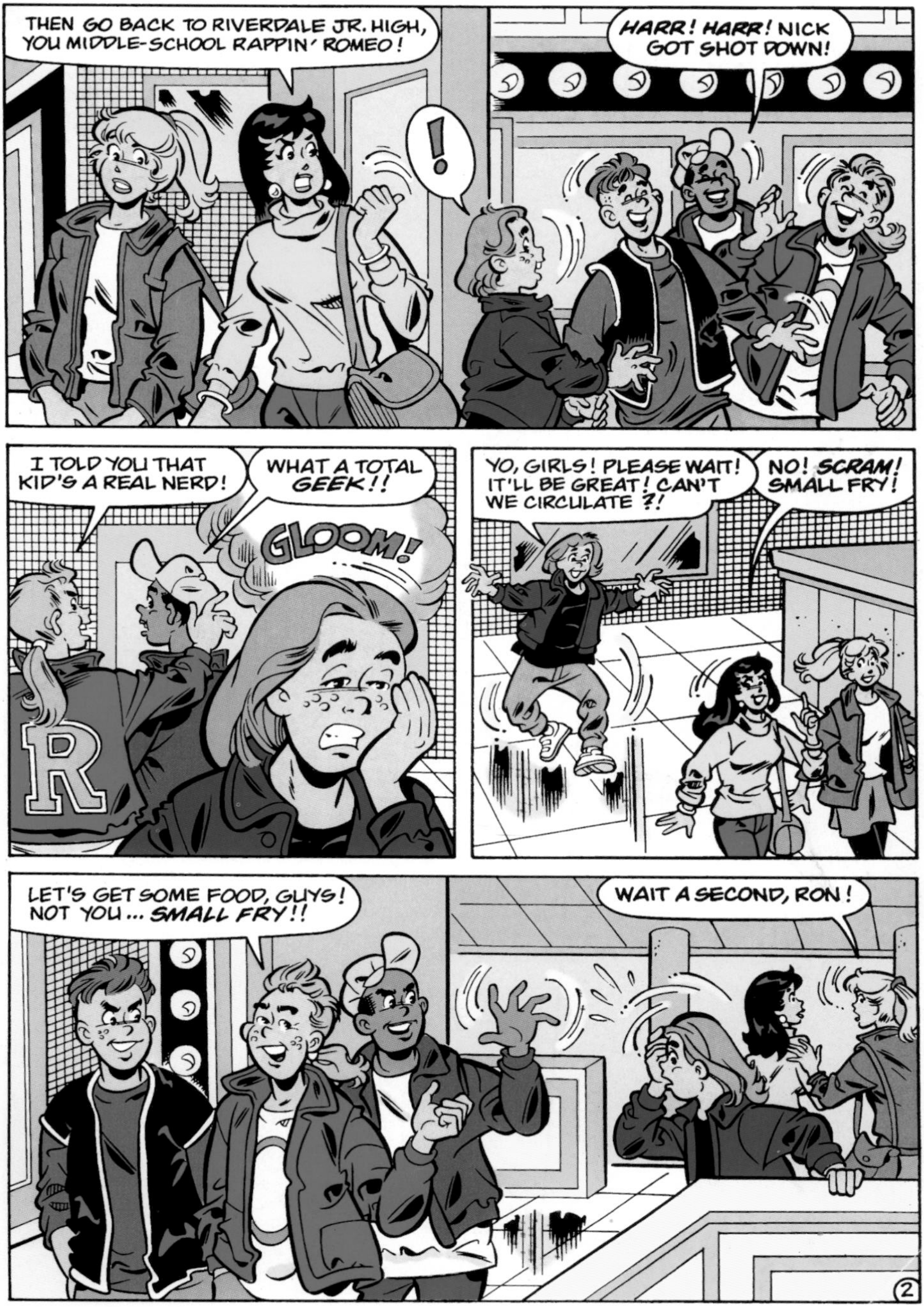
THEN GO BACK TO RIVERDALE JR. HIGH, YOU MIDDLE-SCHOOL RAPPIN' ROMEO!
!
HARR! HARR! NICK GOT SHOT DOWN!
I TOLD YOU THAT KID'S A REAL NERD!
WHAT A TOTAL GEEK!!
GLOOM!
YO, GIRLS! PLEASE WAIT! IT'LL BE GREAT! CAN'T WE CIRCULATE ?!
NO! SCRAM! SMALL FRY!
LET'S GET SOME FOOD, GUYS! NOT YOU... SMALL FRY!!
WAIT A SECOND, RON!
2

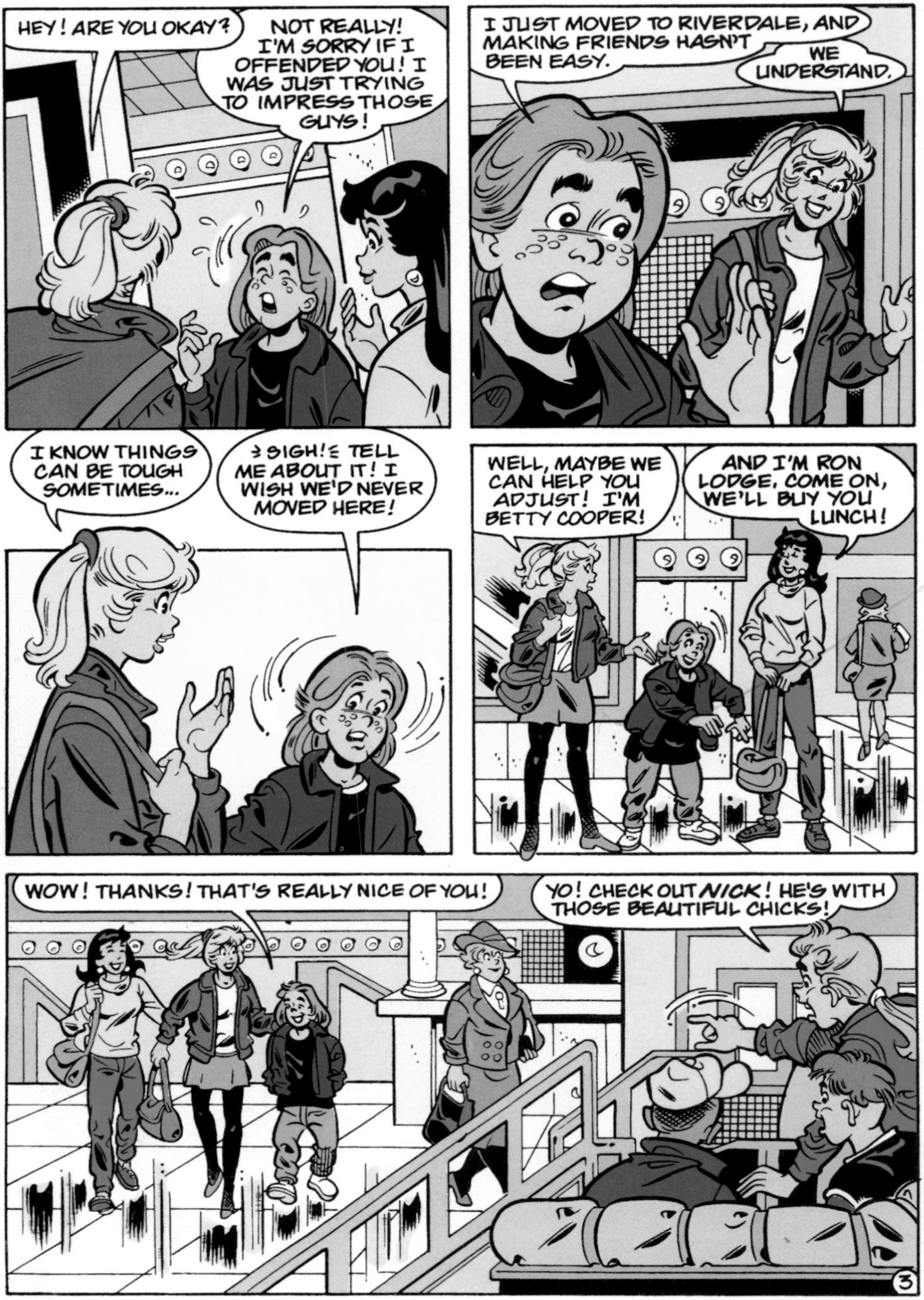
HEY! ARE YOU OKAY?
NOT REALLY! I'M SORRY IF I OFFENDED YOU! I WAS JUST TRYING TO IMPRESS THOSE GUYS!
I JUST MOVED TO RIVERDALE, AND MAKING FRIENDS HASN'T BEEN EASY.
WE UNDERSTAND.
I KNOW THINGS CAN BE TOUGH SOMETIMES...
SIGH! TELL ME ABOUT IT! I WISH WE'D NEVER MOVED HERE!
WELL, MAYBE WE CAN HELP YOU ADJUST! I'M BETTY COOPER!
AND I'M RON LODGE, COME ON, WE'LL BUY YOU LUNCH!
WOW! THANKS! THAT'S REALLY NICE OF YOU!
YO! CHECK OUT NICK! HE'S WITH THOSE BEAUTIFUL CHICKS!
3

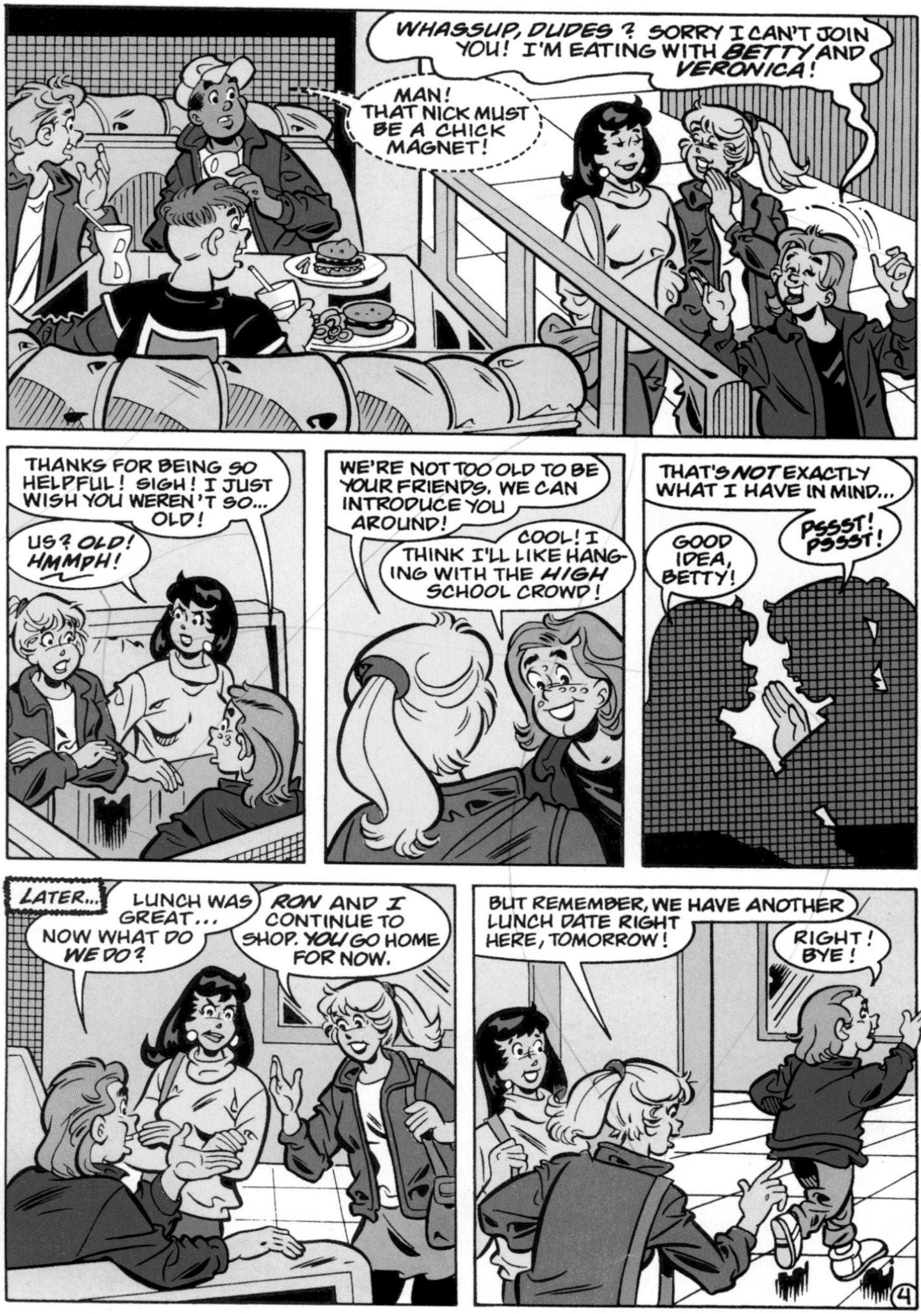
MAN! THAT NICK MUST BE A CHICK MAGNET!
WHASSUP, DUDES? SORRY I CAN'T JOIN YOU! I'M EATING WITH BETTY AND VERONICA!
THANKS FOR BEING SO HELPFUL! SIGH! I JUST WISH YOU WEREN'T SO... OLD!
US? OLD! HMMPH!
WE'RE NOT TOO OLD TO BE YOUR FRIENDS. WE CAN INTRODUCE YOU AROUND!
COOL! I THINK I'LL LIKE HANGING WITH THE HIGH SCHOOL CROWD!
THAT'S NOT EXACTLY WHAT I HAVE IN MIND...
GOOD IDEA, BETTY!
PSSST! PSSST!
LATER...
LUNCH WAS GREAT... NOW WHAT DO WE DO?
RON AND I CONTINUE TO SHOP. YOU GO HOME FOR NOW.
BUT REMEMBER, WE HAVE ANOTHER LUNCH DATE RIGHT HERE, TOMORROW!
RIGHT! BYE!
4

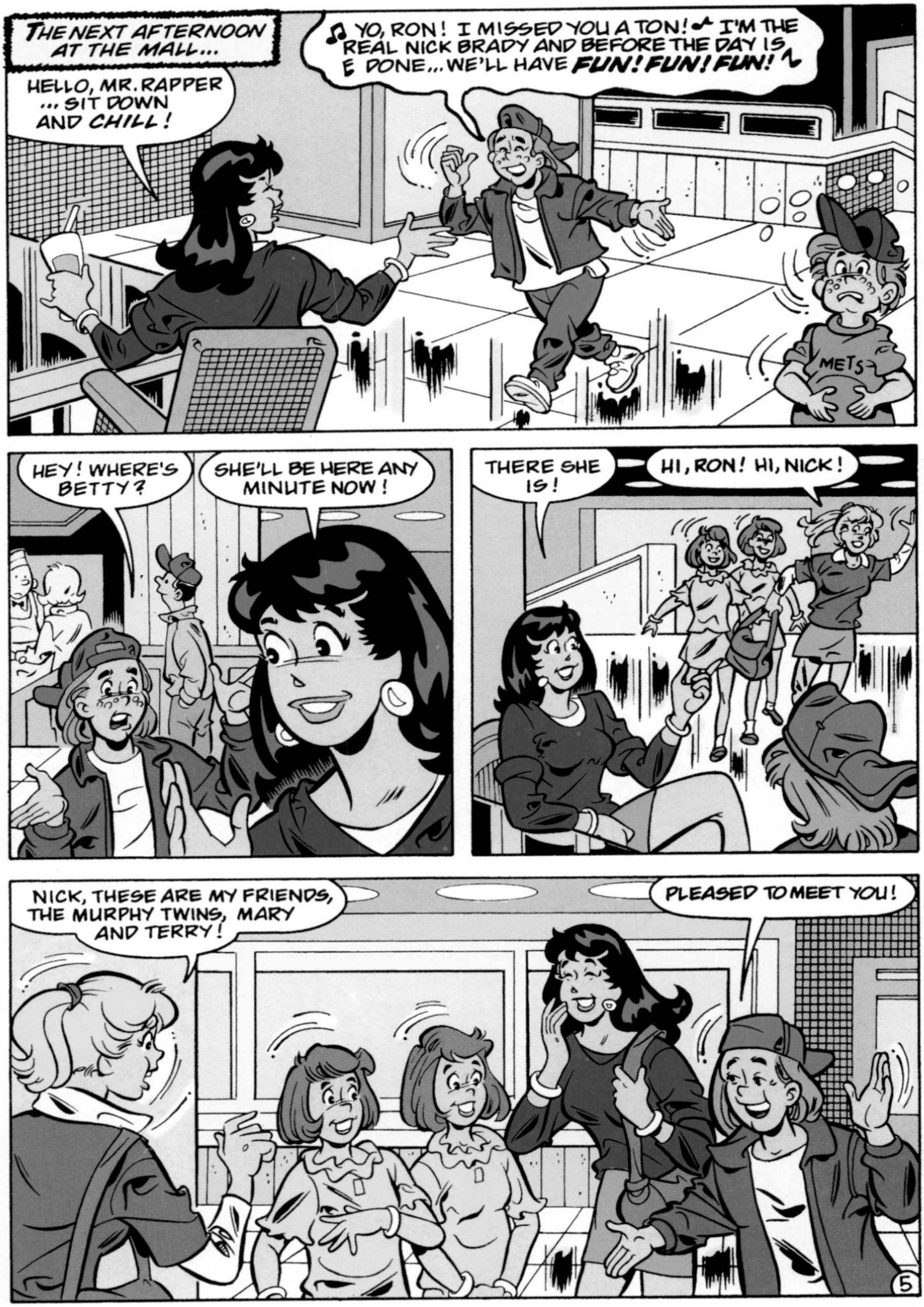
THE NEXT AFTERNOON AT THE MALL...
YO, RON! I MISSED YOU A TON! I'M THE REAL NICK BRADY AND BEFORE THE DAY IS DONE... WE'LL HAVE FUN! FUN! FUN!
HELLO, MR. RAPPER ... SIT DOWN AND CHILL!
METS
HEY! WHERE'S BETTY?
SHE'LL BE HERE ANY MINUTE NOW!
THERE SHE IS!
HI, RON! HI, NICK!
NICK, THESE ARE MY FRIENDS, THE MURPHY TWINS, MARY AND TERRY!
PLEASED TO MEET YOU!
5

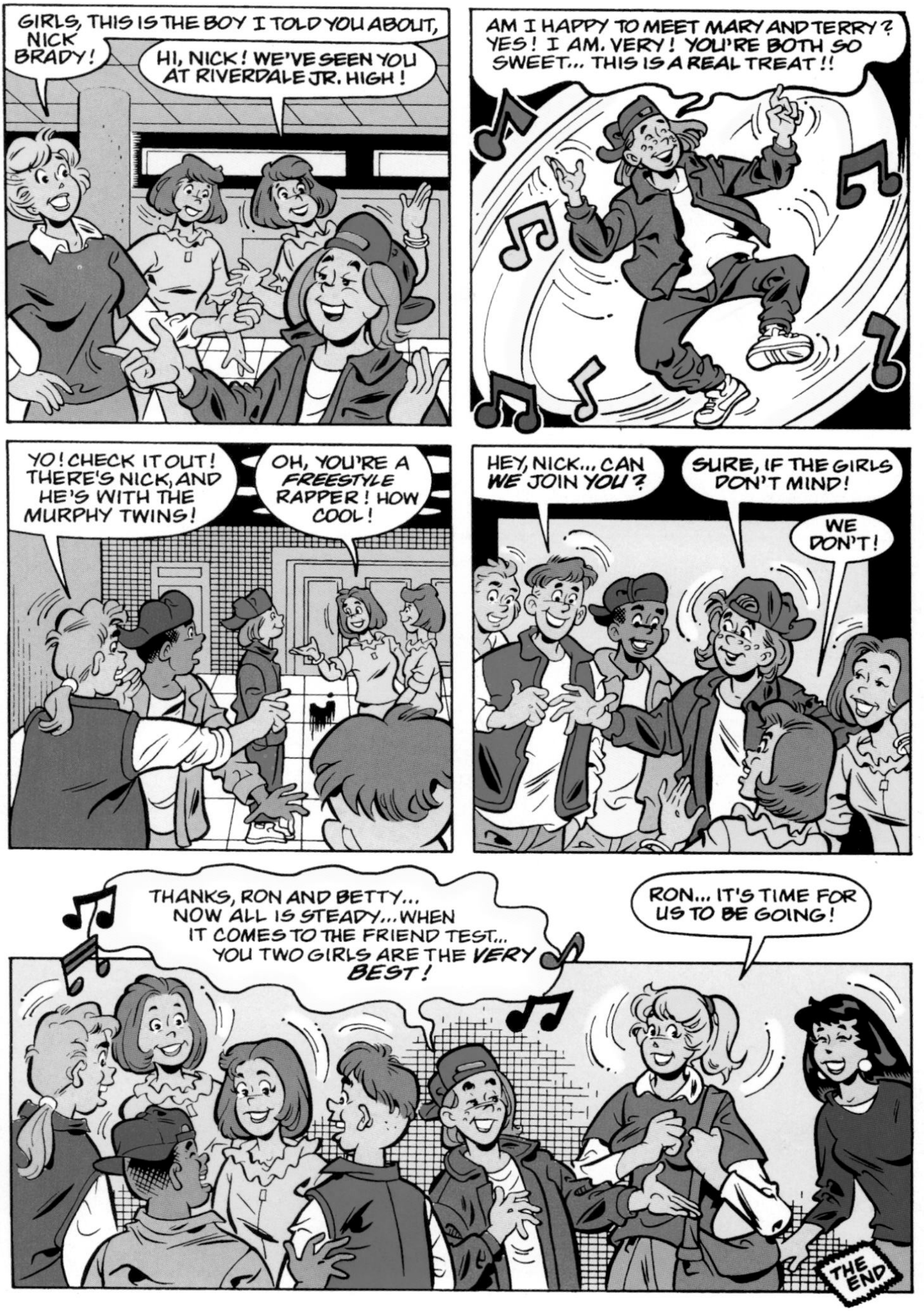
GIRLS, THIS IS THE BOY I TOLD YOU ABOUT, NICK BRADY!
HI, NICK! WE'VE SEEN YOU AT RIVERDALE JR. HIGH!
AM I HAPPY TO MEET MARY AND TERRY? YES! I AM. VERY! YOU'RE BOTH SO SWEET... THIS IS A REAL TREAT!!
YO! CHECK IT OUT! THERE'S NICK, AND HE'S WITH THE MURPHY TWINS!
OH, YOU'RE A FREESTYLE RAPPER! HOW COOL!
HEY, NICK... CAN WE JOIN YOU?
SURE, IF THE GIRLS DON'T MIND!
WE DON'T!
THANKS, RON AND BETTY... NOW ALL IS STEADY... WHEN IT COMES TO THE FRIEND TEST... YOU TWO GIRLS ARE THE VERY BEST!
RON... IT'S TIME FOR US TO BE GOING!
THE END

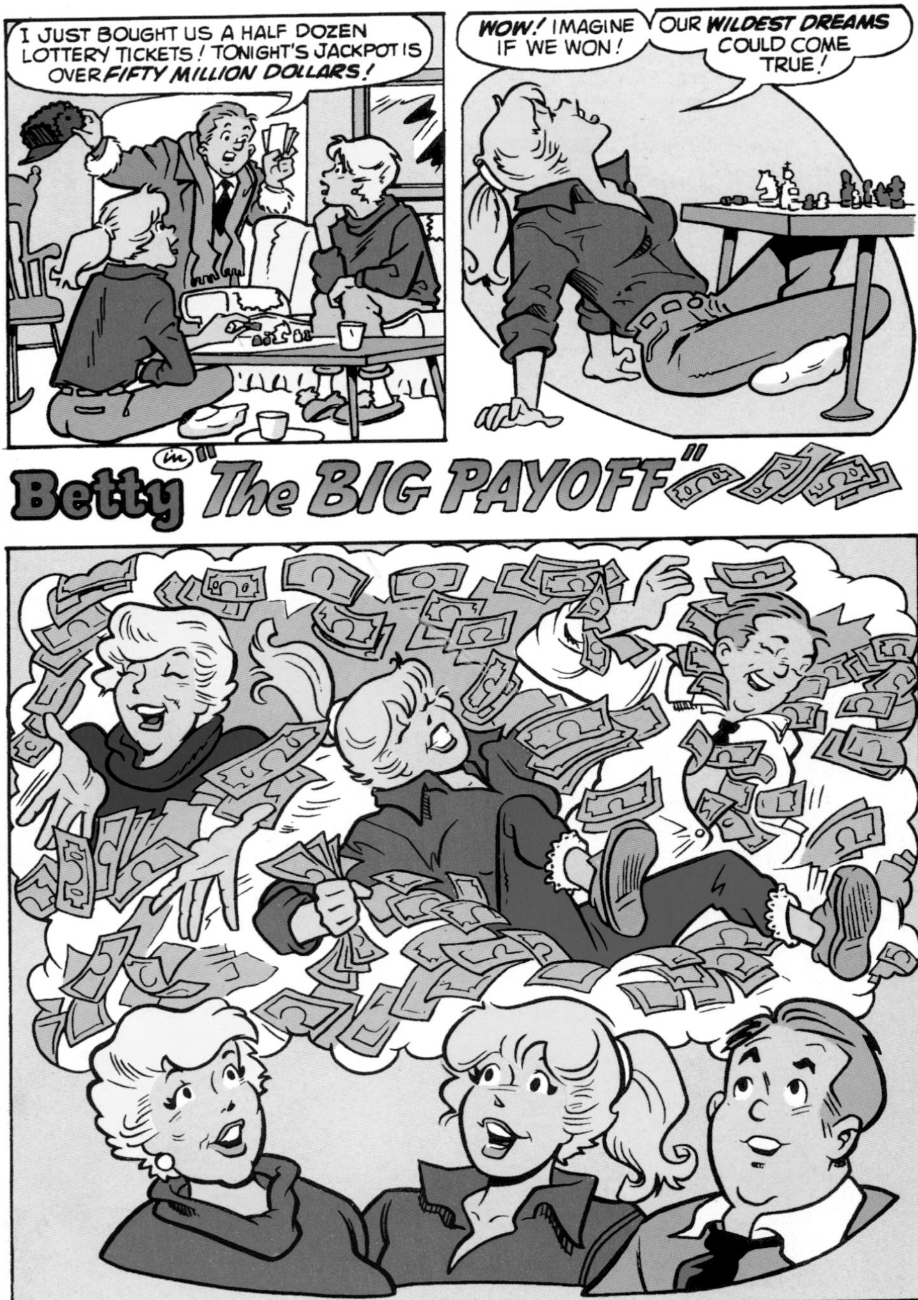
I JUST BOUGHT US A HALF DOZEN LOTTERY TICKETS! TONIGHT'S JACKPOT IS OVER FIFTY MILLION DOLLARS!
WOW! IMAGINE IF WE WON!
OUR WILDEST DREAMS COULD COME TRUE!
Betty in "The BIG PAYOFF"

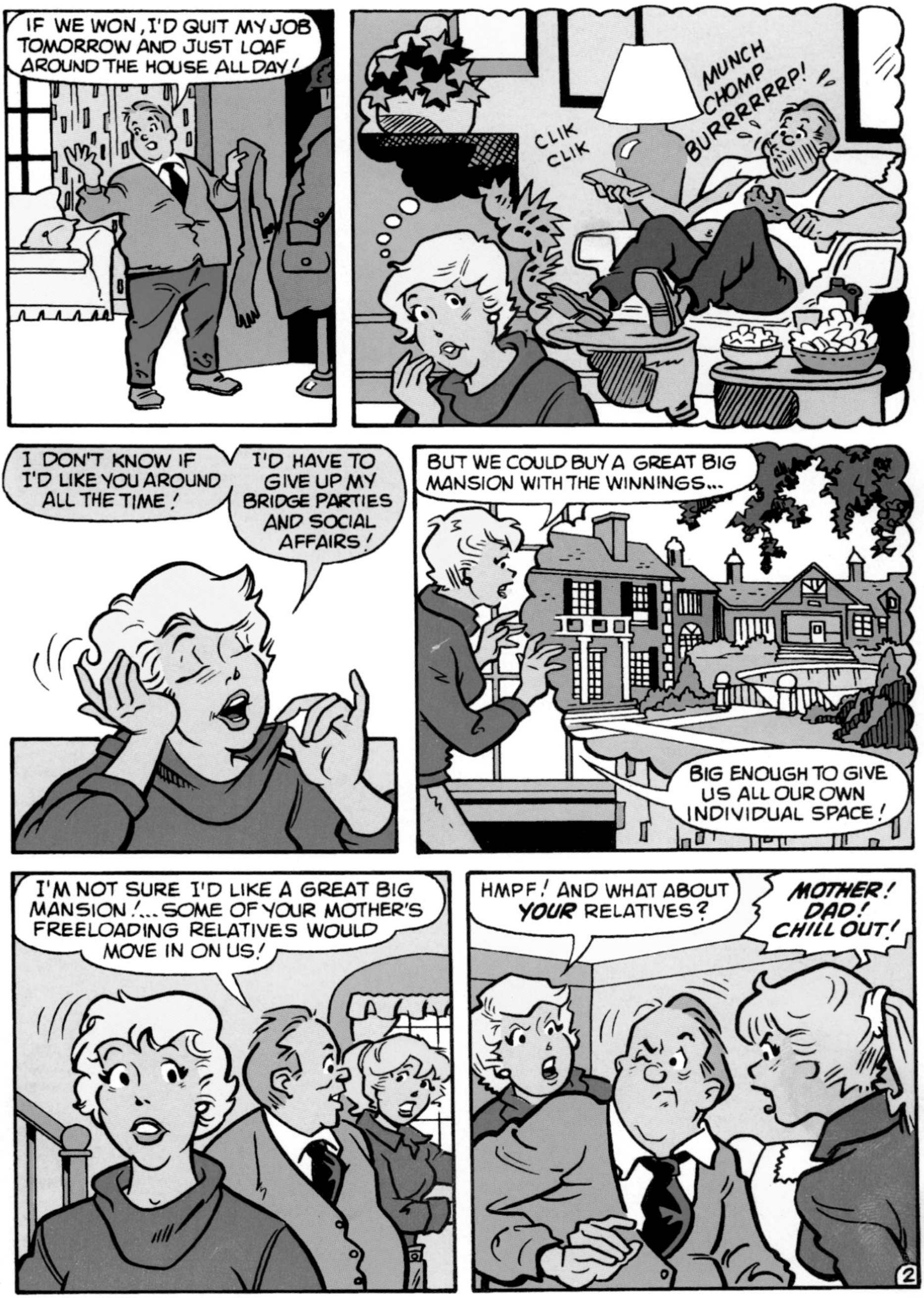
IF WE WON, I'D QUIT MY JOB TOMORROW AND JUST LOAF AROUND THE HOUSE ALL DAY!
CLIK CLIK
MUNCH CHOMP BURRRRRRP!
I DON'T KNOW IF I'D LIKE YOU AROUND ALL THE TIME!
I'D HAVE TO GIVE UP MY BRIDGE PARTIES AND SOCIAL AFFAIRS!
BUT WE COULD BUY A GREAT BIG MANSION WITH THE WINNINGS...
BIG ENOUGH TO GIVE US ALL OUR OWN INDIVIDUAL SPACE!
I'M NOT SURE I'D LIKE A GREAT BIG MANSION!... SOME OF YOUR MOTHER'S FREELOADING RELATIVES WOULD MOVE IN ON US!
HMPF! AND WHAT ABOUT YOUR RELATIVES?
MOTHER! DAD! CHILL OUT!
2

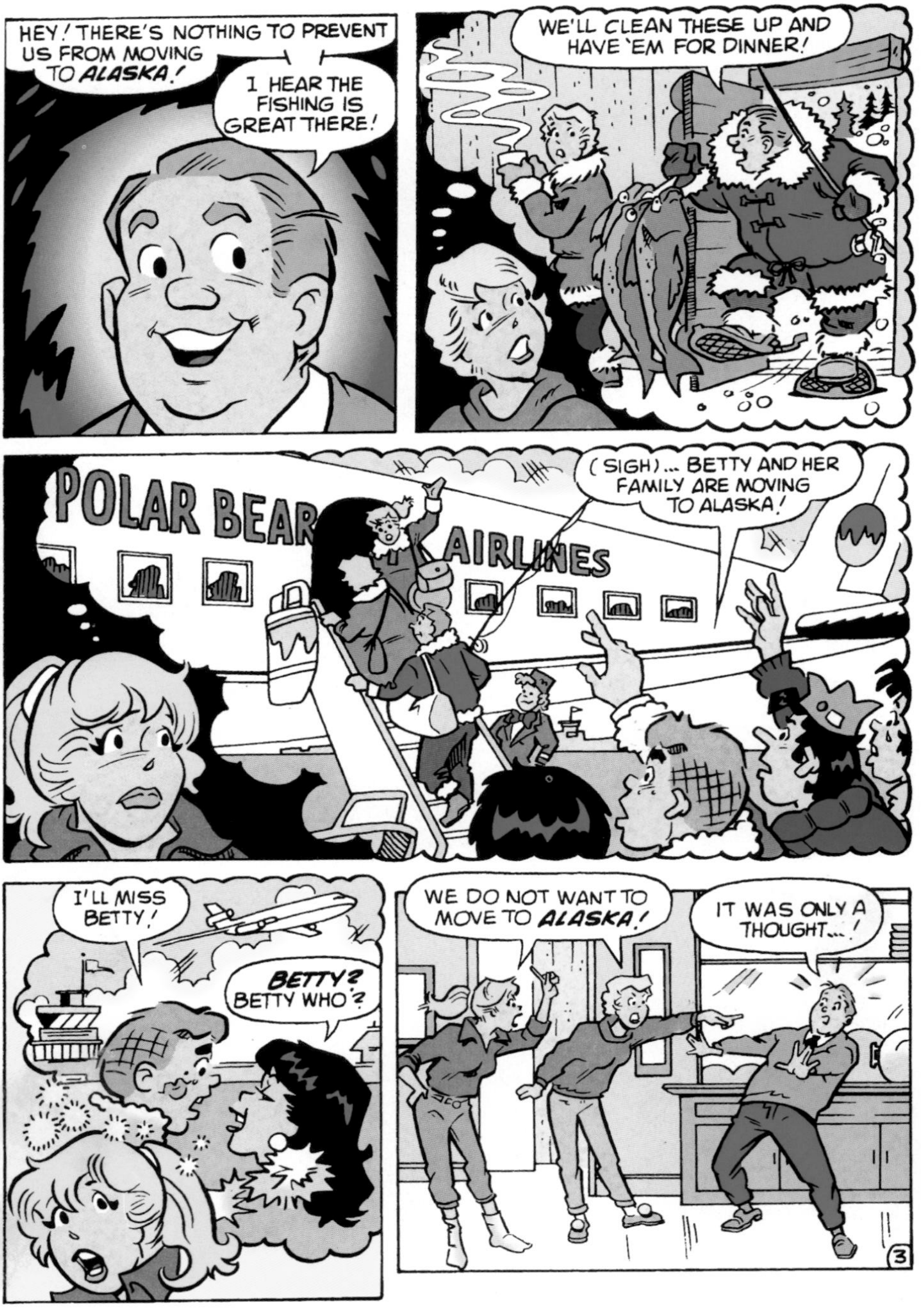
HEY! THERE'S NOTHING TO PREVENT US FROM MOVING TO ALASKA!
I HEAR THE FISHING IS GREAT THERE!
WE'LL CLEAN THESE UP AND HAVE 'EM FOR DINNER!
POLAR BEAR AIRLINES
(SIGH)... BETTY AND HER FAMILY ARE MOVING TO ALASKA!
I'LL MISS BETTY!
BETTY? BETTY WHO?
WE DO NOT WANT TO MOVE TO ALASKA!
IT WAS ONLY A THOUGHT...!
3

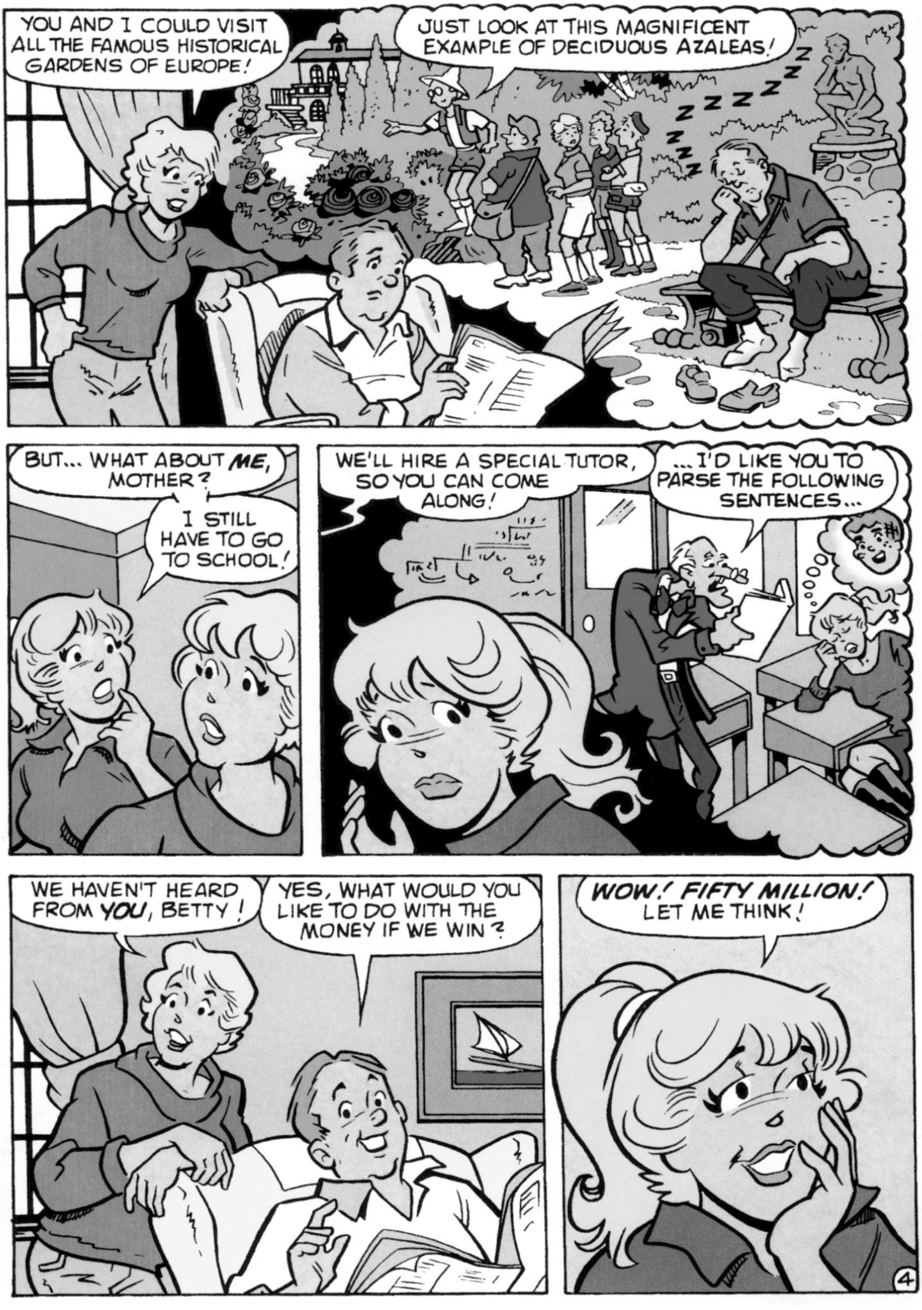
YOU AND I COULD VISIT ALL THE FAMOUS HISTORICAL GARDENS OF EUROPE!
JUST LOOK AT THIS MAGNIFICENT EXAMPLE OF DECIDUOUS AZALEAS!
Z Z Z Z Z Z Z Z Z
BUT... WHAT ABOUT ME, MOTHER?
I STILL HAVE TO GO TO SCHOOL!
WE'LL HIRE A SPECIAL TUTOR, SO YOU CAN COME ALONG!
...I'D LIKE YOU TO PARSE THE FOLLOWING SENTENCES...
WE HAVEN'T HEARD FROM YOU, BETTY!
YES, WHAT WOULD YOU LIKE TO DO WITH THE MONEY IF WE WIN?
WOW! FIFTY MILLION! LET ME THINK!
4

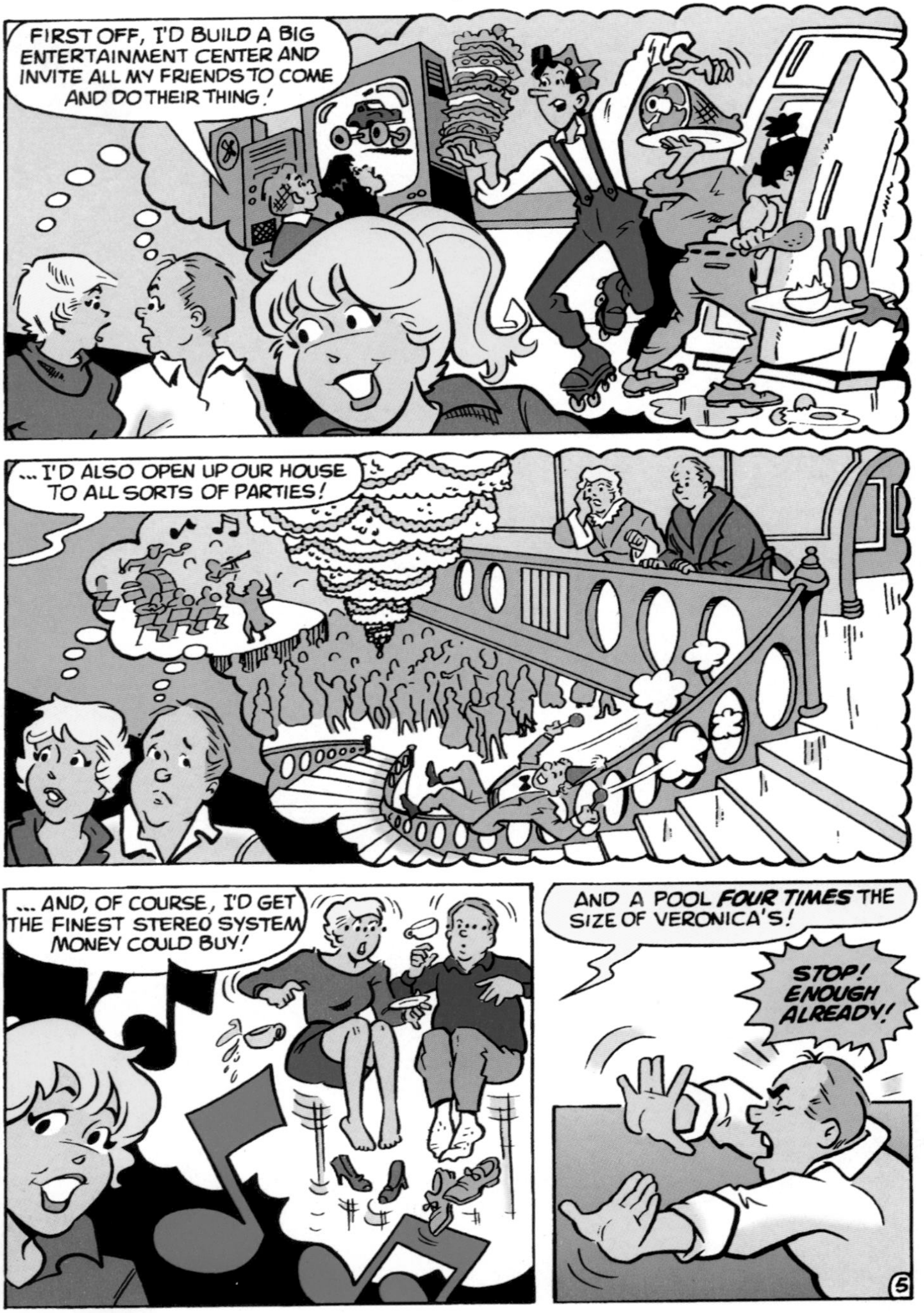
FIRST OFF, I'D BUILD A BIG ENTERTAINMENT CENTER AND INVITE ALL MY FRIENDS TO COME AND DO THEIR THING!
... I'D ALSO OPEN UP OUR HOUSE TO ALL SORTS OF PARTIES!
... AND, OF COURSE, I'D GET THE FINEST STEREO SYSTEM MONEY COULD BUY!
AND A POOL FOUR TIMES THE SIZE OF VERONICA'S!
STOP! ENOUGH ALREADY!
5

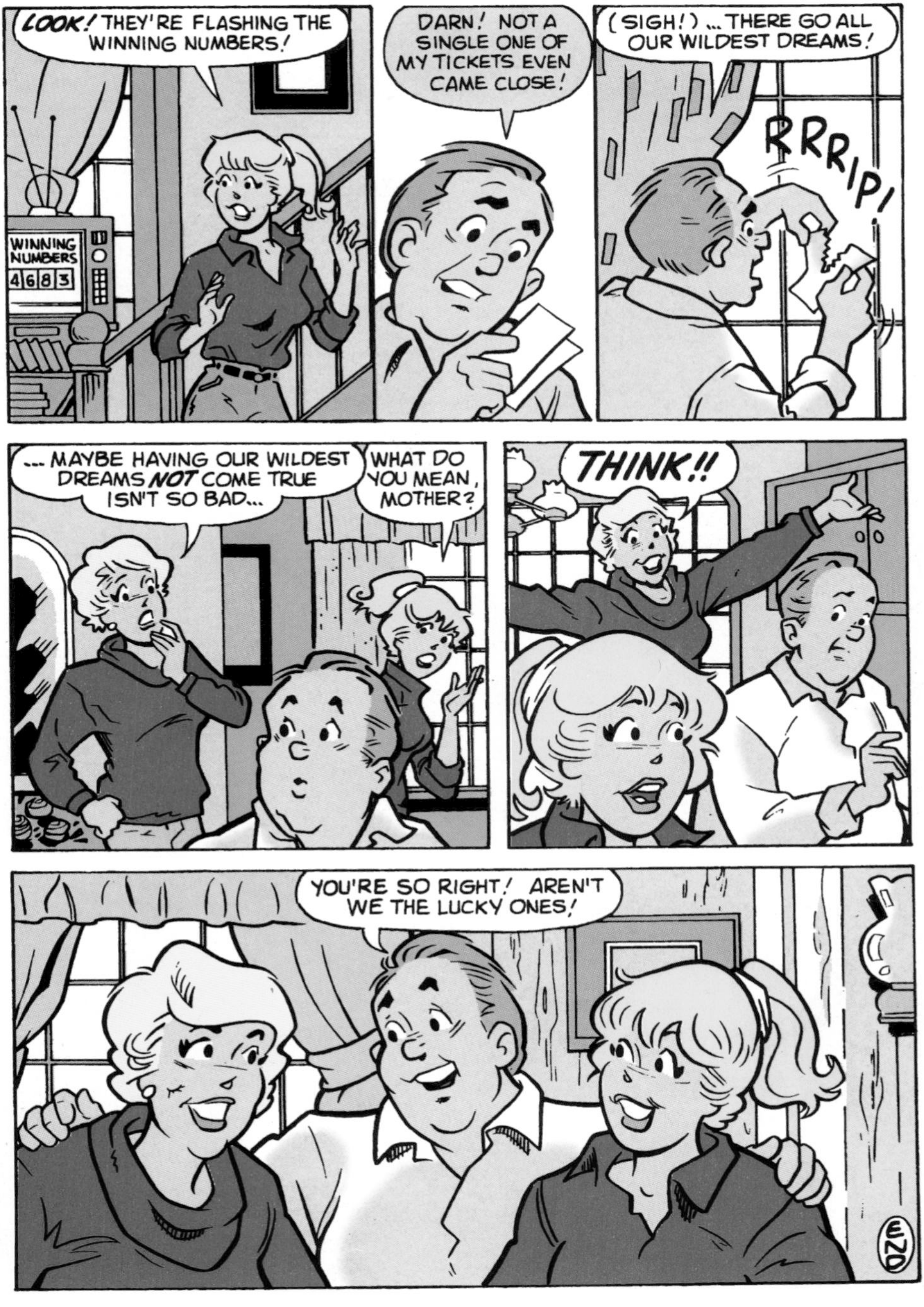
LOOK! THEY'RE FLASHING THE WINNING NUMBERS!
WINNING NUMBERS
4683
DARN! NOT A SINGLE ONE OF MY TICKETS EVEN CAME CLOSE!
(SIGH!) ... THERE GO ALL OUR WILDEST DREAMS!
RRRIP!
... MAYBE HAVING OUR WILDEST DREAMS NOT COME TRUE ISN'T SO BAD...
WHAT DO YOU MEAN, MOTHER?
THINK!!
YOU'RE SO RIGHT! AREN'T WE THE LUCKY ONES!
END

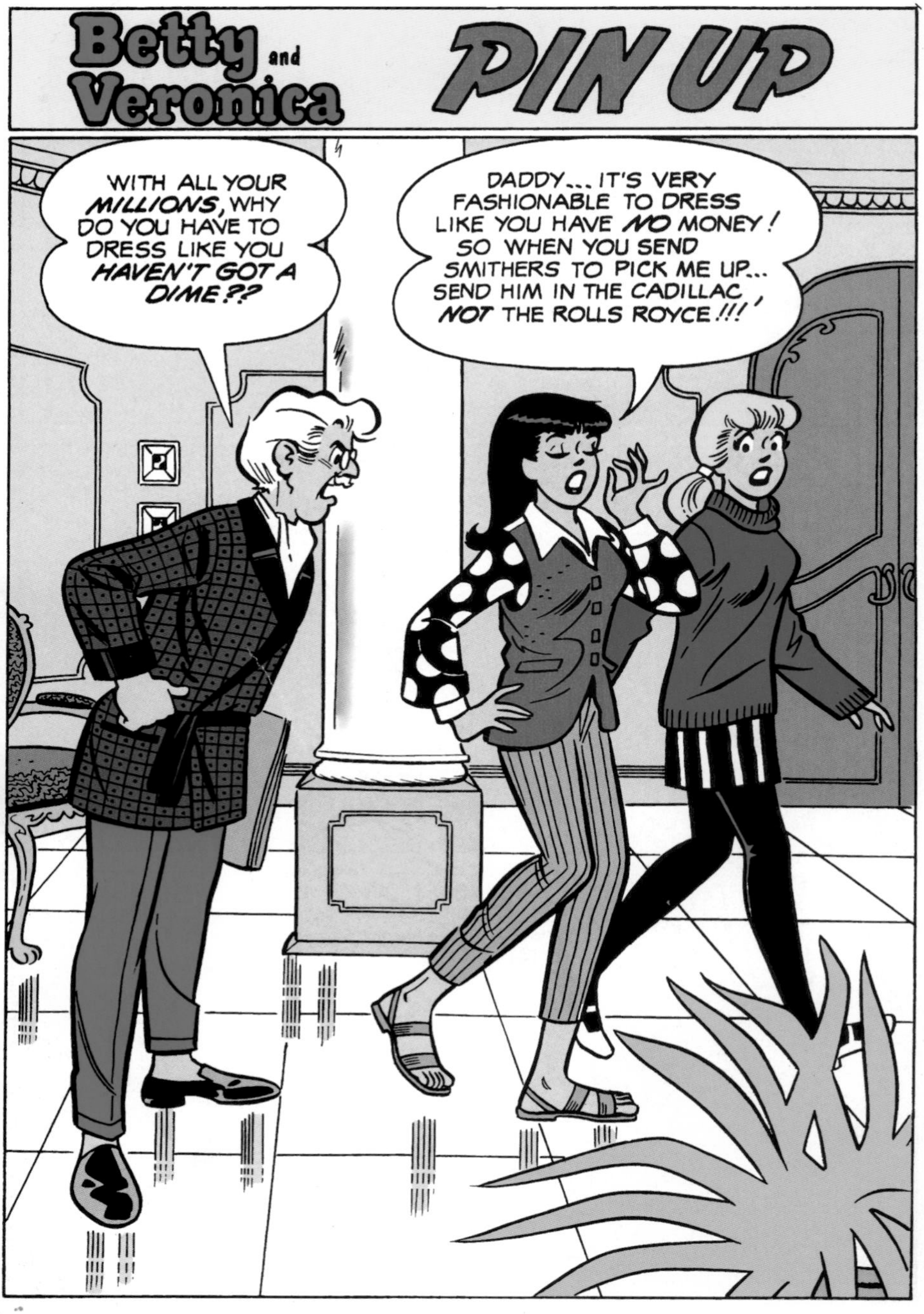
Betty and Veronica
PIN UP
WITH ALL YOUR MILLIONS, WHY DO YOU HAVE TO DRESS LIKE YOU HAVEN'T GOT A DIME??
DADDY... IT'S VERY FASHIONABLE TO DRESS LIKE YOU HAVE NO MONEY! SO WHEN YOU SEND SMITHERS TO PICK ME UP... SEND HIM IN THE CADILLAC, NOT THE ROLLS ROYCE!!!

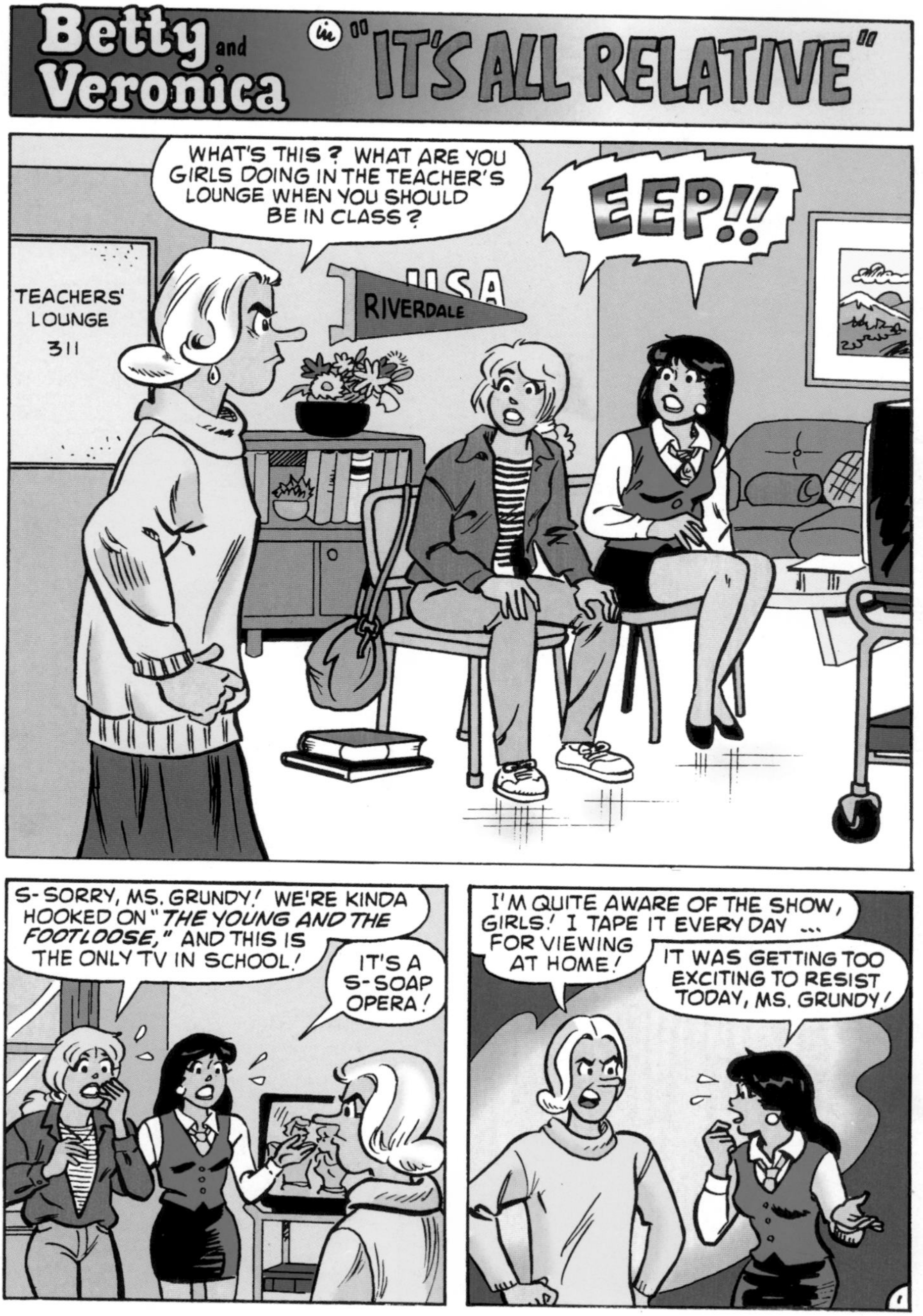
Betty and Veronica in "IT'S ALL RELATIVE"
WHAT'S THIS? WHAT ARE YOU GIRLS DOING IN THE TEACHER'S LOUNGE WHEN YOU SHOULD BE IN CLASS?
EEP!!
TEACHERS' LOUNGE 311
USA
RIVERDALE
S-SORRY, MS. GRUNDY! WE'RE KINDA HOOKED ON "THE YOUNG AND THE FOOTLOOSE," AND THIS IS THE ONLY TV IN SCHOOL!
IT'S A S-SOAP OPERA!
I'M QUITE AWARE OF THE SHOW, GIRLS! I TAPE IT EVERY DAY ... FOR VIEWING AT HOME!
IT WAS GETTING TOO EXCITING TO RESIST TODAY, MS. GRUNDY!

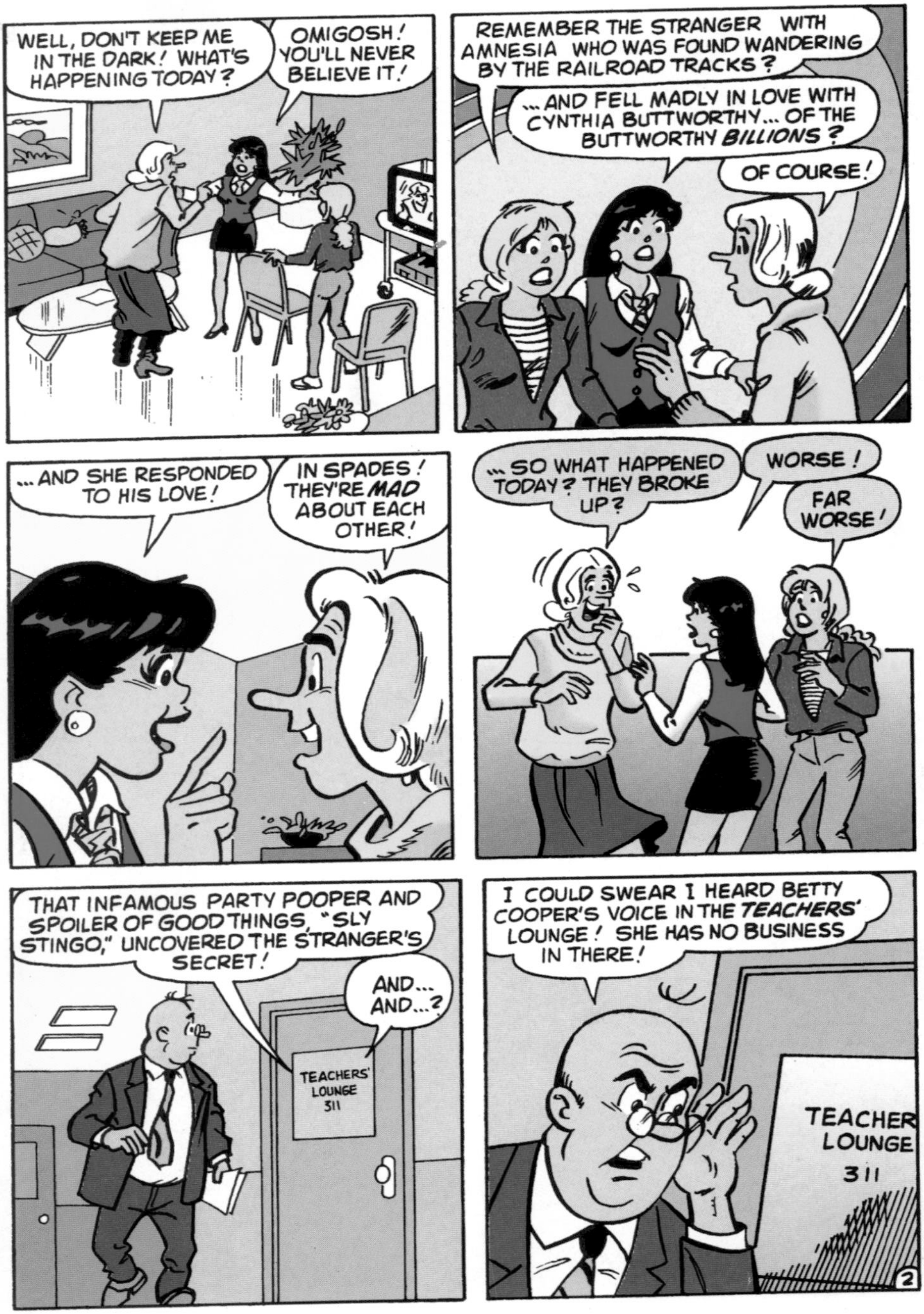
WELL, DON'T KEEP ME IN THE DARK! WHAT'S HAPPENING TODAY?
OMIGOSH! YOU'LL NEVER BELIEVE IT!
REMEMBER THE STRANGER WITH AMNESIA WHO WAS FOUND WANDERING BY THE RAILROAD TRACKS?
...AND FELL MADLY IN LOVE WITH CYNTHIA BUTTWORTHY... OF THE BUTTWORTHY BILLIONS?
OF COURSE!
...AND SHE RESPONDED TO HIS LOVE!
IN SPADES! THEY'RE MAD ABOUT EACH OTHER!
...SO WHAT HAPPENED TODAY? THEY BROKE UP?
WORSE!
FAR WORSE!
THAT INFAMOUS PARTY POOPER AND SPOILER OF GOOD THINGS, "SLY STINGO," UNCOVERED THE STRANGER'S SECRET!
AND... AND...?
TEACHERS' LOUNGE 311
I COULD SWEAR I HEARD BETTY COOPER'S VOICE IN THE TEACHERS' LOUNGE! SHE HAS NO BUSINESS IN THERE!
TEACHER LOUNGE 311
2

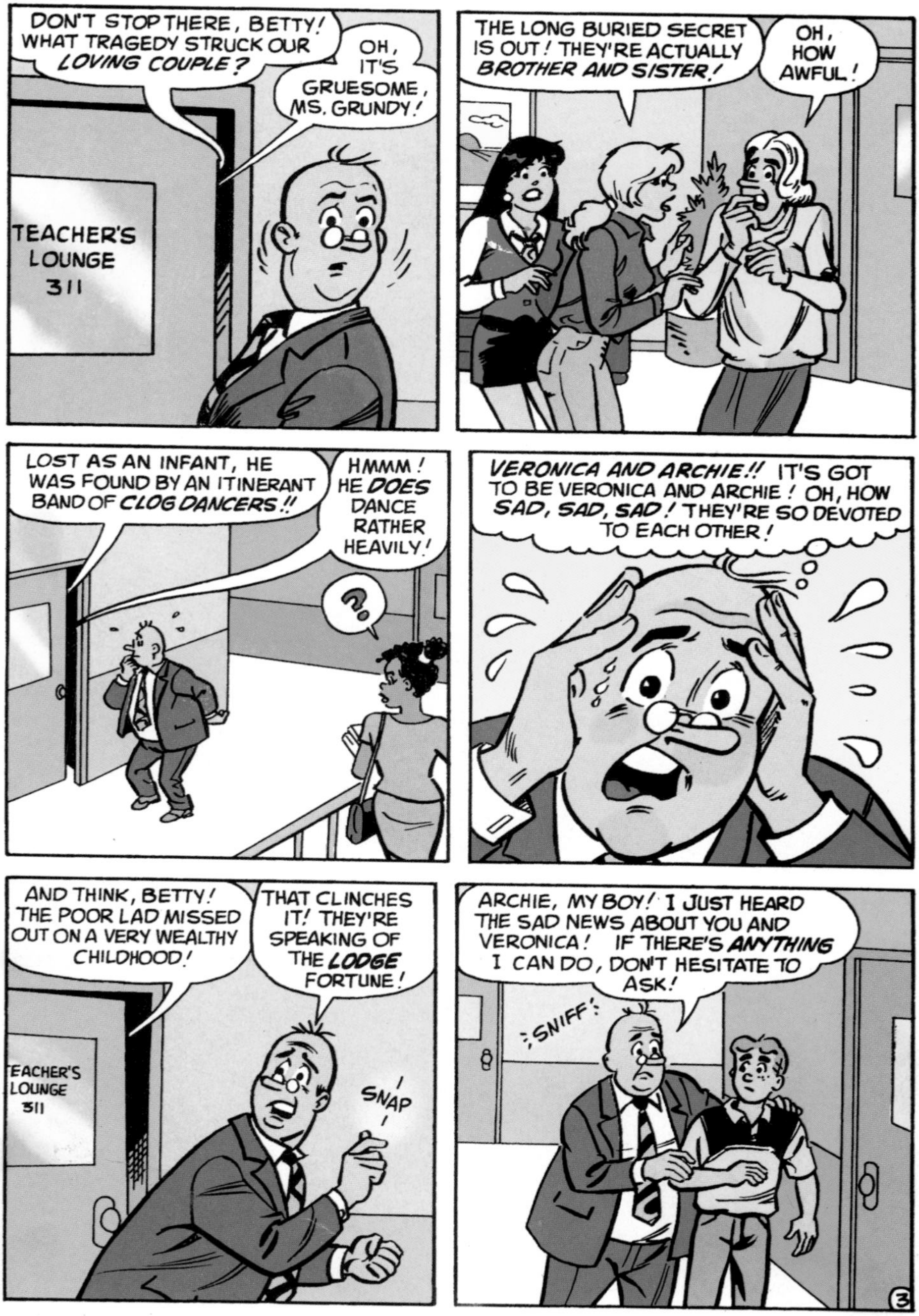
DON'T STOP THERE, BETTY! WHAT TRAGEDY STRUCK OUR LOVING COUPLE?
OH, IT'S GRUESOME, MS. GRUNDY!
TEACHER'S LOUNGE 311
THE LONG BURIED SECRET IS OUT! THEY'RE ACTUALLY BROTHER AND SISTER!
OH, HOW AWFUL!
LOST AS AN INFANT, HE WAS FOUND BY AN ITINERANT BAND OF CLOG DANCERS!!
HMMM! HE DOES DANCE RATHER HEAVILY!
?
VERONICA AND ARCHIE!! IT'S GOT TO BE VERONICA AND ARCHIE! OH, HOW SAD, SAD, SAD! THEY'RE SO DEVOTED TO EACH OTHER!
AND THINK, BETTY! THE POOR LAD MISSED OUT ON A VERY WEALTHY CHILDHOOD!
THAT CLINCHES IT! THEY'RE SPEAKING OF THE LODGE FORTUNE!
TEACHER'S LOUNGE 311
SNAP
ARCHIE, MY BOY! I JUST HEARD THE SAD NEWS ABOUT YOU AND VERONICA! IF THERE'S ANYTHING I CAN DO, DON'T HESITATE TO ASK!
SNIFF
3

JEEPERS! HE HEARD ABOUT OUR LITTLE *SPAT* YESTERDAY! I DIDN'T THINK HE CARED!

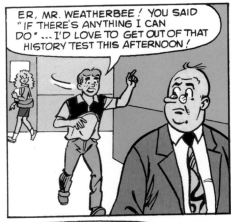

ER, MR. WEATHERBEE! YOU SAID "IF THERE'S ANYTHING I CAN DO"... I'D LOVE TO GET OUT OF THAT HISTORY TEST THIS AFTERNOON!

SAY NO MORE, SON! YOU DON'T WANT TO DWELL ON THE *PAST* RIGHT NOW!!

ULP! GEE, THANKS!!

YOU GOT EXCUSED FROM THAT TEST? HOW DID YOU MANAGE *THAT*?

BEATS ME, JUG!

SOMEHOW THE "BEE" IS SUDDENLY ACTING LIKE HE'S MY *DAD*!

HOW GROSS!

...BUT, HEY, IF IT GOT *ME* OUT OF A HISTORY TEST, I'D BE HIS LOVING SON!

④

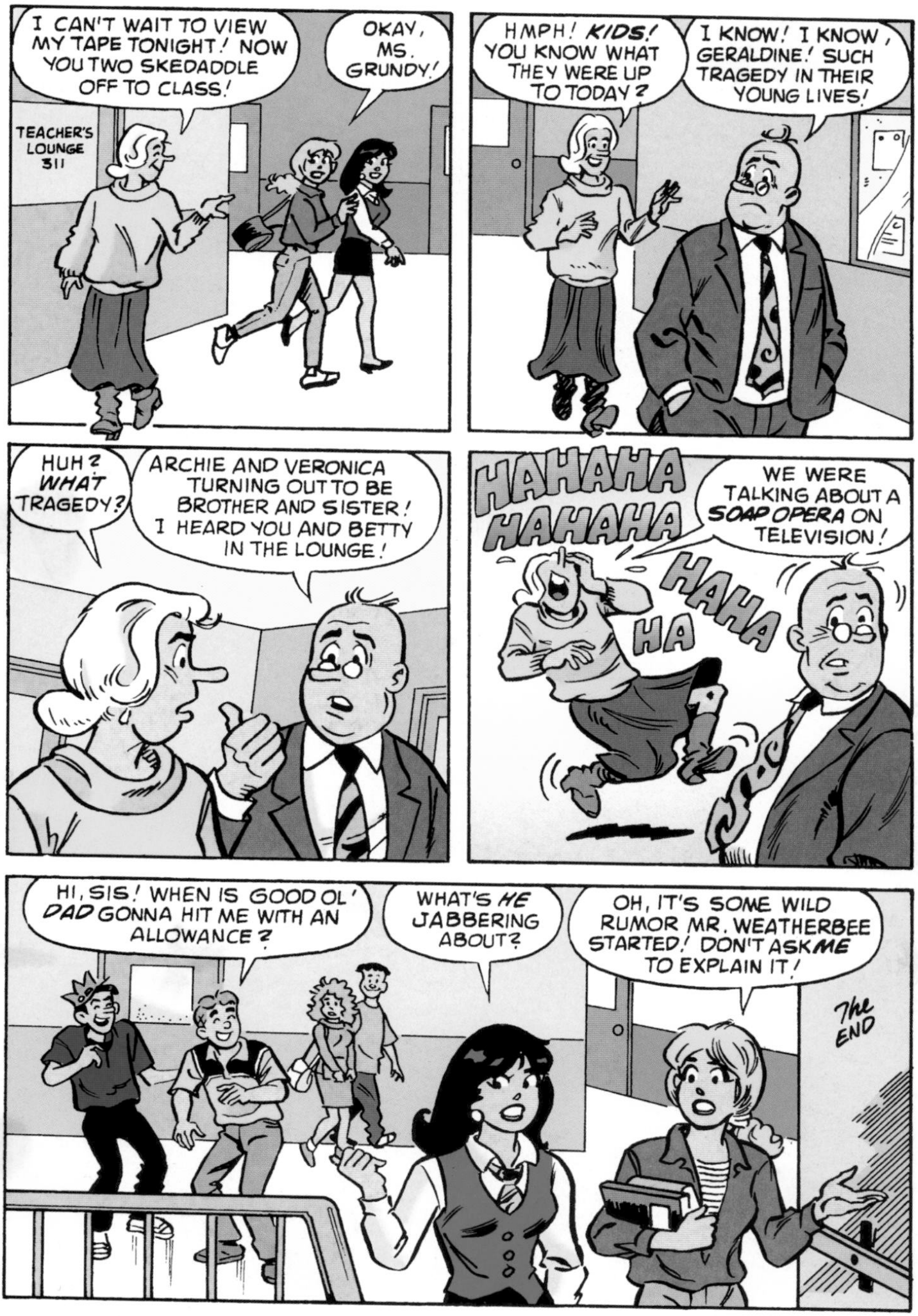
I CAN'T WAIT TO VIEW MY TAPE TONIGHT! NOW YOU TWO SKEDADDLE OFF TO CLASS!
OKAY, MS. GRUNDY!
TEACHER'S LOUNGE 311
HMPH! KIDS! YOU KNOW WHAT THEY WERE UP TO TODAY?
I KNOW! I KNOW, GERALDINE! SUCH TRAGEDY IN THEIR YOUNG LIVES!
HUH? WHAT TRAGEDY?
ARCHIE AND VERONICA TURNING OUT TO BE BROTHER AND SISTER! I HEARD YOU AND BETTY IN THE LOUNGE!
HAHAHA HAHAHA
WE WERE TALKING ABOUT A SOAP OPERA ON TELEVISION!
HAHAHA HA
HI, SIS! WHEN IS GOOD OL' DAD GONNA HIT ME WITH AN ALLOWANCE?
WHAT'S HE JABBERING ABOUT?
OH, IT'S SOME WILD RUMOR MR. WEATHERBEE STARTED! DON'T ASK ME TO EXPLAIN IT!
The END

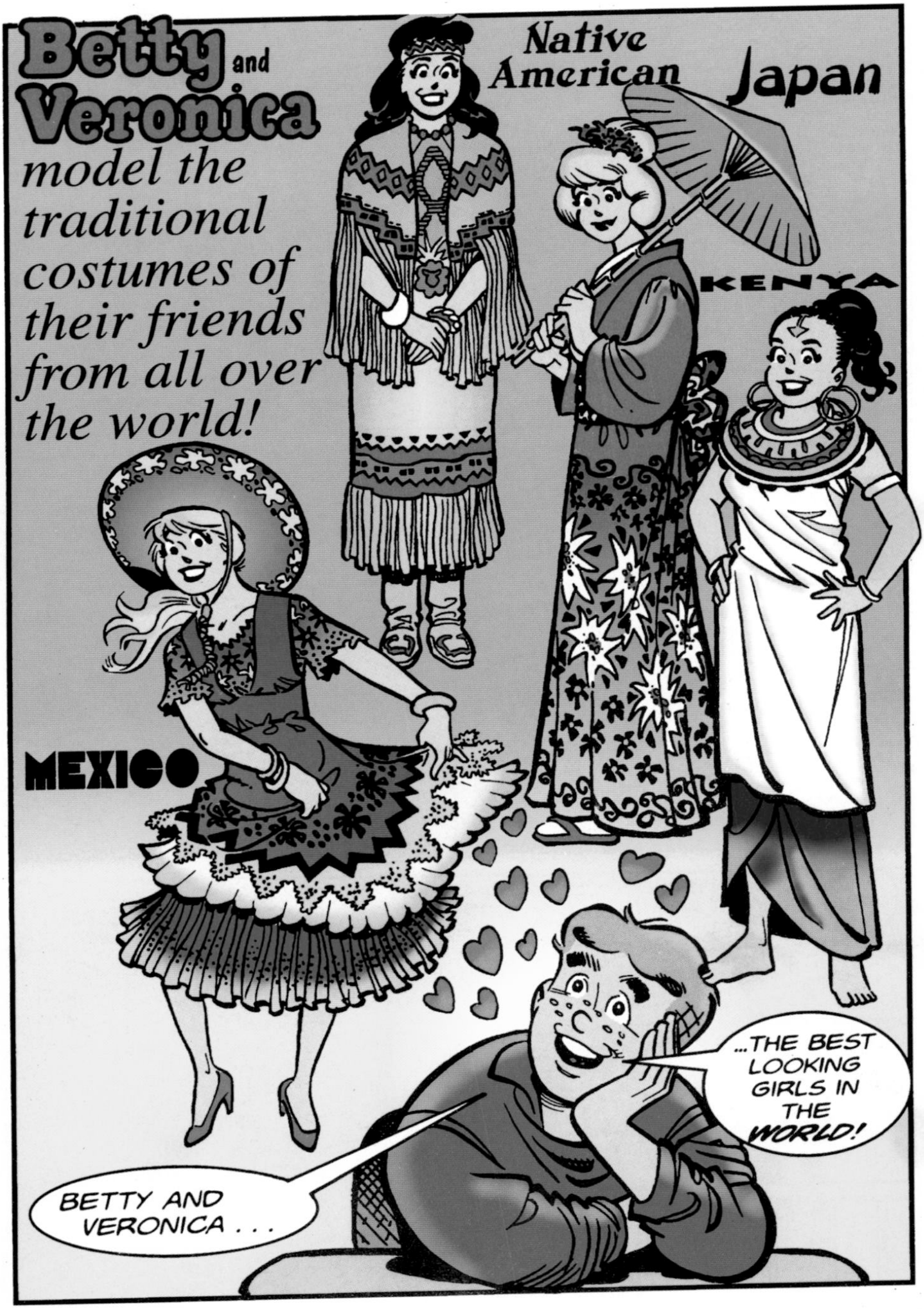
Betty and Veronica model the traditional costumes of their friends from all over the world!
Native American
Japan
KENYA
MEXICO
BETTY AND VERONICA . . .
...THE BEST LOOKING GIRLS IN THE WORLD!

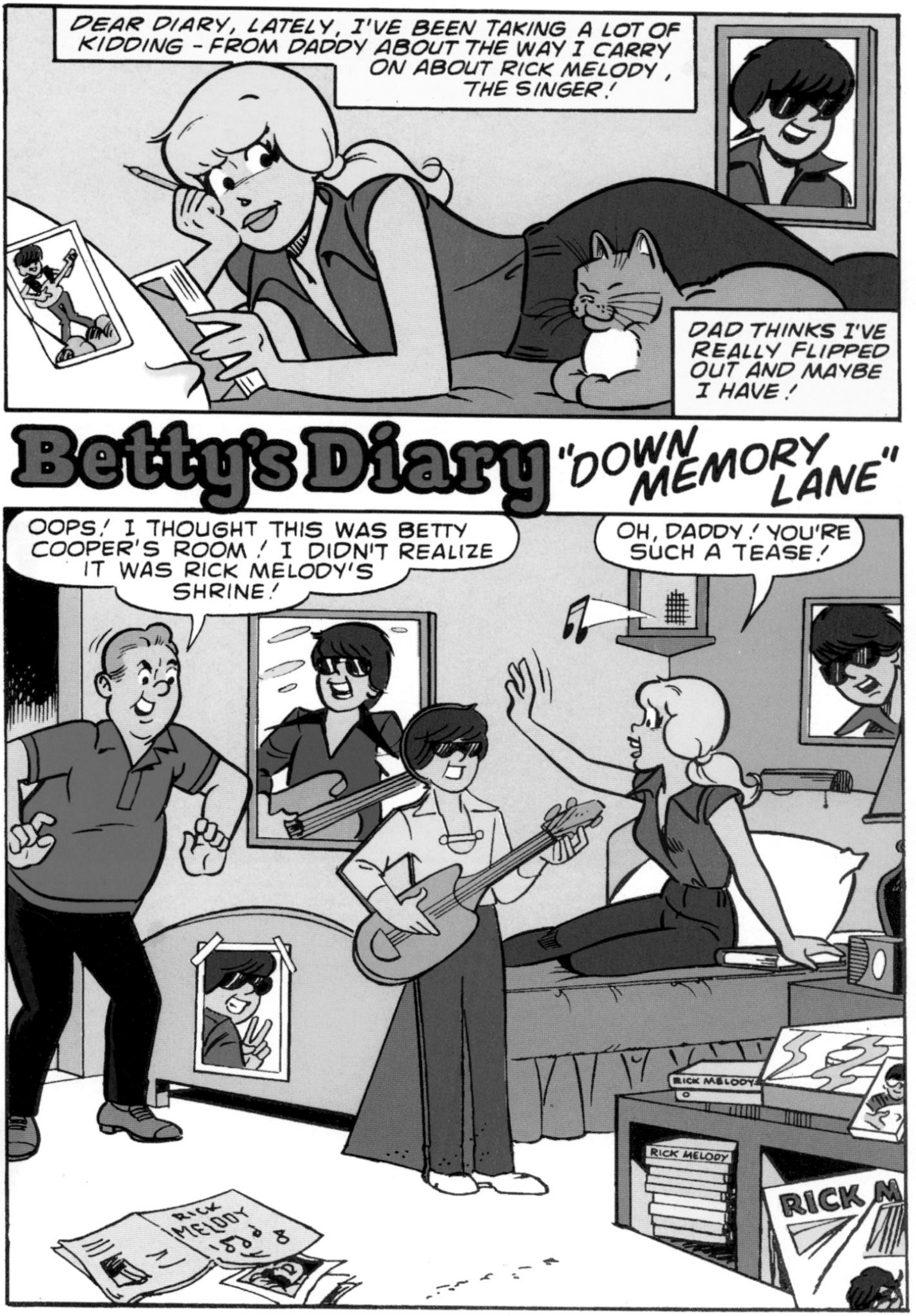
DEAR DIARY, LATELY, I'VE BEEN TAKING A LOT OF KIDDING - FROM DADDY ABOUT THE WAY I CARRY ON ABOUT RICK MELODY, THE SINGER!
DAD THINKS I'VE REALLY FLIPPED OUT AND MAYBE I HAVE!
Betty's Diary
"DOWN MEMORY LANE"
OOPS! I THOUGHT THIS WAS BETTY COOPER'S ROOM! I DIDN'T REALIZE IT WAS RICK MELODY'S SHRINE!
OH, DADDY! YOU'RE SUCH A TEASE!
RICK MELODY
RICK MELODY
RICK M
RICK MELODY

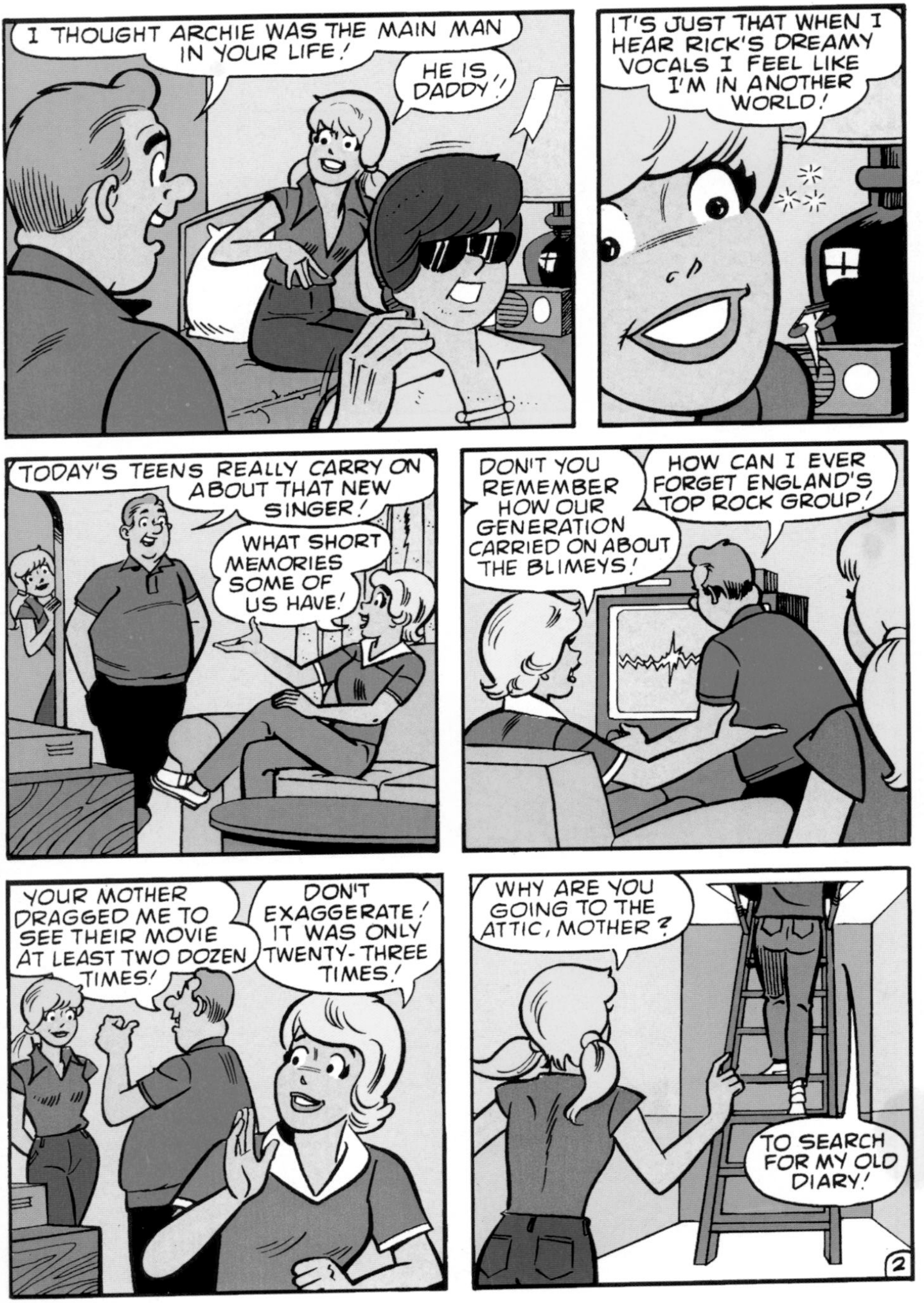
I THOUGHT ARCHIE WAS THE MAIN MAN IN YOUR LIFE!
HE IS DADDY!
IT'S JUST THAT WHEN I HEAR RICK'S DREAMY VOCALS I FEEL LIKE I'M IN ANOTHER WORLD!
TODAY'S TEENS REALLY CARRY ON ABOUT THAT NEW SINGER!
WHAT SHORT MEMORIES SOME OF US HAVE!
DON'T YOU REMEMBER HOW OUR GENERATION CARRIED ON ABOUT THE BLIMEYS!
HOW CAN I EVER FORGET ENGLAND'S TOP ROCK GROUP!
YOUR MOTHER DRAGGED ME TO SEE THEIR MOVIE AT LEAST TWO DOZEN TIMES!
DON'T EXAGGERATE! IT WAS ONLY TWENTY-THREE TIMES!
WHY ARE YOU GOING TO THE ATTIC, MOTHER?
TO SEARCH FOR MY OLD DIARY!
2

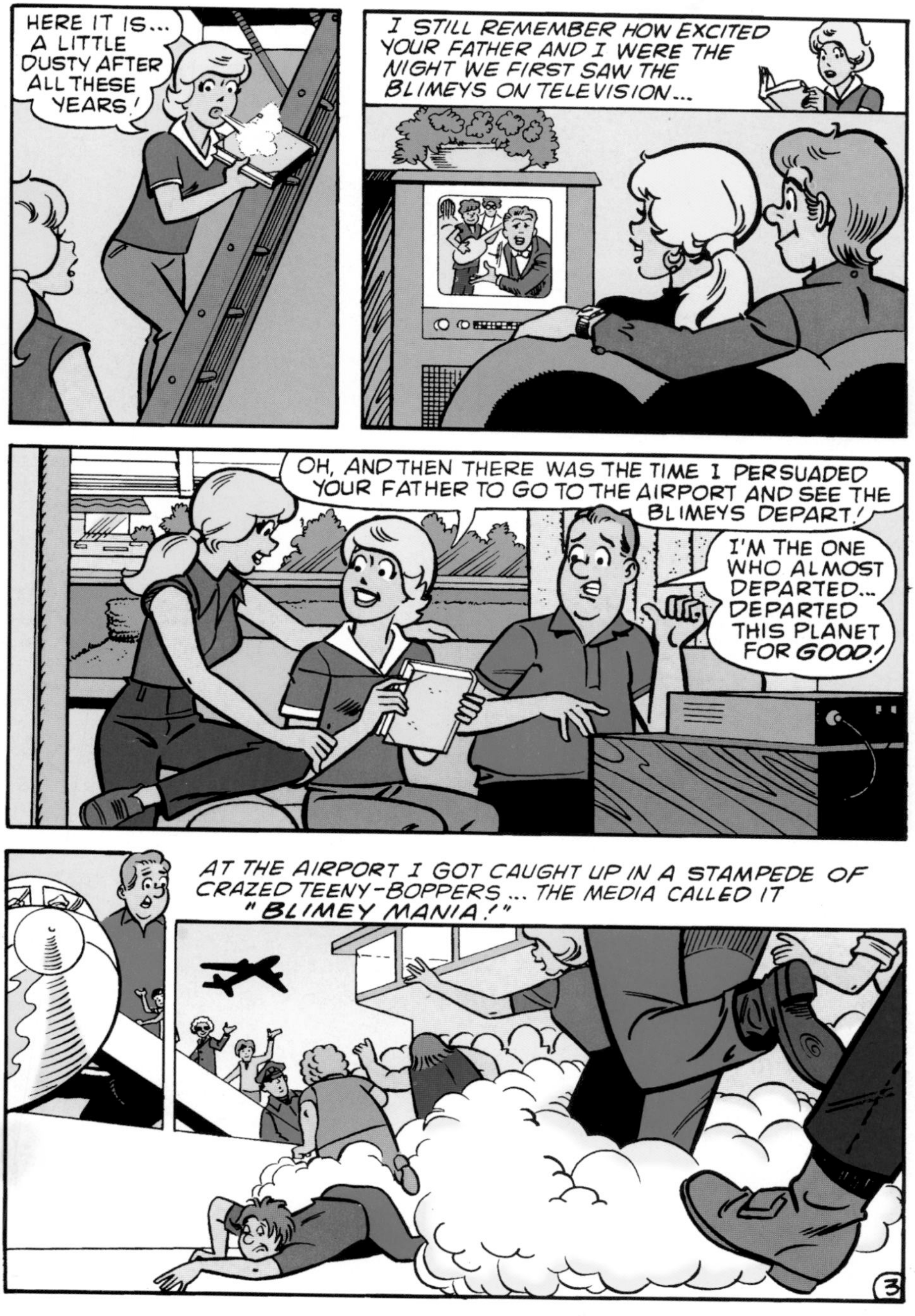
HERE IT IS... A LITTLE DUSTY AFTER ALL THESE YEARS!
I STILL REMEMBER HOW EXCITED YOUR FATHER AND I WERE THE NIGHT WE FIRST SAW THE BLIMEYS ON TELEVISION...
OH, AND THEN THERE WAS THE TIME I PERSUADED YOUR FATHER TO GO TO THE AIRPORT AND SEE THE BLIMEYS DEPART!
I'M THE ONE WHO ALMOST DEPARTED... DEPARTED THIS PLANET FOR GOOD!
AT THE AIRPORT I GOT CAUGHT UP IN A STAMPEDE OF CRAZED TEENY-BOPPERS ... THE MEDIA CALLED IT "BLIMEY MANIA!"
3

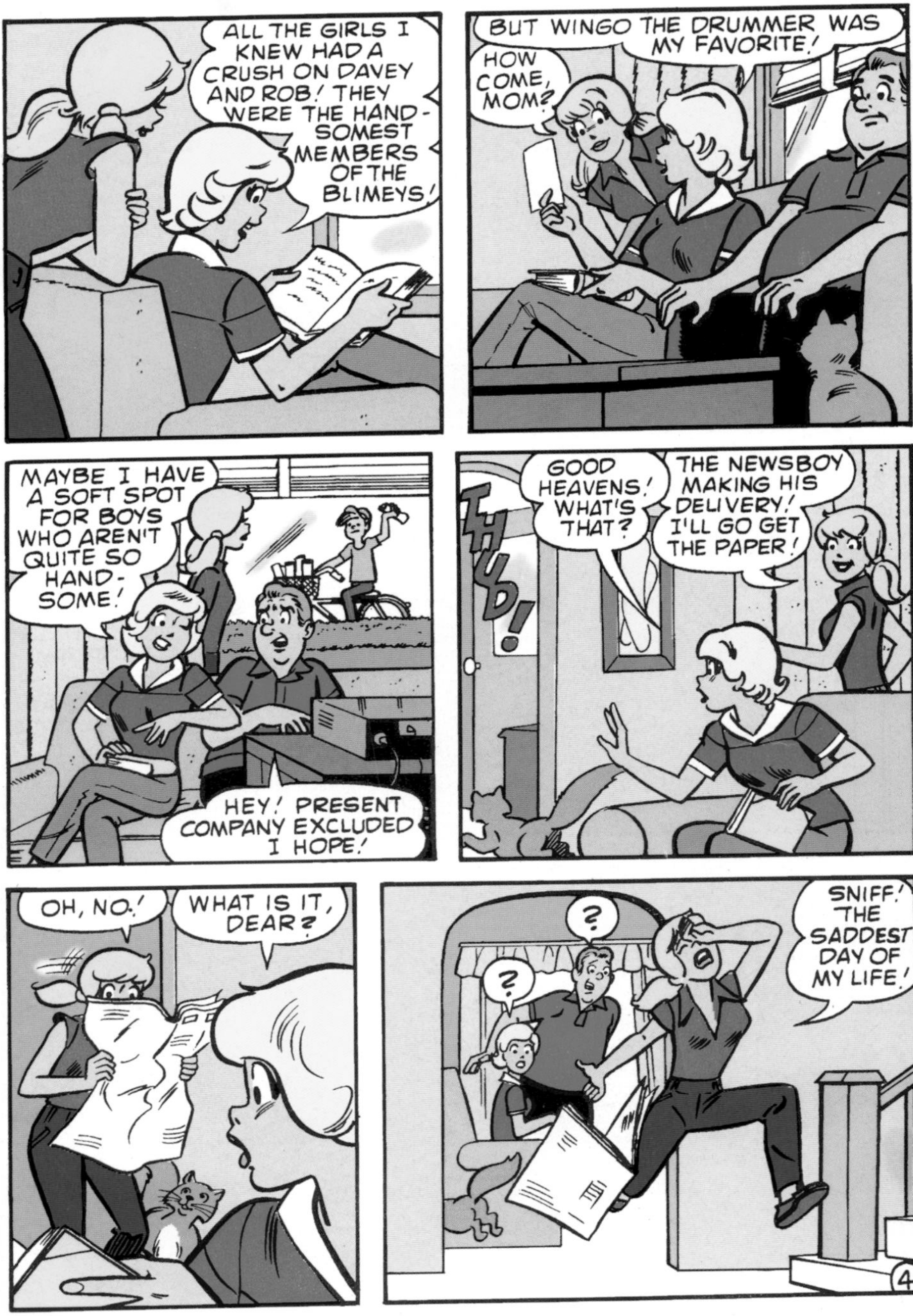

ALL THE GIRLS I KNEW HAD A CRUSH ON DAVEY AND ROB! THEY WERE THE HAND-SOMEST MEMBERS OF THE BLIMEYS!
BUT WINGO THE DRUMMER WAS MY FAVORITE!
HOW COME, MOM?
MAYBE I HAVE A SOFT SPOT FOR BOYS WHO AREN'T QUITE SO HAND-SOME!
HEY! PRESENT COMPANY EXCLUDED I HOPE!
THUD!
GOOD HEAVENS! WHAT'S THAT?
THE NEWSBOY MAKING HIS DELIVERY! I'LL GO GET THE PAPER!
OH, NO!
WHAT IS IT, DEAR?
?
?
SNIFF! THE SADDEST DAY OF MY LIFE!
4

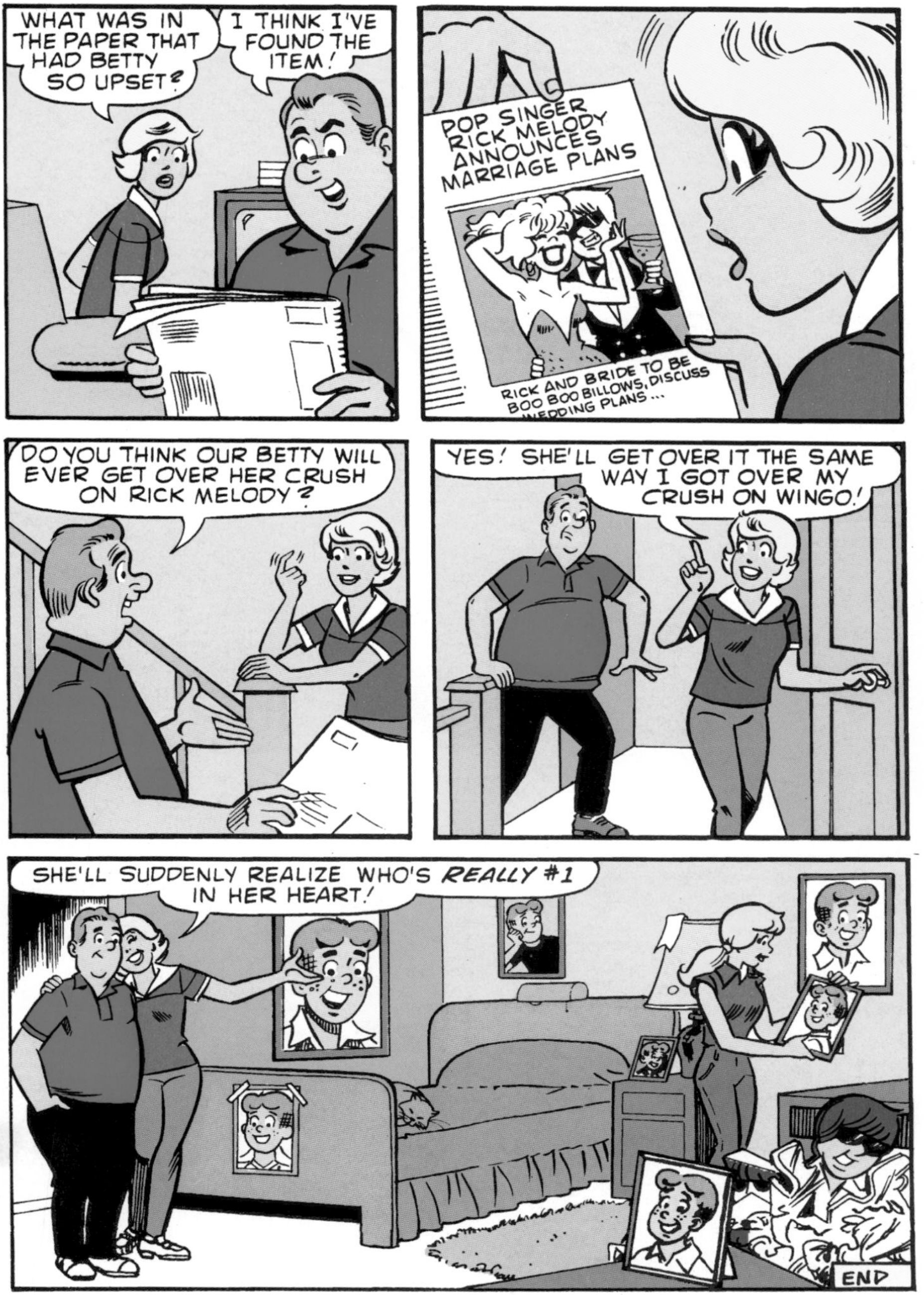
WHAT WAS IN THE PAPER THAT HAD BETTY SO UPSET?
I THINK I'VE FOUND THE ITEM!
POP SINGER RICK MELODY ANNOUNCES MARRIAGE PLANS
RICK AND BRIDE TO BE BOO BOO BILLOWS, DISCUSS WEDDING PLANS...
DO YOU THINK OUR BETTY WILL EVER GET OVER HER CRUSH ON RICK MELODY?
YES! SHE'LL GET OVER IT THE SAME WAY I GOT OVER MY CRUSH ON WINGO!
SHE'LL SUDDENLY REALIZE WHO'S *REALLY* #1 IN HER HEART!
END

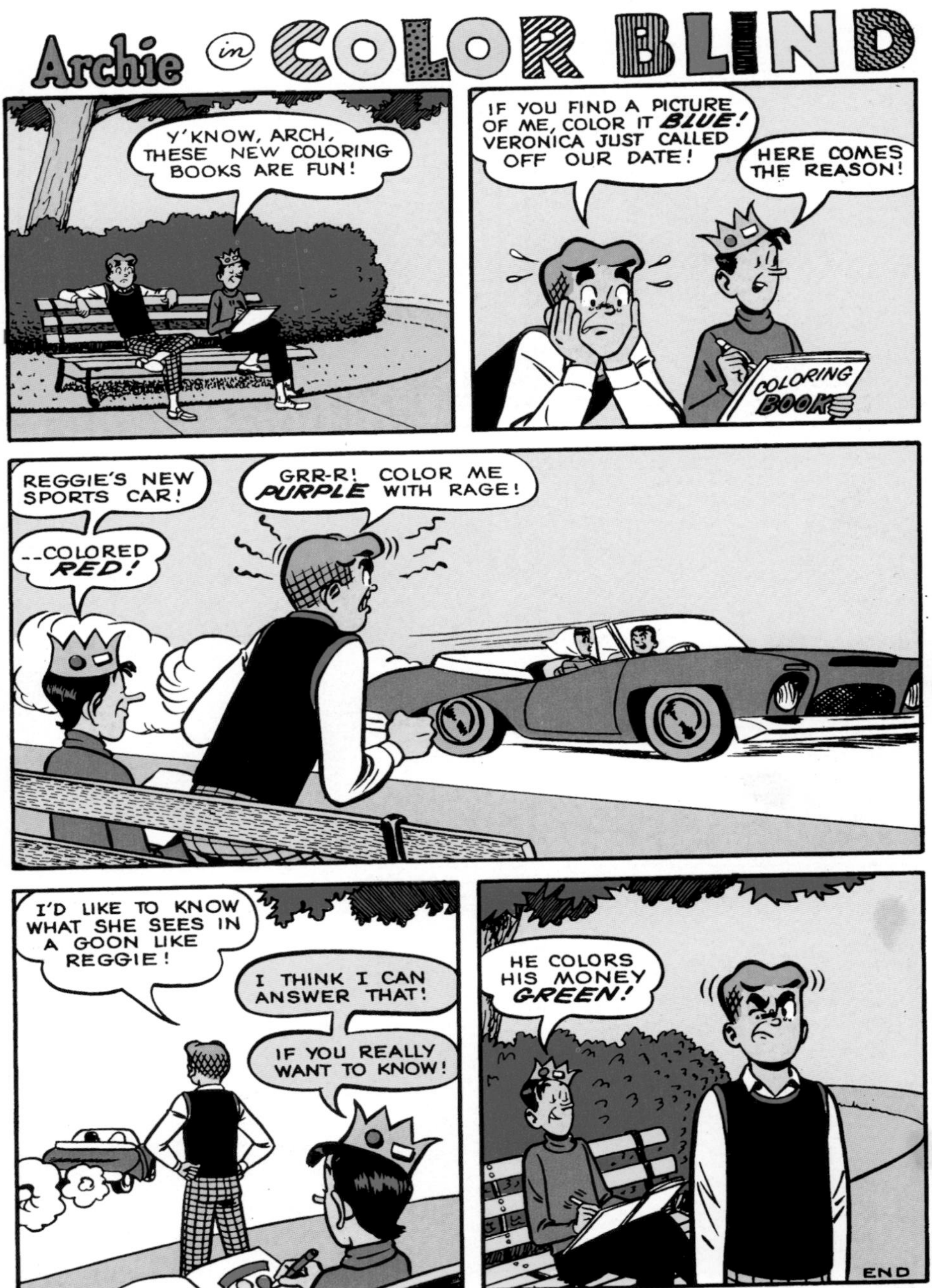
Archie in COLOR BLIND
Y'KNOW, ARCH, THESE NEW COLORING BOOKS ARE FUN!
IF YOU FIND A PICTURE OF ME, COLOR IT BLUE! VERONICA JUST CALLED OFF OUR DATE!
HERE COMES THE REASON!
COLORING BOOK
REGGIE'S NEW SPORTS CAR!
--COLORED RED!
GRR-R! COLOR ME PURPLE WITH RAGE!
I'D LIKE TO KNOW WHAT SHE SEES IN A GOON LIKE REGGIE!
I THINK I CAN ANSWER THAT!
IF YOU REALLY WANT TO KNOW!
HE COLORS HIS MONEY GREEN!
END

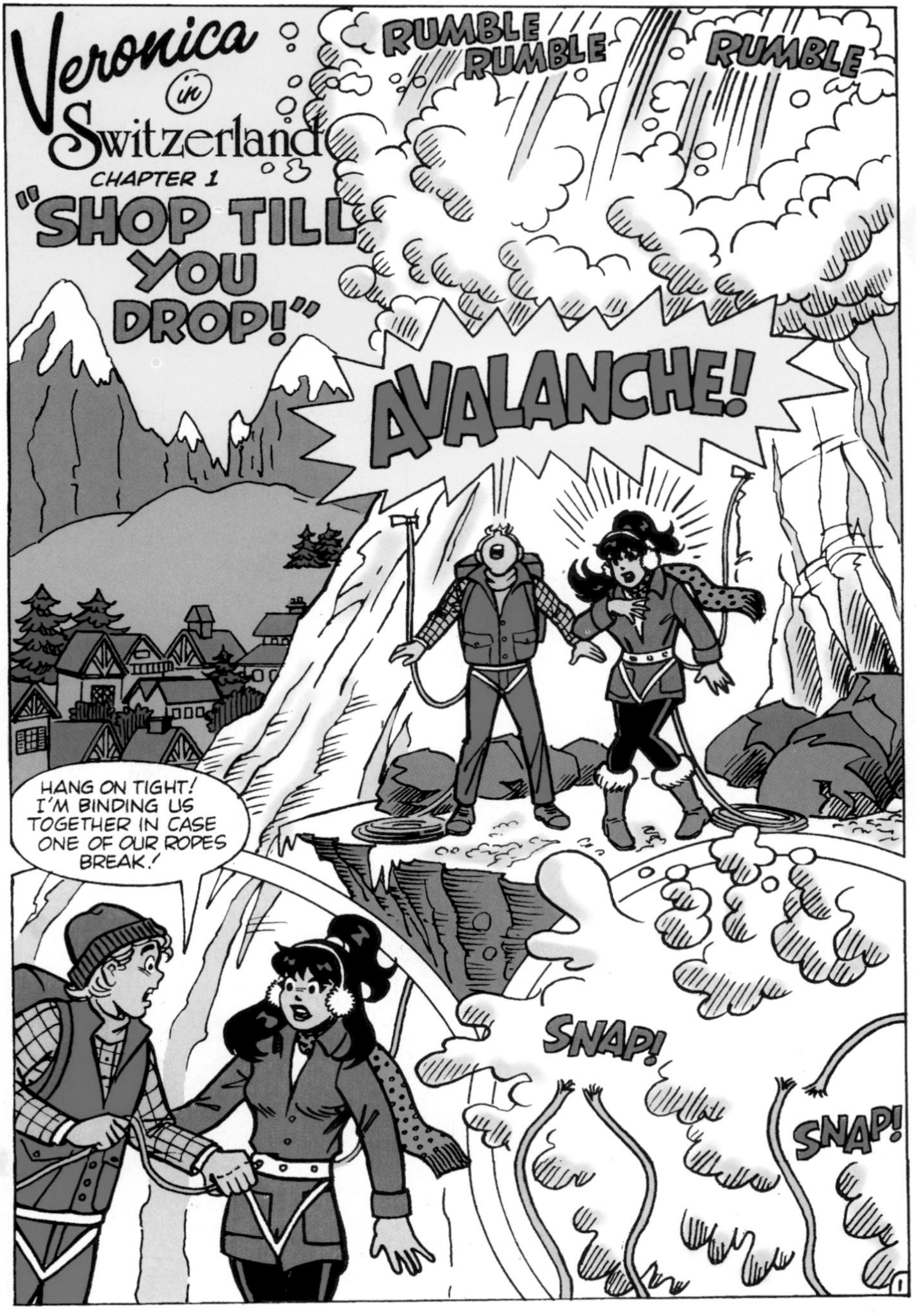
Veronica in Switzerland
CHAPTER 1
"SHOP TILL YOU DROP!"
RUMBLE RUMBLE
RUMBLE
AVALANCHE!
HANG ON TIGHT! I'M BINDING US TOGETHER IN CASE ONE OF OUR ROPES BREAK!
SNAP!
SNAP!
1

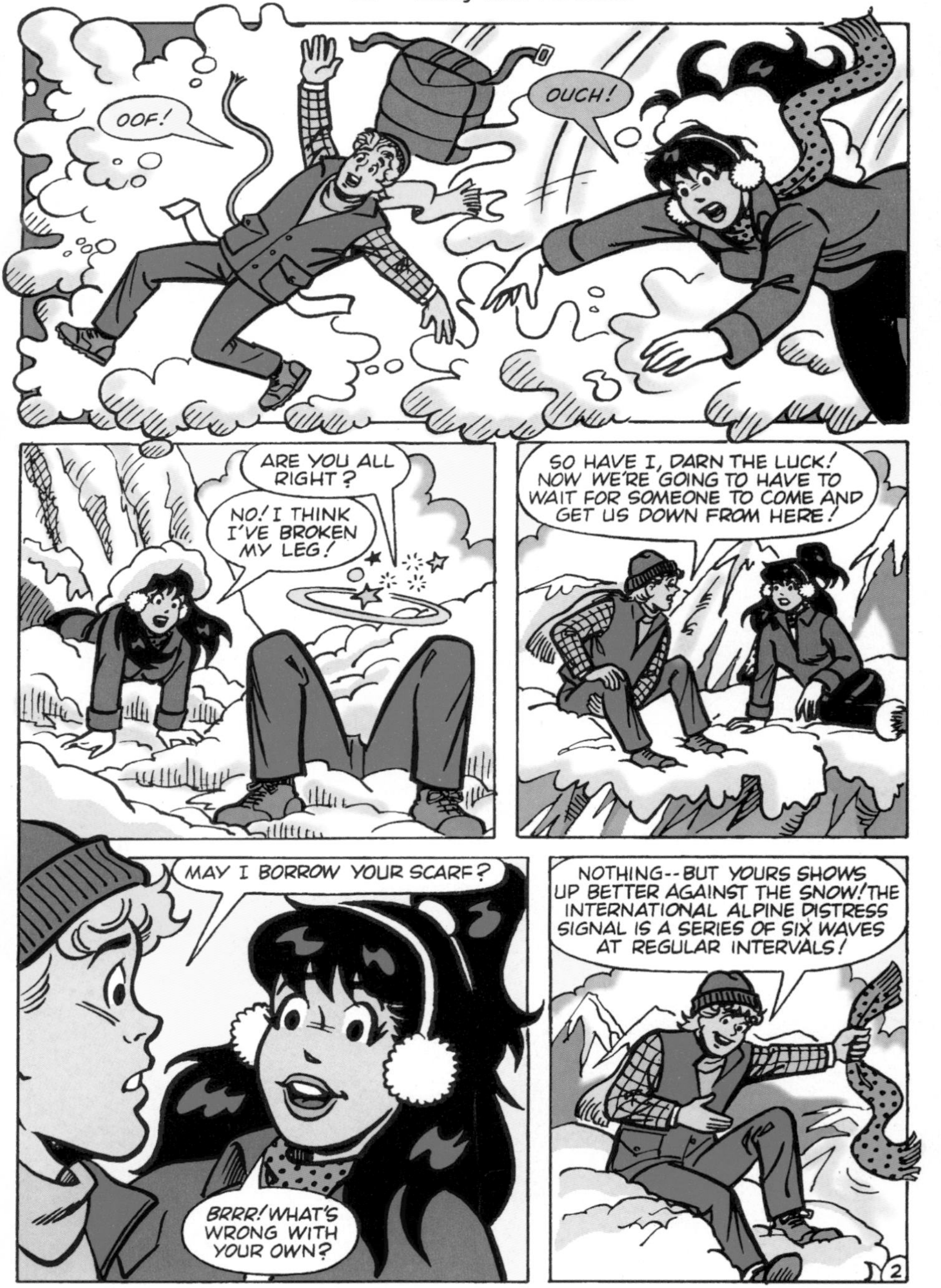
OOF!
OUCH!
ARE YOU ALL RIGHT?
NO! I THINK I'VE BROKEN MY LEG!
SO HAVE I, DARN THE LUCK! NOW WE'RE GOING TO HAVE TO WAIT FOR SOMEONE TO COME AND GET US DOWN FROM HERE!
MAY I BORROW YOUR SCARF?
BRRR! WHAT'S WRONG WITH YOUR OWN?
NOTHING--BUT YOURS SHOWS UP BETTER AGAINST THE SNOW! THE INTERNATIONAL ALPINE DISTRESS SIGNAL IS A SERIES OF SIX WAVES AT REGULAR INTERVALS!
2

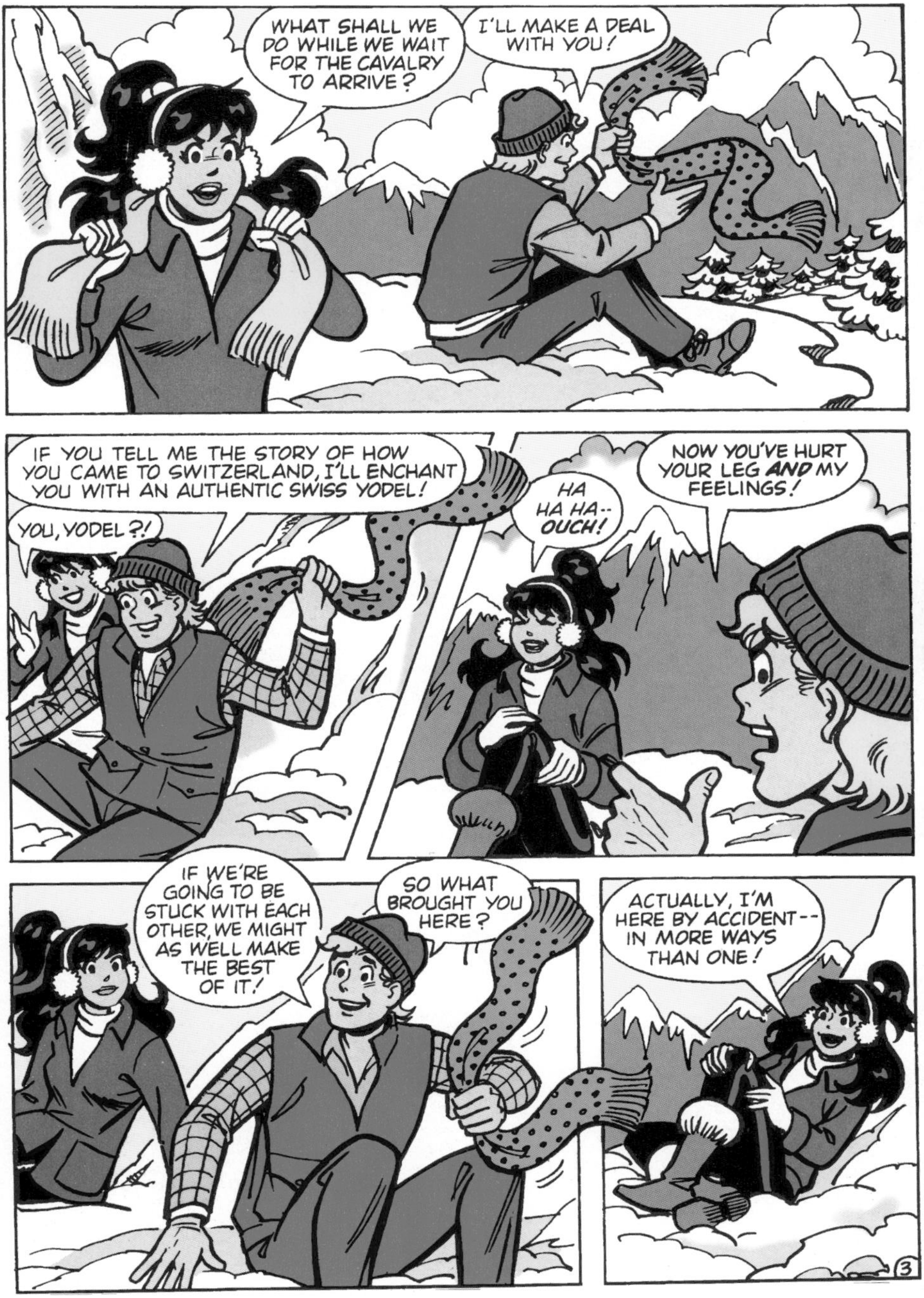
WHAT SHALL WE DO WHILE WE WAIT FOR THE CAVALRY TO ARRIVE?
I'LL MAKE A DEAL WITH YOU!
IF YOU TELL ME THE STORY OF HOW YOU CAME TO SWITZERLAND, I'LL ENCHANT YOU WITH AN AUTHENTIC SWISS YODEL!
YOU, YODEL?!
HA HA HA-- OUCH!
NOW YOU'VE HURT YOUR LEG AND MY FEELINGS!
IF WE'RE GOING TO BE STUCK WITH EACH OTHER, WE MIGHT AS WELL MAKE THE BEST OF IT!
SO WHAT BROUGHT YOU HERE?
ACTUALLY, I'M HERE BY ACCIDENT-- IN MORE WAYS THAN ONE!
3

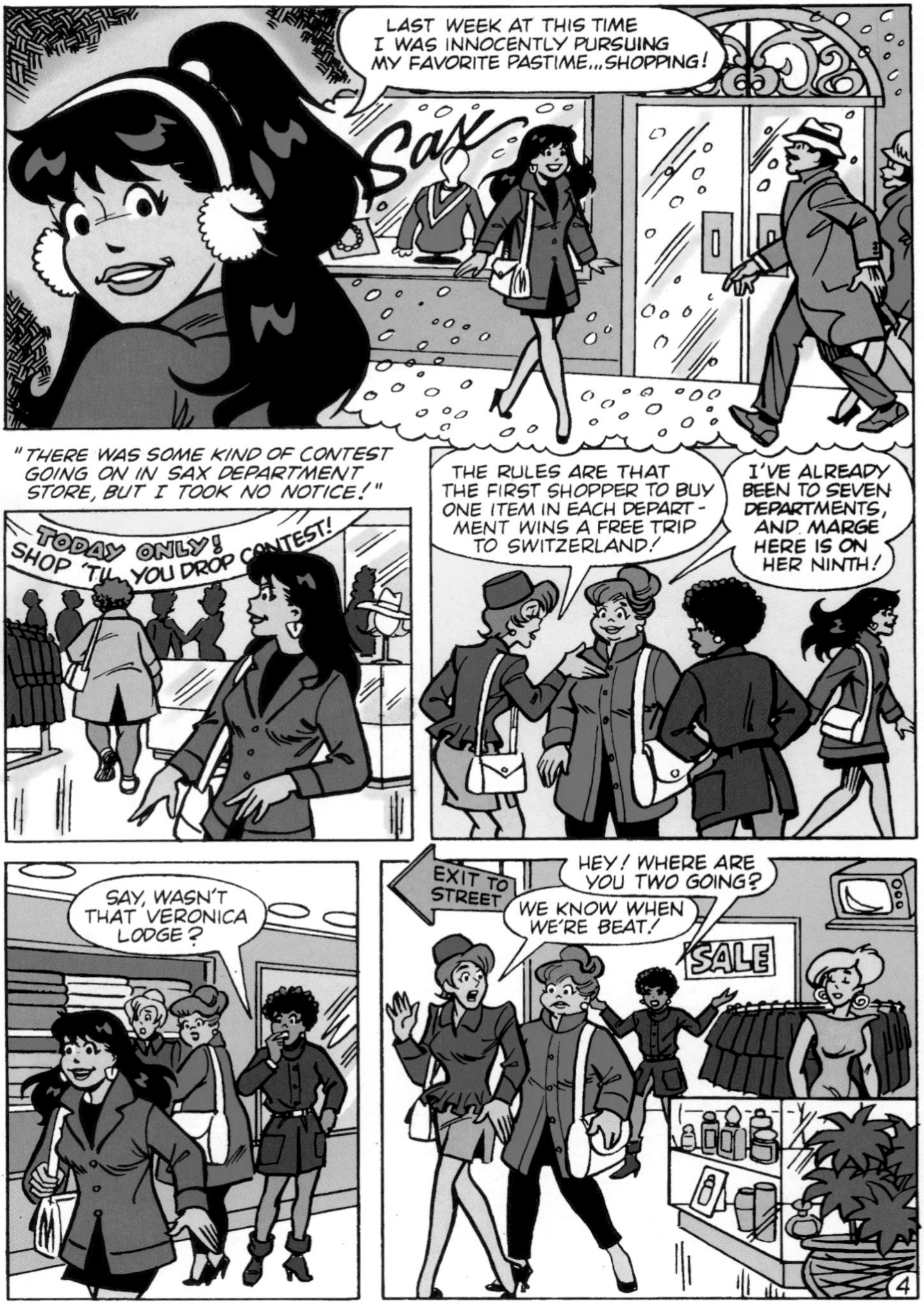
LAST WEEK AT THIS TIME I WAS INNOCENTLY PURSUING MY FAVORITE PASTIME... SHOPPING!
Sax
"THERE WAS SOME KIND OF CONTEST GOING ON IN SAX DEPARTMENT STORE, BUT I TOOK NO NOTICE!"
TODAY ONLY! SHOP 'TIL YOU DROP CONTEST!
THE RULES ARE THAT THE FIRST SHOPPER TO BUY ONE ITEM IN EACH DEPARTMENT WINS A FREE TRIP TO SWITZERLAND!
I'VE ALREADY BEEN TO SEVEN DEPARTMENTS, AND MARGE HERE IS ON HER NINTH!
SAY, WASN'T THAT VERONICA LODGE?
EXIT TO STREET
HEY! WHERE ARE YOU TWO GOING?
WE KNOW WHEN WE'RE BEAT!
SALE
4

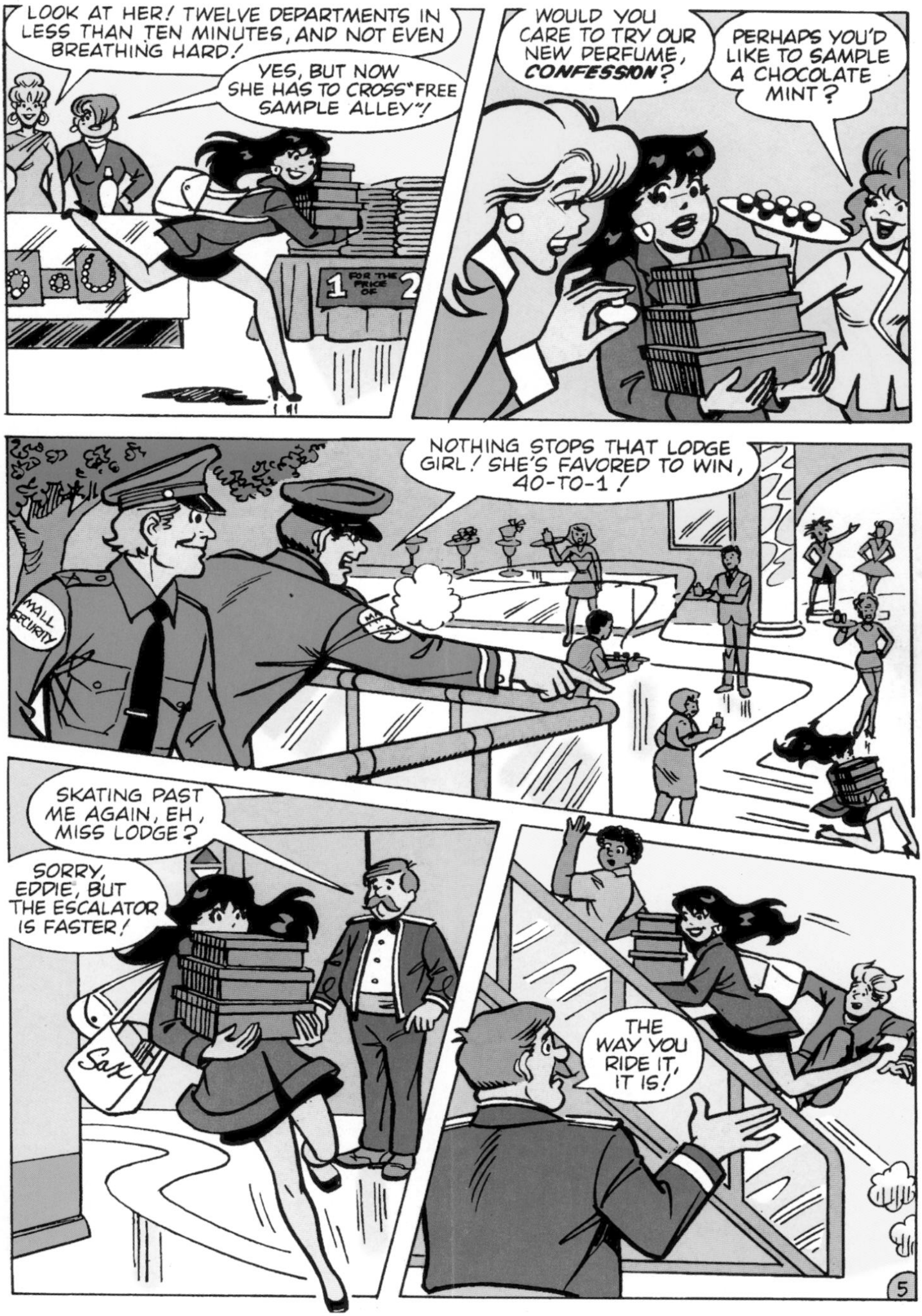
LOOK AT HER! TWELVE DEPARTMENTS IN LESS THAN TEN MINUTES, AND NOT EVEN BREATHING HARD!
YES, BUT NOW SHE HAS TO CROSS "FREE SAMPLE ALLEY"!
1 FOR THE PRICE OF 2
WOULD YOU CARE TO TRY OUR NEW PERFUME, CONFESSION?
PERHAPS YOU'D LIKE TO SAMPLE A CHOCOLATE MINT?
NOTHING STOPS THAT LODGE GIRL! SHE'S FAVORED TO WIN, 40-TO-1!
MALL SECURITY
SKATING PAST ME AGAIN, EH, MISS LODGE?
SORRY, EDDIE, BUT THE ESCALATOR IS FASTER!
Sax
THE WAY YOU RIDE IT, IT IS!
5

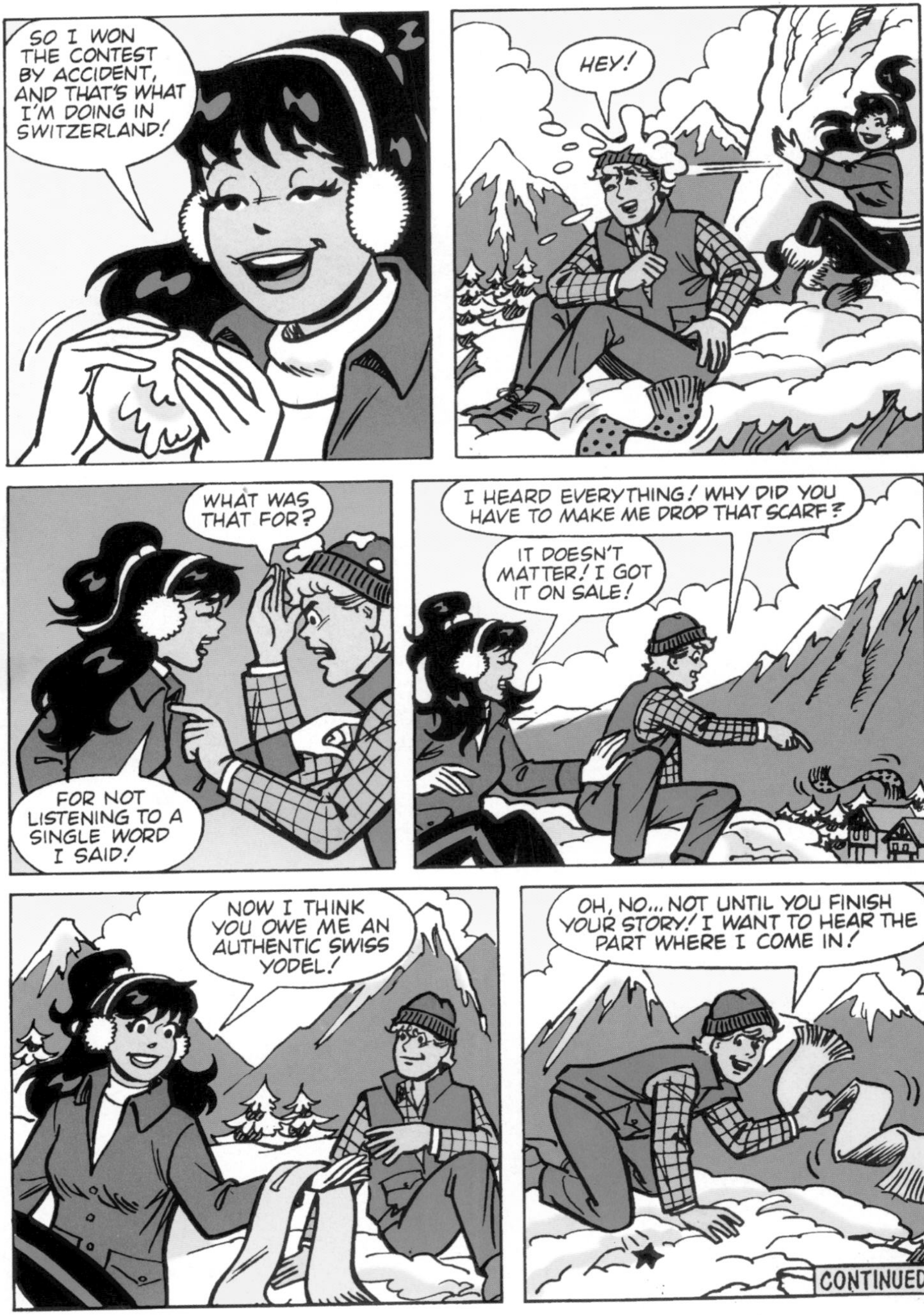
SO I WON THE CONTEST BY ACCIDENT, AND THAT'S WHAT I'M DOING IN SWITZERLAND!
HEY!
WHAT WAS THAT FOR?
FOR NOT LISTENING TO A SINGLE WORD I SAID!
I HEARD EVERYTHING! WHY DID YOU HAVE TO MAKE ME DROP THAT SCARF?
IT DOESN'T MATTER! I GOT IT ON SALE!
NOW I THINK YOU OWE ME AN AUTHENTIC SWISS YODEL!
OH, NO... NOT UNTIL YOU FINISH YOUR STORY! I WANT TO HEAR THE PART WHERE I COME IN!
CONTINUED

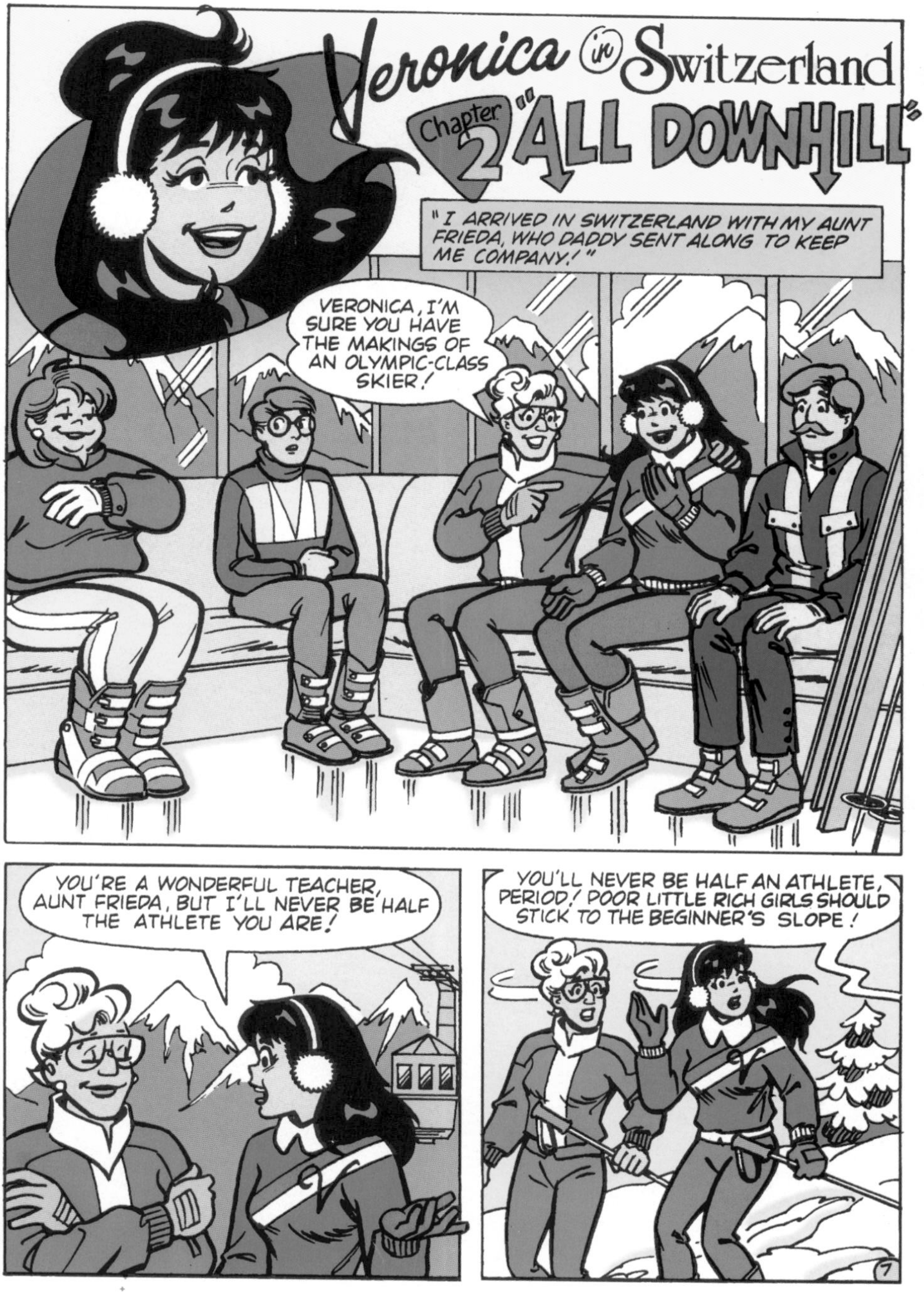
Veronica in Switzerland
Chapter 2 "ALL DOWNHILL"
"I ARRIVED IN SWITZERLAND WITH MY AUNT FRIEDA, WHO DADDY SENT ALONG TO KEEP ME COMPANY!"
VERONICA, I'M SURE YOU HAVE THE MAKINGS OF AN OLYMPIC-CLASS SKIER!
YOU'RE A WONDERFUL TEACHER, AUNT FRIEDA, BUT I'LL NEVER BE HALF THE ATHLETE YOU ARE!
YOU'LL NEVER BE HALF AN ATHLETE, PERIOD! POOR LITTLE RICH GIRLS SHOULD STICK TO THE BEGINNER'S SLOPE!
7

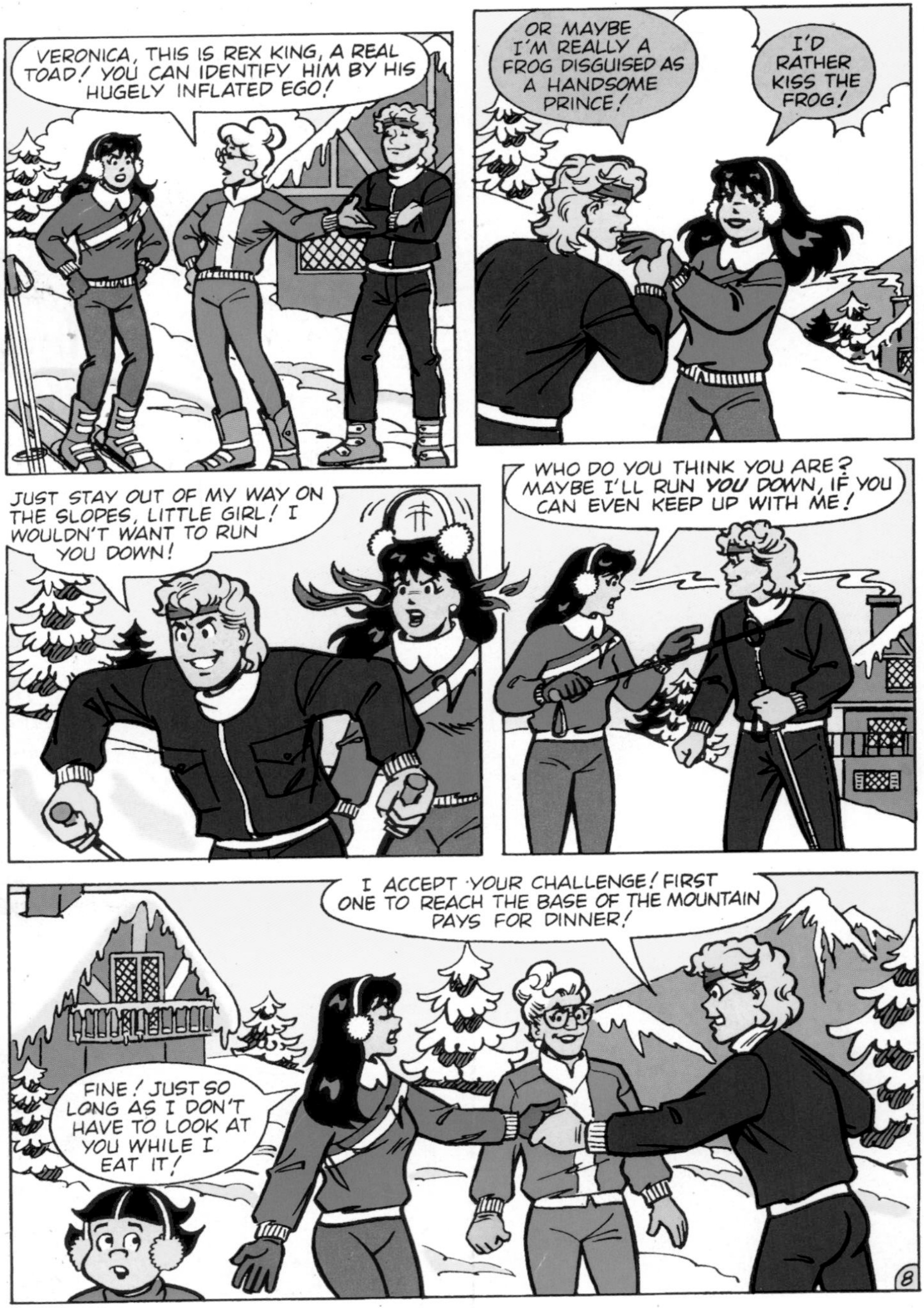
VERONICA, THIS IS REX KING, A REAL TOAD! YOU CAN IDENTIFY HIM BY HIS HUGELY INFLATED EGO!
OR MAYBE I'M REALLY A FROG DISGUISED AS A HANDSOME PRINCE!
I'D RATHER KISS THE FROG!
JUST STAY OUT OF MY WAY ON THE SLOPES, LITTLE GIRL! I WOULDN'T WANT TO RUN YOU DOWN!
WHO DO YOU THINK YOU ARE? MAYBE I'LL RUN **YOU DOWN**, IF YOU CAN EVEN KEEP UP WITH ME!
I ACCEPT YOUR CHALLENGE! FIRST ONE TO REACH THE BASE OF THE MOUNTAIN PAYS FOR DINNER!
FINE! JUST SO LONG AS I DON'T HAVE TO LOOK AT YOU WHILE I EAT IT!
8

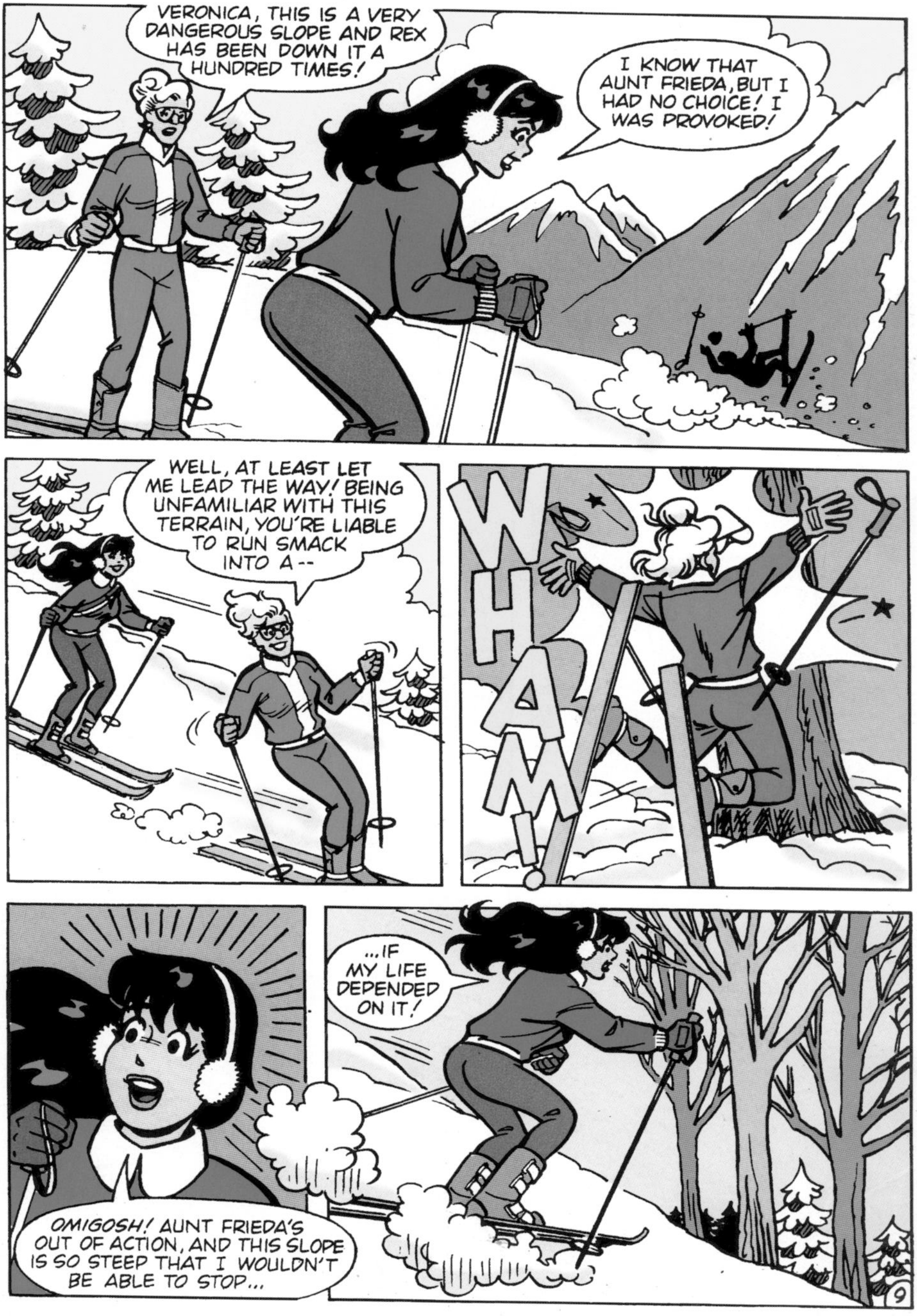
VERONICA, THIS IS A VERY DANGEROUS SLOPE AND REX HAS BEEN DOWN IT A HUNDRED TIMES!
I KNOW THAT AUNT FRIEDA, BUT I HAD NO CHOICE! I WAS PROVOKED!
WELL, AT LEAST LET ME LEAD THE WAY! BEING UNFAMILIAR WITH THIS TERRAIN, YOU'RE LIABLE TO RUN SMACK INTO A--
WHAM!
OMIGOSH! AUNT FRIEDA'S OUT OF ACTION, AND THIS SLOPE IS SO STEEP THAT I WOULDN'T BE ABLE TO STOP...
...IF MY LIFE DEPENDED ON IT!
9

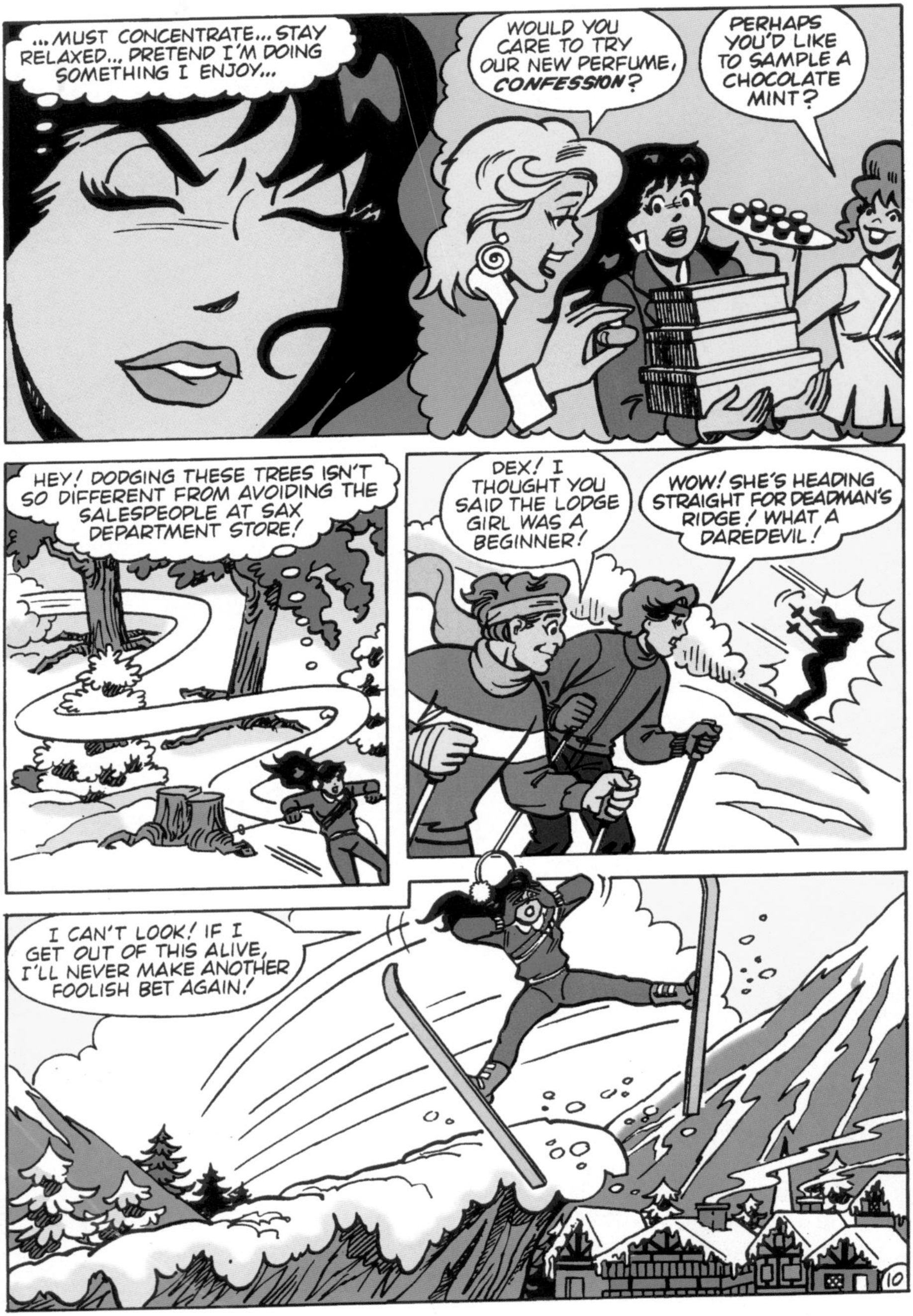
...MUST CONCENTRATE... STAY RELAXED... PRETEND I'M DOING SOMETHING I ENJOY...
WOULD YOU CARE TO TRY OUR NEW PERFUME, CONFESSION?
PERHAPS YOU'D LIKE TO SAMPLE A CHOCOLATE MINT?
HEY! DODGING THESE TREES ISN'T SO DIFFERENT FROM AVOIDING THE SALESPEOPLE AT SAX DEPARTMENT STORE!
DEX! I THOUGHT YOU SAID THE LODGE GIRL WAS A BEGINNER!
WOW! SHE'S HEADING STRAIGHT FOR DEADMAN'S RIDGE! WHAT A DAREDEVIL!
I CAN'T LOOK! IF I GET OUT OF THIS ALIVE, I'LL NEVER MAKE ANOTHER FOOLISH BET AGAIN!
10

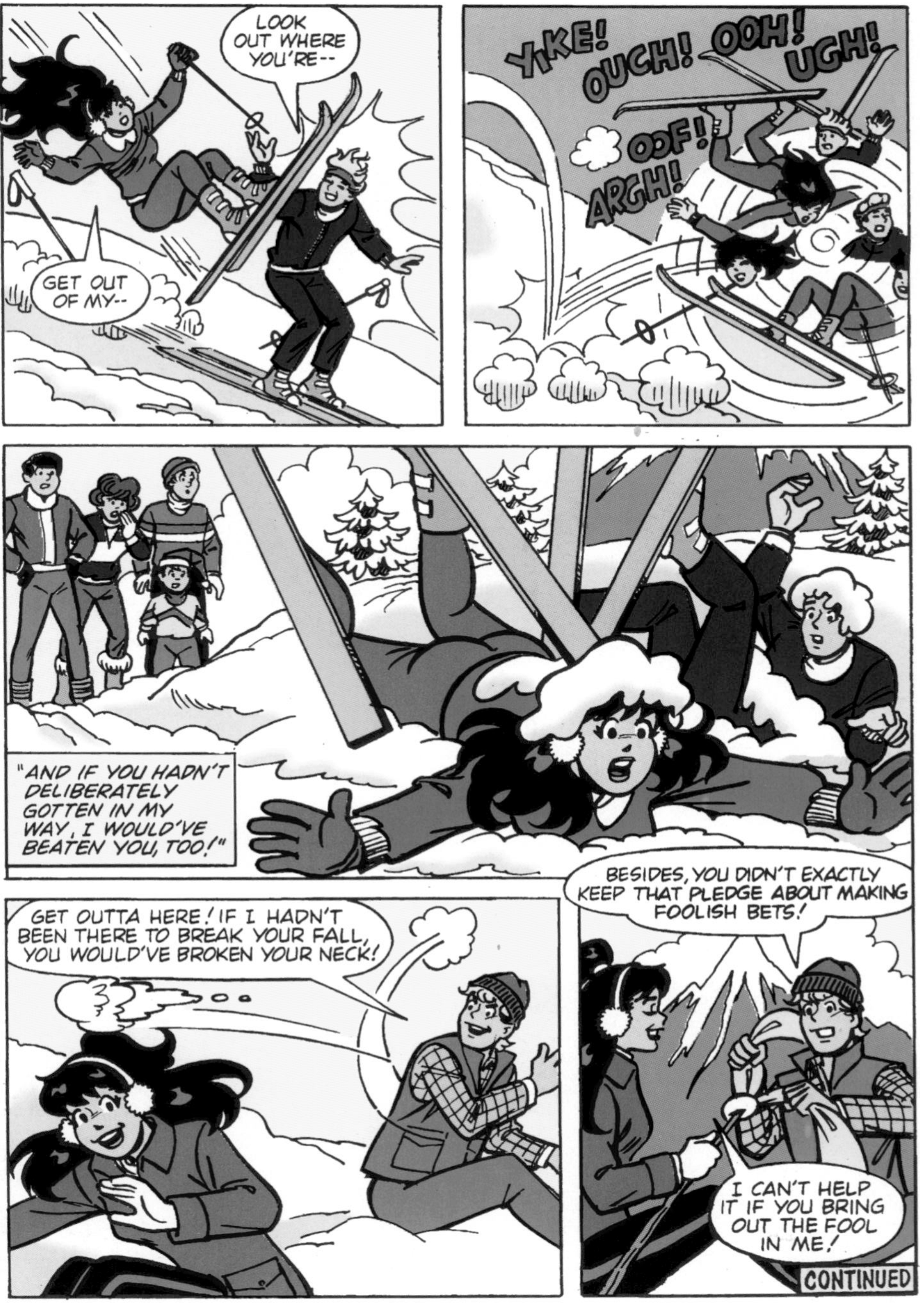
LOOK OUT WHERE YOU'RE--
GET OUT OF MY--
YIKE! OUCH! OOH! UGH!
OOF! ARGH!
"AND IF YOU HADN'T DELIBERATELY GOTTEN IN MY WAY, I WOULD'VE BEATEN YOU, TOO!"
GET OUTTA HERE! IF I HADN'T BEEN THERE TO BREAK YOUR FALL, YOU WOULD'VE BROKEN YOUR NECK!
BESIDES, YOU DIDN'T EXACTLY KEEP THAT PLEDGE ABOUT MAKING FOOLISH BETS!
I CAN'T HELP IT IF YOU BRING OUT THE FOOL IN ME!
CONTINUED

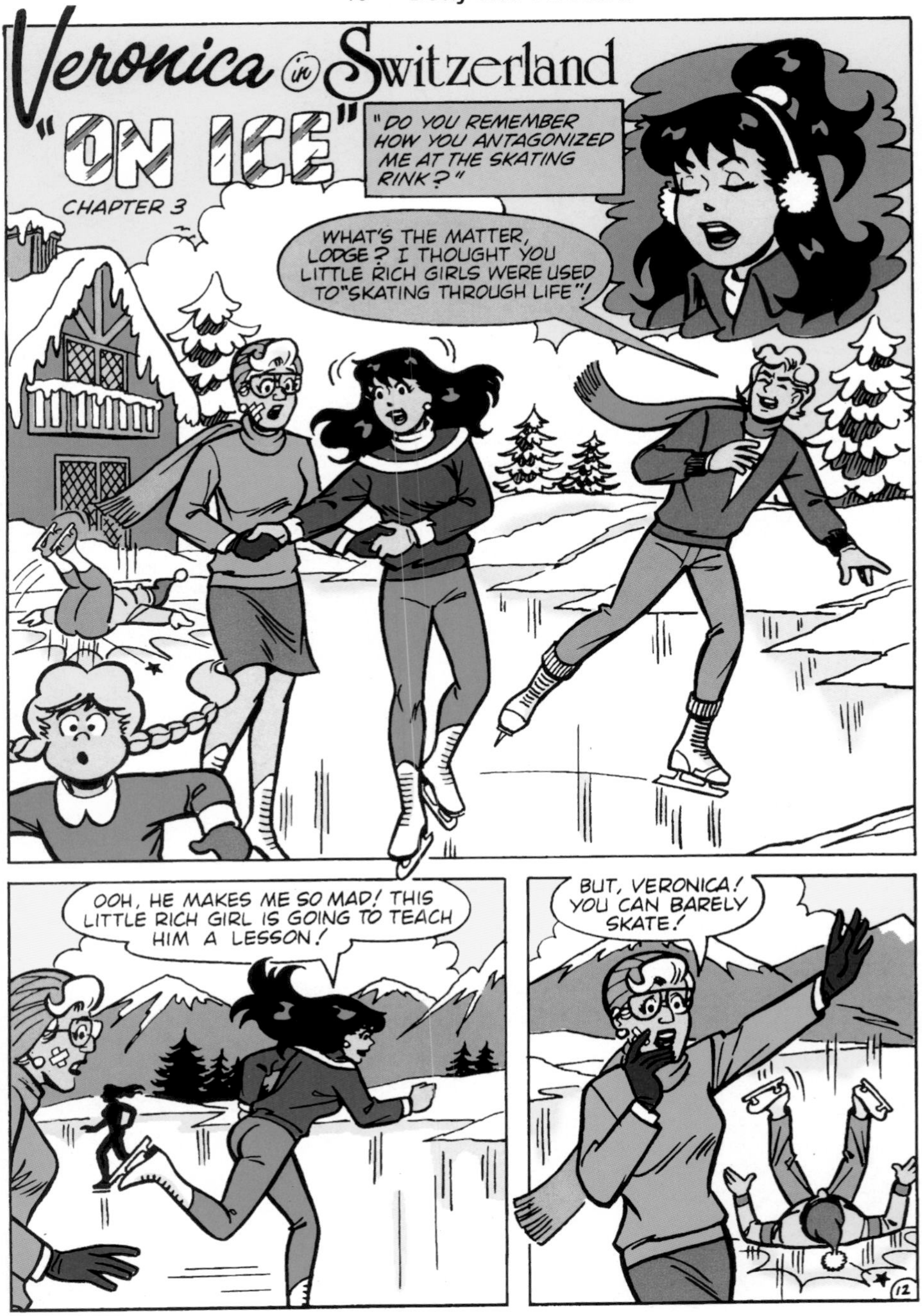
Veronica in Switzerland
"ON ICE"
CHAPTER 3
"DO YOU REMEMBER HOW YOU ANTAGONIZED ME AT THE SKATING RINK?"
WHAT'S THE MATTER, LODGE? I THOUGHT YOU LITTLE RICH GIRLS WERE USED TO "SKATING THROUGH LIFE"!
OOH, HE MAKES ME SO MAD! THIS LITTLE RICH GIRL IS GOING TO TEACH HIM A LESSON!
BUT, VERONICA! YOU CAN BARELY SKATE!
12

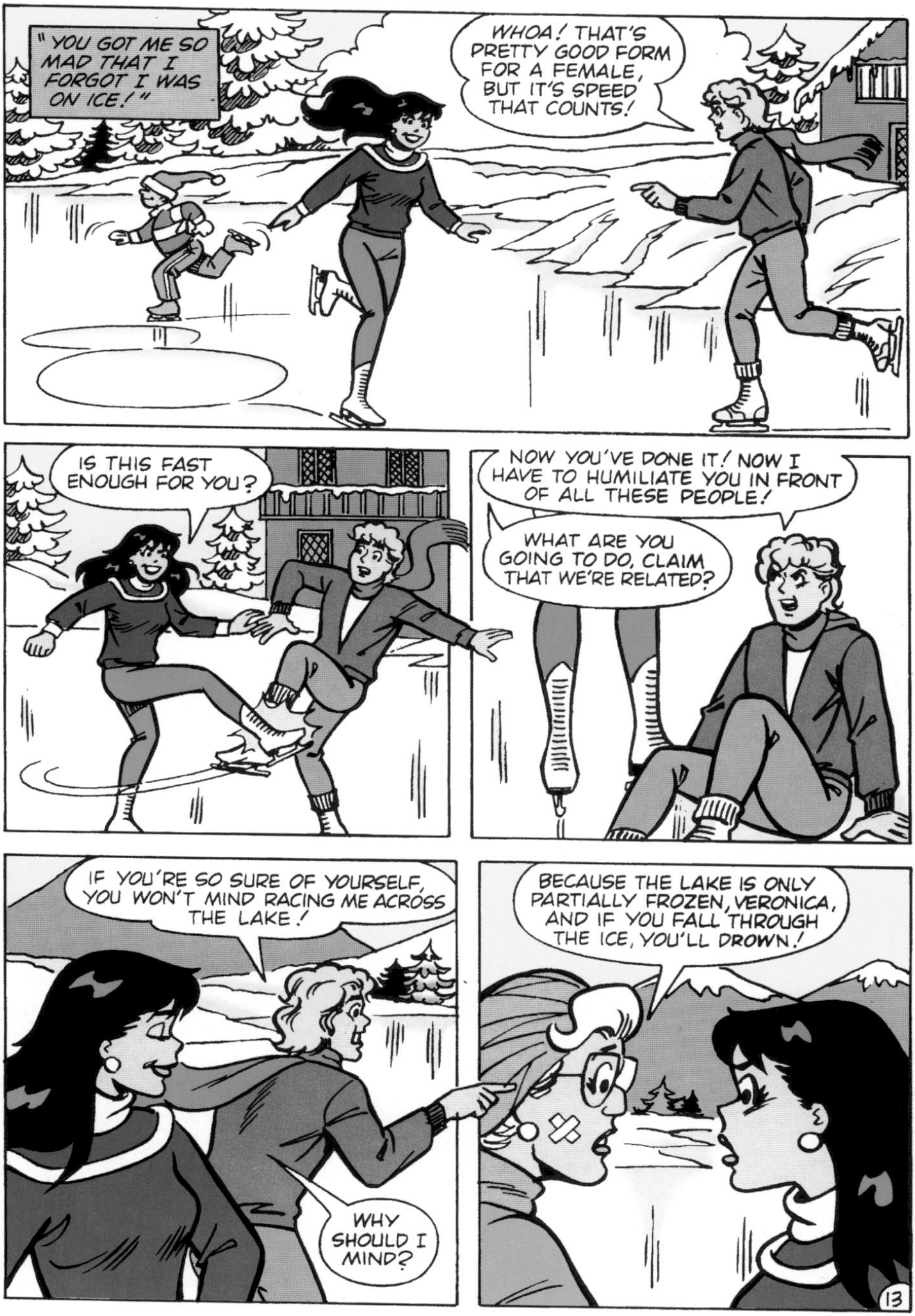
"YOU GOT ME SO MAD THAT I FORGOT I WAS ON ICE!"
WHOA! THAT'S PRETTY GOOD FORM FOR A FEMALE, BUT IT'S SPEED THAT COUNTS!
IS THIS FAST ENOUGH FOR YOU?
NOW YOU'VE DONE IT! NOW I HAVE TO HUMILIATE YOU IN FRONT OF ALL THESE PEOPLE!
WHAT ARE YOU GOING TO DO, CLAIM THAT WE'RE RELATED?
IF YOU'RE SO SURE OF YOURSELF, YOU WON'T MIND RACING ME ACROSS THE LAKE!
WHY SHOULD I MIND?
BECAUSE THE LAKE IS ONLY PARTIALLY FROZEN, VERONICA, AND IF YOU FALL THROUGH THE ICE, YOU'LL DROWN!
13

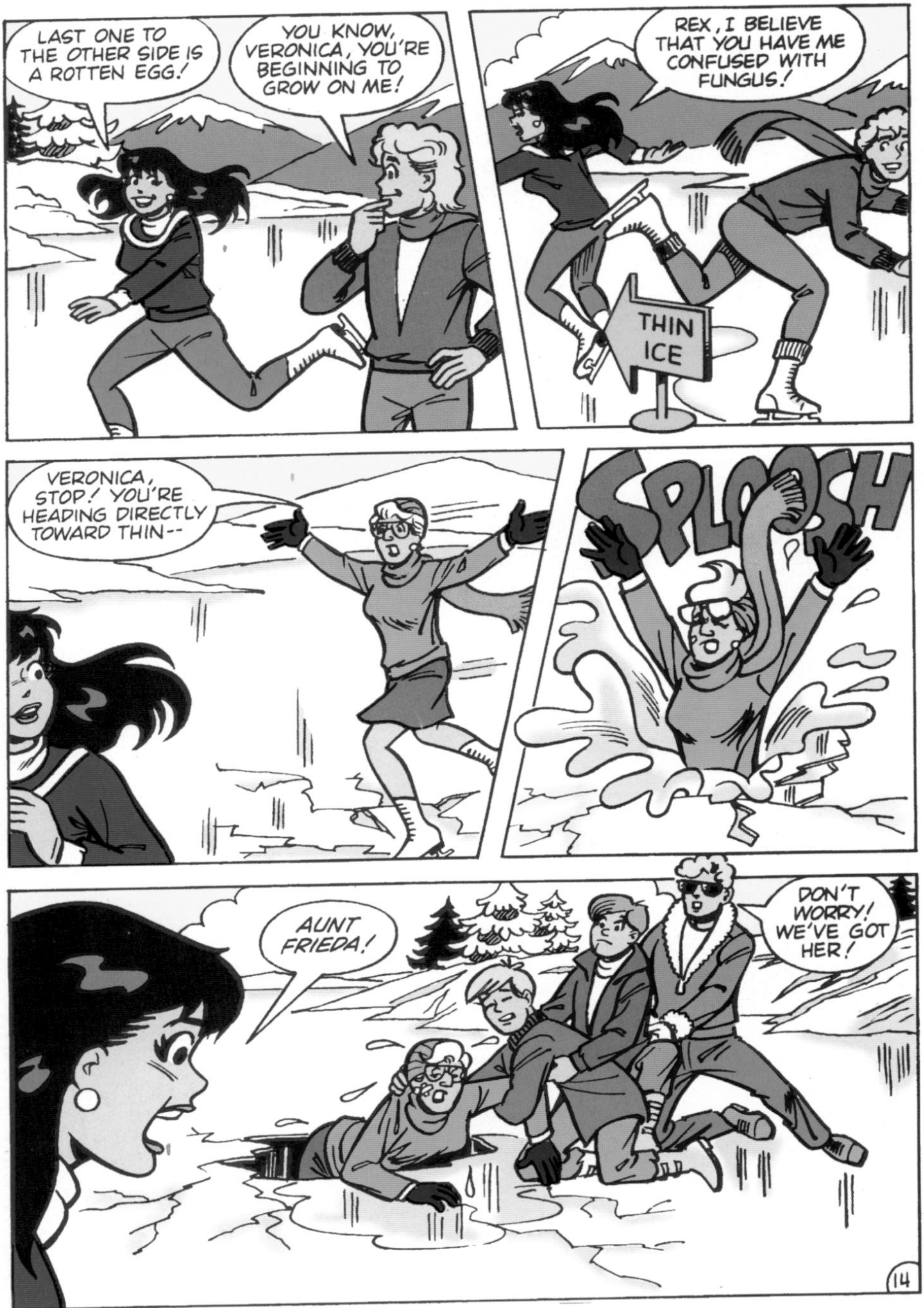
LAST ONE TO THE OTHER SIDE IS A ROTTEN EGG!
YOU KNOW, VERONICA, YOU'RE BEGINNING TO GROW ON ME!
REX, I BELIEVE THAT YOU HAVE ME CONFUSED WITH FUNGUS!
THIN ICE
VERONICA, STOP! YOU'RE HEADING DIRECTLY TOWARD THIN--
SPLOOSH
AUNT FRIEDA!
DON'T WORRY! WE'VE GOT HER!
14

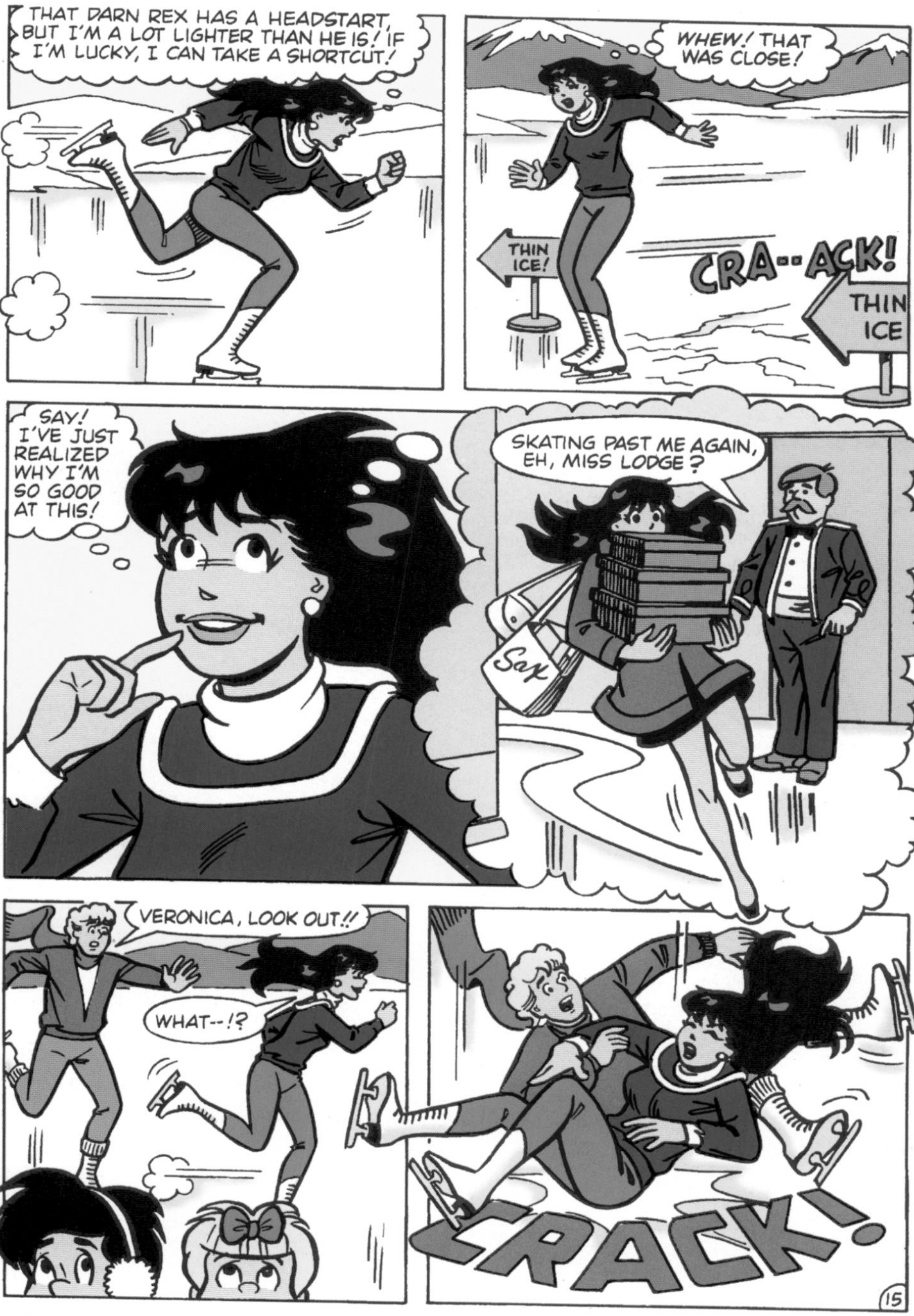
THAT DARN REX HAS A HEADSTART, BUT I'M A LOT LIGHTER THAN HE IS! IF I'M LUCKY, I CAN TAKE A SHORTCUT!
WHEW! THAT WAS CLOSE!
THIN ICE!
CRA--ACK!
THIN ICE
SAY! I'VE JUST REALIZED WHY I'M SO GOOD AT THIS!
SKATING PAST ME AGAIN, EH, MISS LODGE?
VERONICA, LOOK OUT!!
WHAT--!?
CRACK!
15

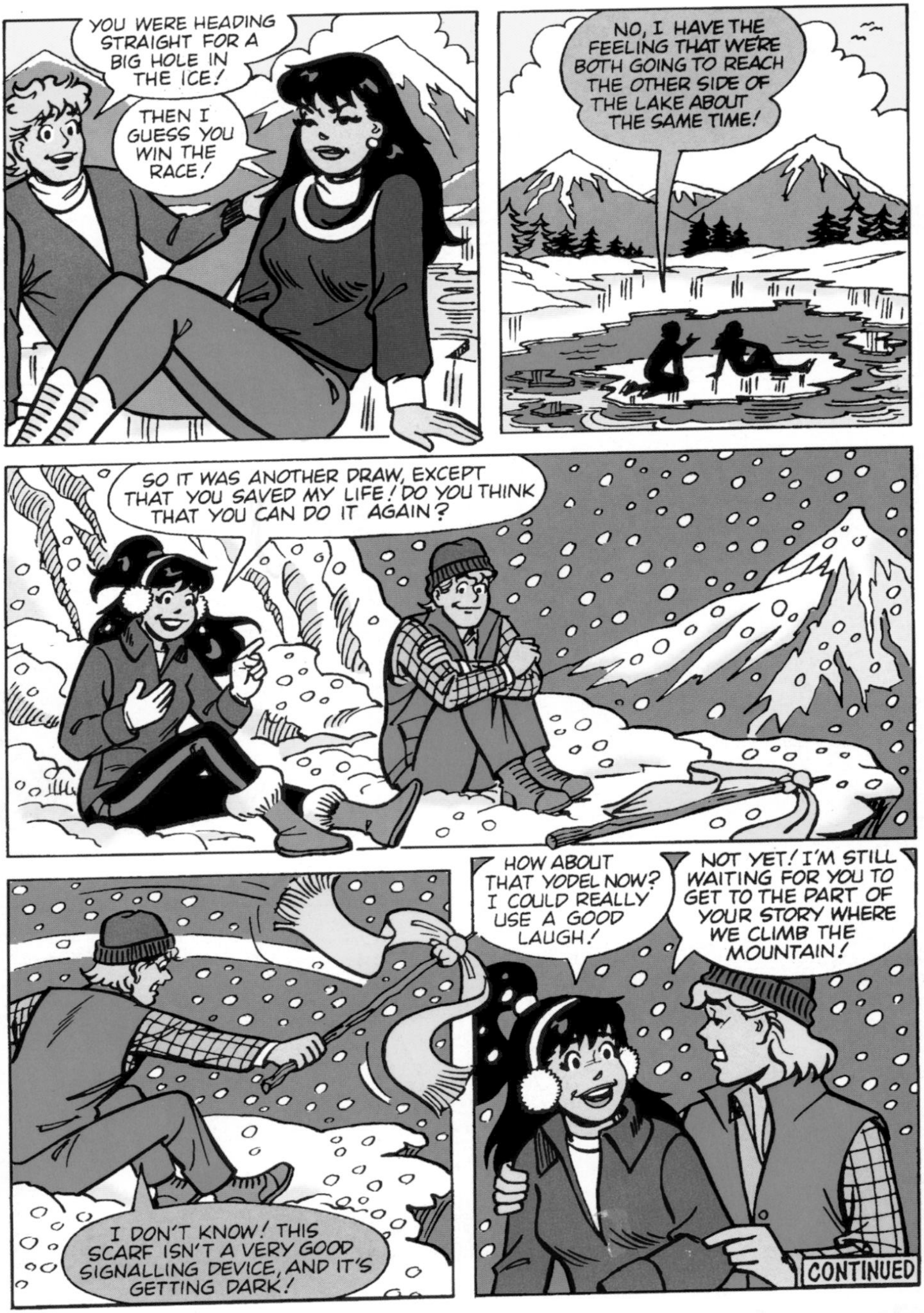
YOU WERE HEADING STRAIGHT FOR A BIG HOLE IN THE ICE!
THEN I GUESS YOU WIN THE RACE!
NO, I HAVE THE FEELING THAT WE'RE BOTH GOING TO REACH THE OTHER SIDE OF THE LAKE ABOUT THE SAME TIME!
SO IT WAS ANOTHER DRAW, EXCEPT THAT YOU SAVED MY LIFE! DO YOU THINK THAT YOU CAN DO IT AGAIN?
I DON'T KNOW! THIS SCARF ISN'T A VERY GOOD SIGNALLING DEVICE, AND IT'S GETTING DARK!
HOW ABOUT THAT YODEL NOW? I COULD REALLY USE A GOOD LAUGH!
NOT YET! I'M STILL WAITING FOR YOU TO GET TO THE PART OF YOUR STORY WHERE WE CLIMB THE MOUNTAIN!
CONTINUED

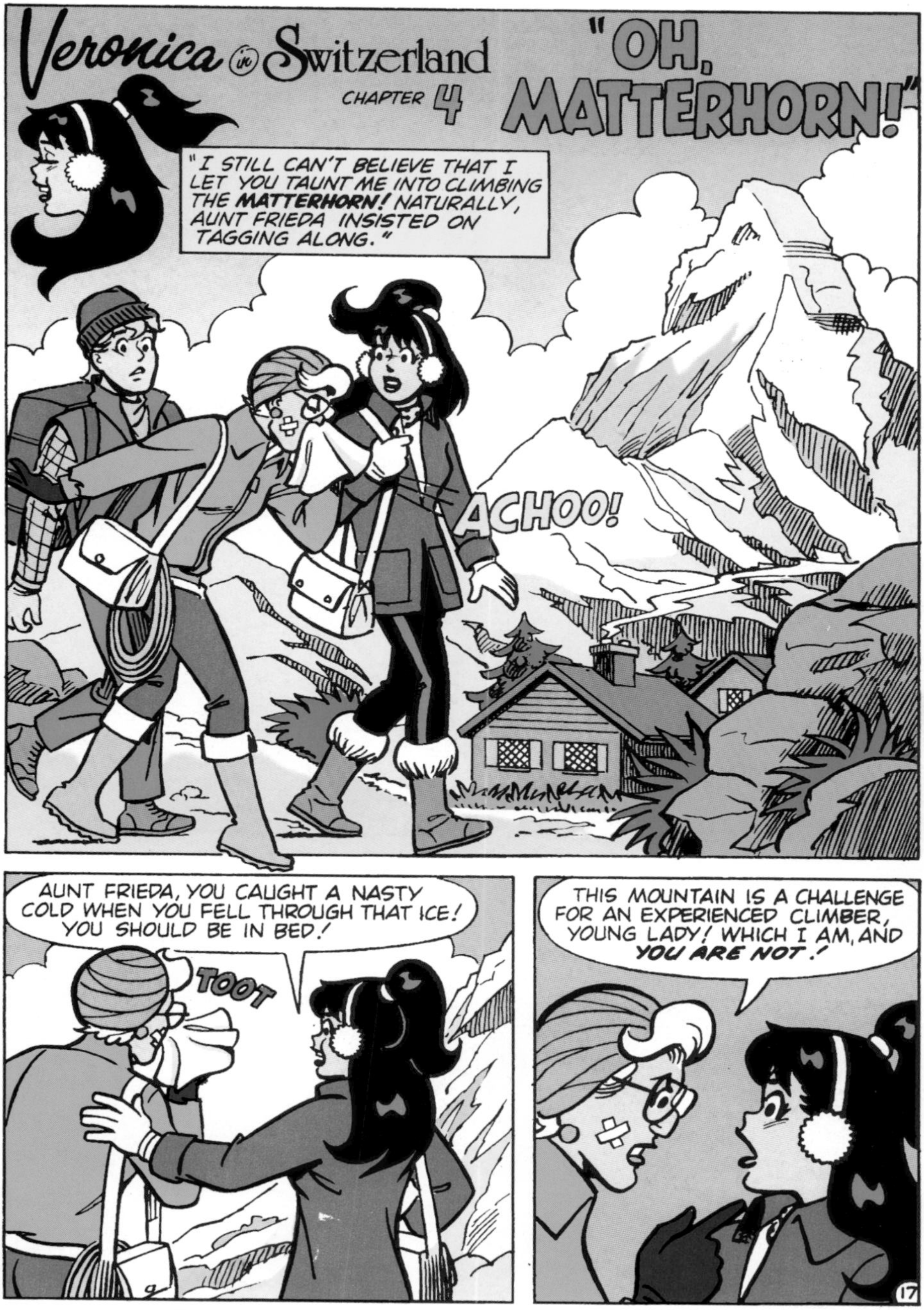
Veronica in Switzerland
CHAPTER 4
"OH, MATTERHORN!"
"I STILL CAN'T BELIEVE THAT I LET YOU TAUNT ME INTO CLIMBING THE MATTERHORN! NATURALLY, AUNT FRIEDA INSISTED ON TAGGING ALONG."
ACHOO!
AUNT FRIEDA, YOU CAUGHT A NASTY COLD WHEN YOU FELL THROUGH THAT ICE! YOU SHOULD BE IN BED!
TOOT
THIS MOUNTAIN IS A CHALLENGE FOR AN EXPERIENCED CLIMBER, YOUNG LADY! WHICH I AM, AND YOU ARE NOT!
17

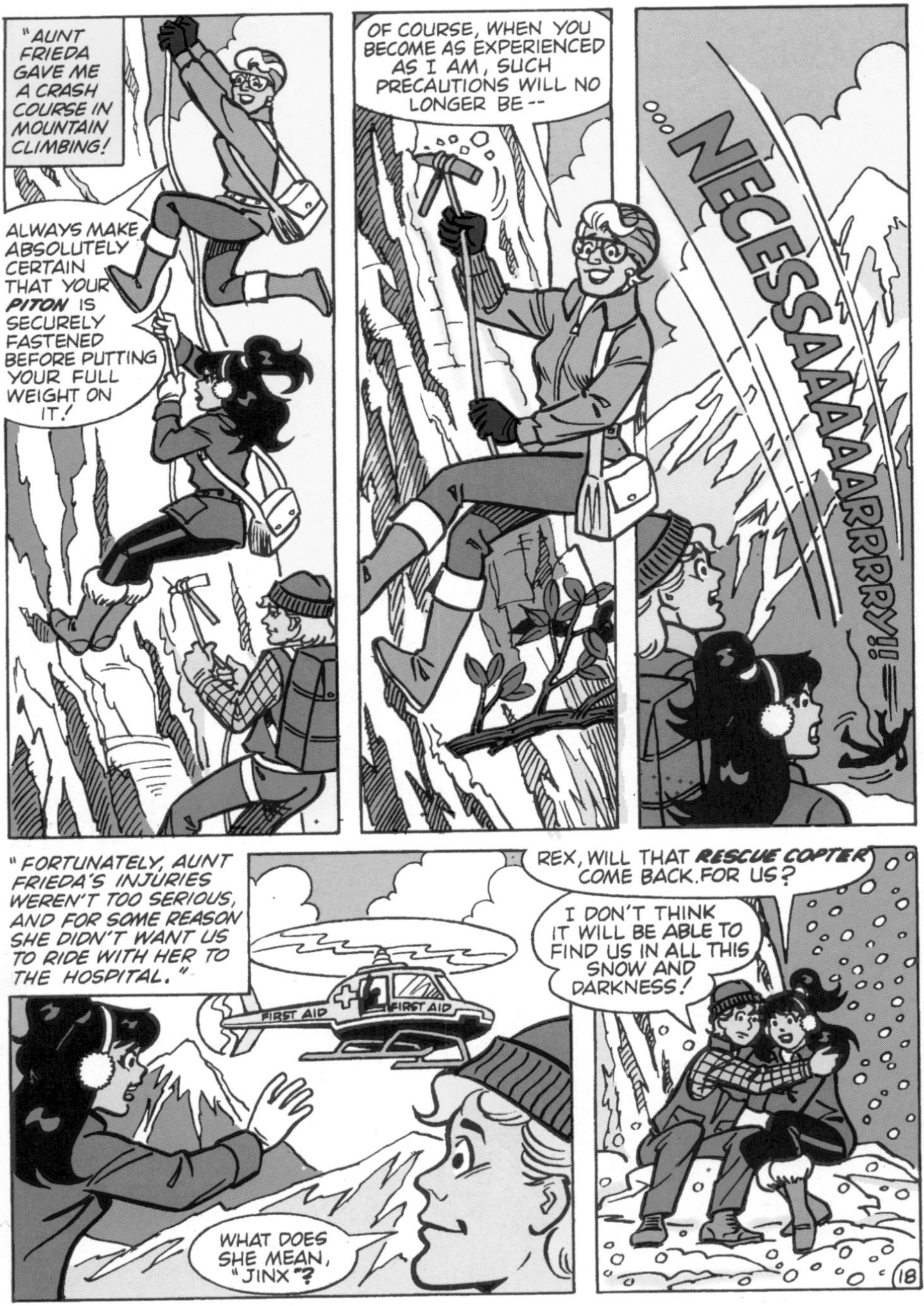
"AUNT FRIEDA GAVE ME A CRASH COURSE IN MOUNTAIN CLIMBING!
ALWAYS MAKE ABSOLUTELY CERTAIN THAT YOUR PITON IS SECURELY FASTENED BEFORE PUTTING YOUR FULL WEIGHT ON IT!
OF COURSE, WHEN YOU BECOME AS EXPERIENCED AS I AM, SUCH PRECAUTIONS WILL NO LONGER BE--
NECESSAAAAARRRY!!
"FORTUNATELY, AUNT FRIEDA'S INJURIES WEREN'T TOO SERIOUS, AND FOR SOME REASON SHE DIDN'T WANT US TO RIDE WITH HER TO THE HOSPITAL."
FIRST AID
FIRST AID
WHAT DOES SHE MEAN, "JINX"?
REX, WILL THAT RESCUE COPTER COME BACK FOR US?
I DON'T THINK IT WILL BE ABLE TO FIND US IN ALL THIS SNOW AND DARKNESS!
18

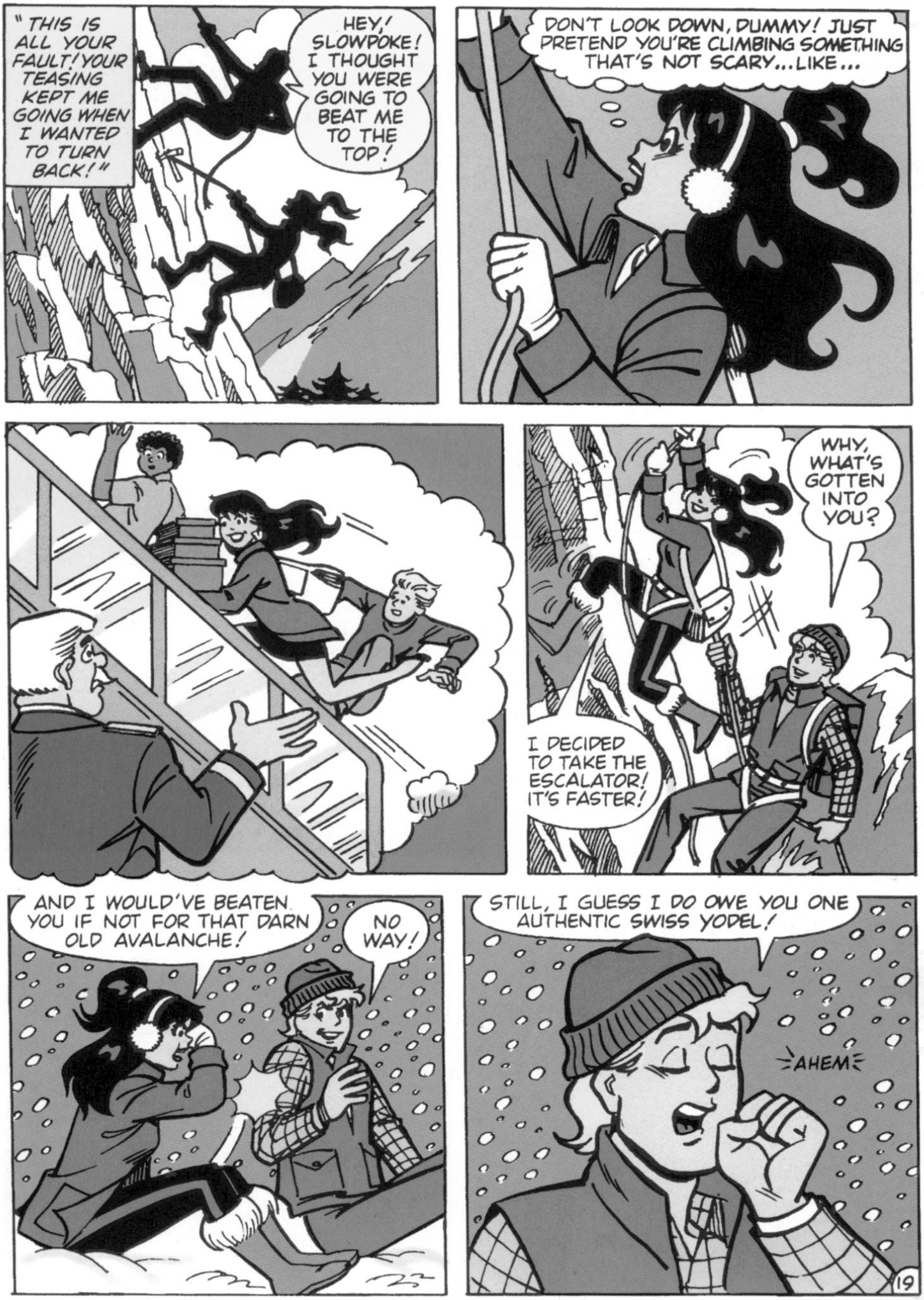
"THIS IS ALL YOUR FAULT! YOUR TEASING KEPT ME GOING WHEN I WANTED TO TURN BACK!"
HEY! SLOWPOKE! I THOUGHT YOU WERE GOING TO BEAT ME TO THE TOP!
DON'T LOOK DOWN, DUMMY! JUST PRETEND YOU'RE CLIMBING SOMETHING THAT'S NOT SCARY...LIKE...
WHY, WHAT'S GOTTEN INTO YOU?
I DECIDED TO TAKE THE ESCALATOR! IT'S FASTER!
AND I WOULD'VE BEATEN YOU IF NOT FOR THAT DARN OLD AVALANCHE!
NO WAY!
STILL, I GUESS I DO OWE YOU ONE AUTHENTIC SWISS YODEL!
AHEM
19

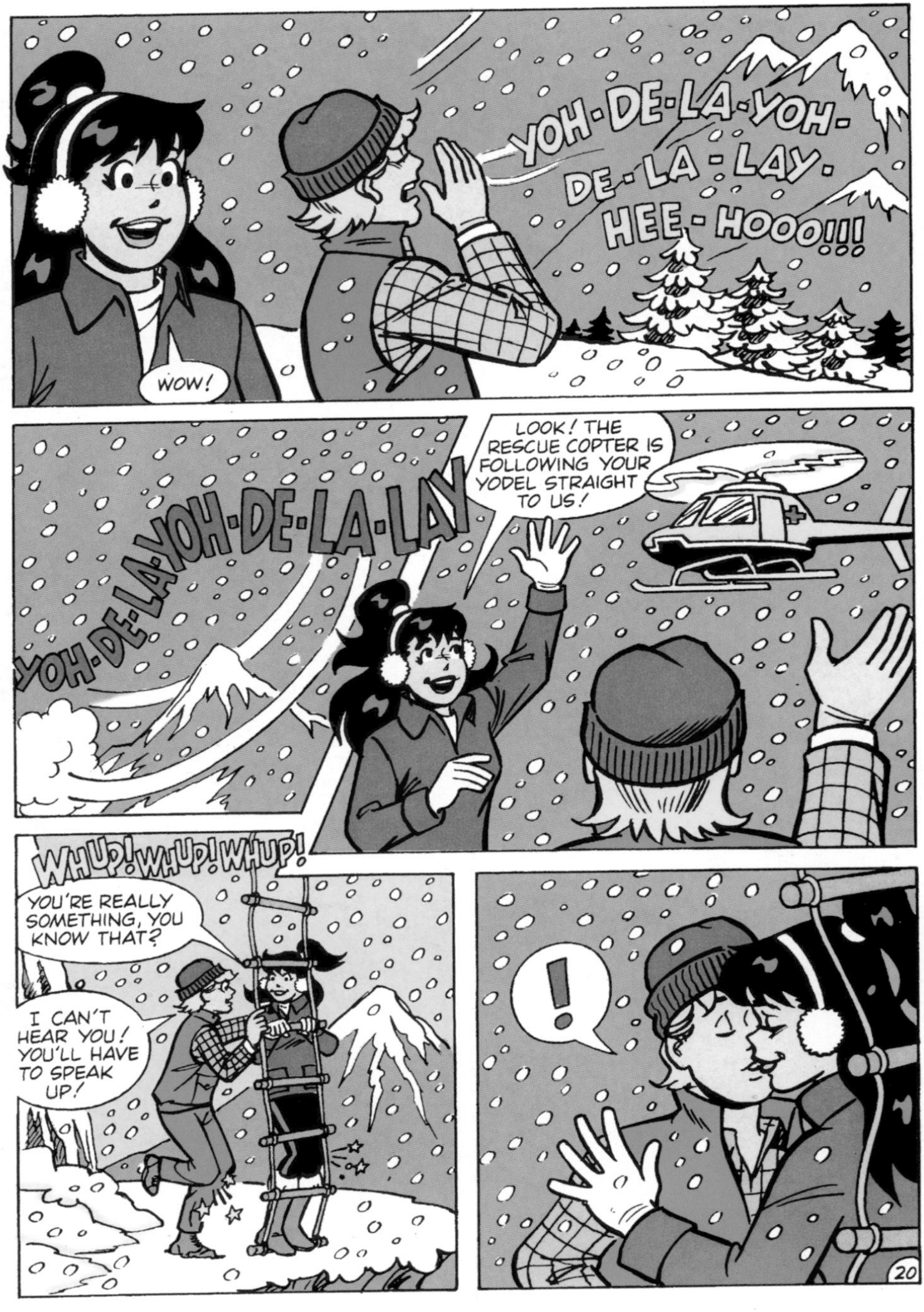
YOH-DE-LA-YOH-
DE-LA-LAY-
HEE-HOOO!!!
WOW!
LOOK! THE RESCUE COPTER IS FOLLOWING YOUR YODEL STRAIGHT TO US!
YOH-DE-LA-YOH-DE-LA-LAY
WHUP! WHUP! WHUP!
YOU'RE REALLY SOMETHING, YOU KNOW THAT?
I CAN'T HEAR YOU! YOU'LL HAVE TO SPEAK UP!
!
20

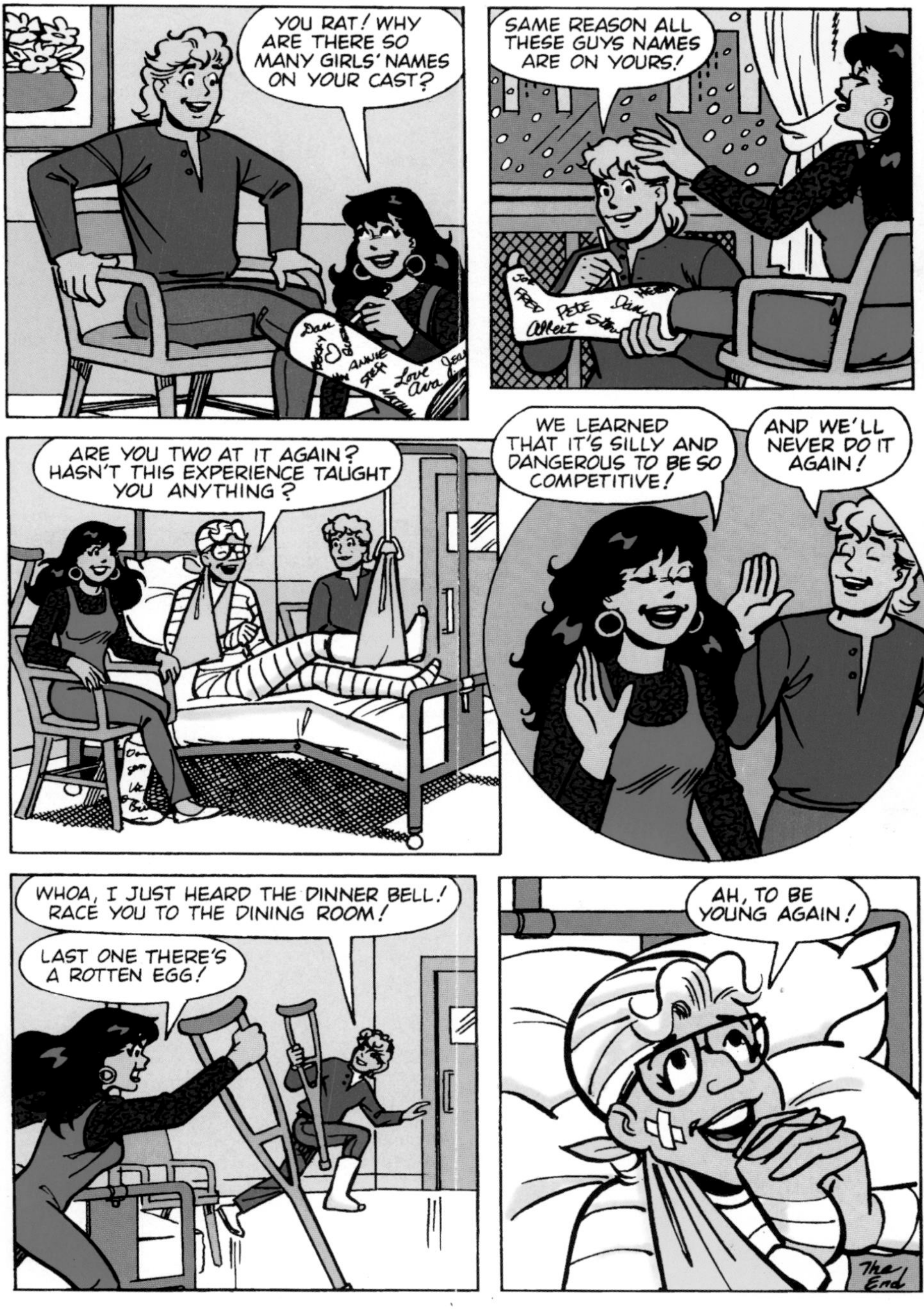
YOU RAT! WHY ARE THERE SO MANY GIRLS' NAMES ON YOUR CAST?
SAME REASON ALL THESE GUYS NAMES ARE ON YOURS!
ARE YOU TWO AT IT AGAIN? HASN'T THIS EXPERIENCE TAUGHT YOU ANYTHING?
WE LEARNED THAT IT'S SILLY AND DANGEROUS TO BE SO COMPETITIVE!
AND WE'LL NEVER DO IT AGAIN!
WHOA, I JUST HEARD THE DINNER BELL! RACE YOU TO THE DINING ROOM!
LAST ONE THERE'S A ROTTEN EGG!
AH, TO BE YOUNG AGAIN!
The End

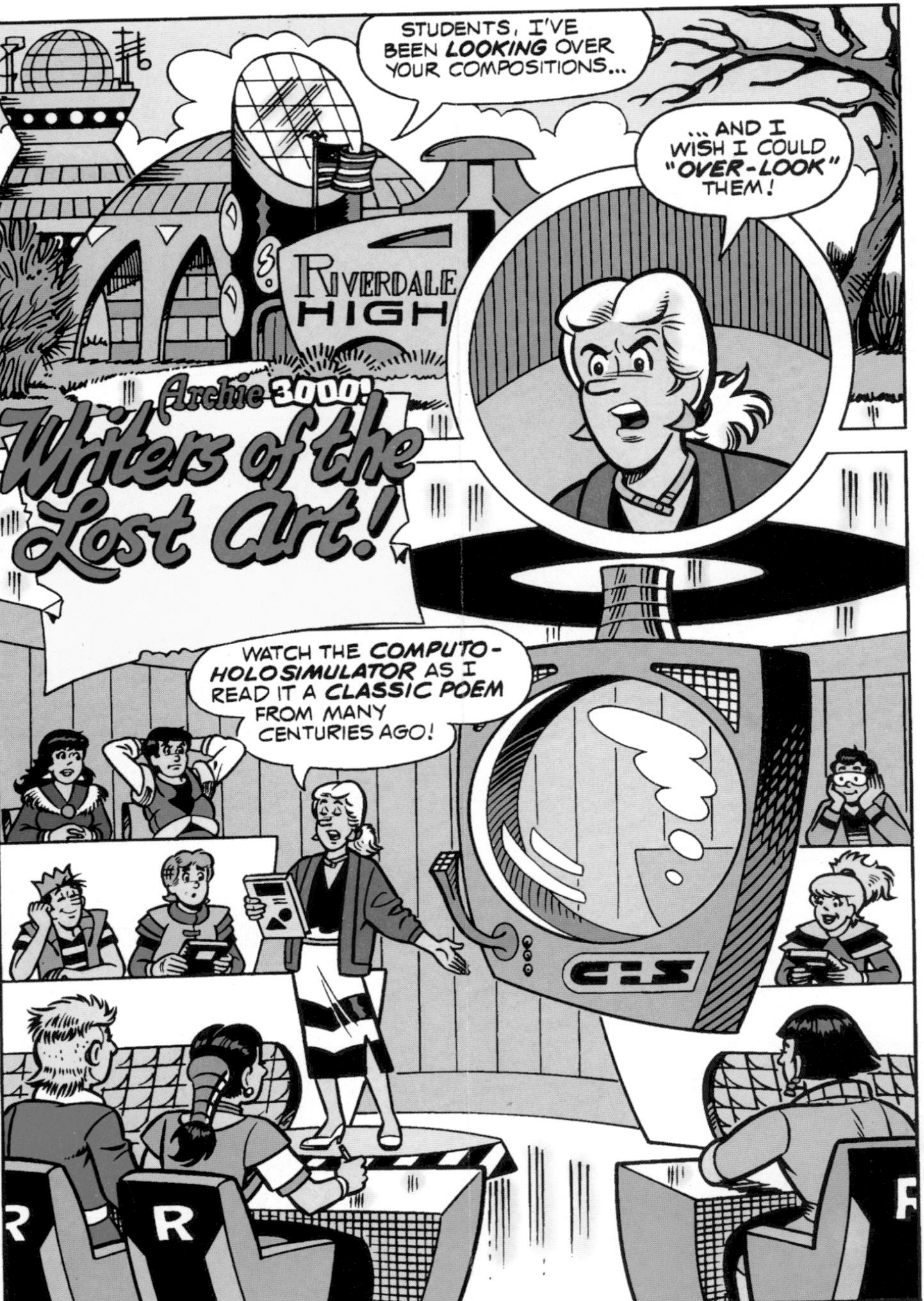
STUDENTS, I'VE BEEN LOOKING OVER YOUR COMPOSITIONS...
...AND I WISH I COULD "OVER-LOOK" THEM!
RIVERDALE HIGH
Archie 3000!
Writers of the Lost Art!
WATCH THE COMPUTO-HOLOSIMULATOR AS I READ IT A CLASSIC POEM FROM MANY CENTURIES AGO!
CHS
R
R

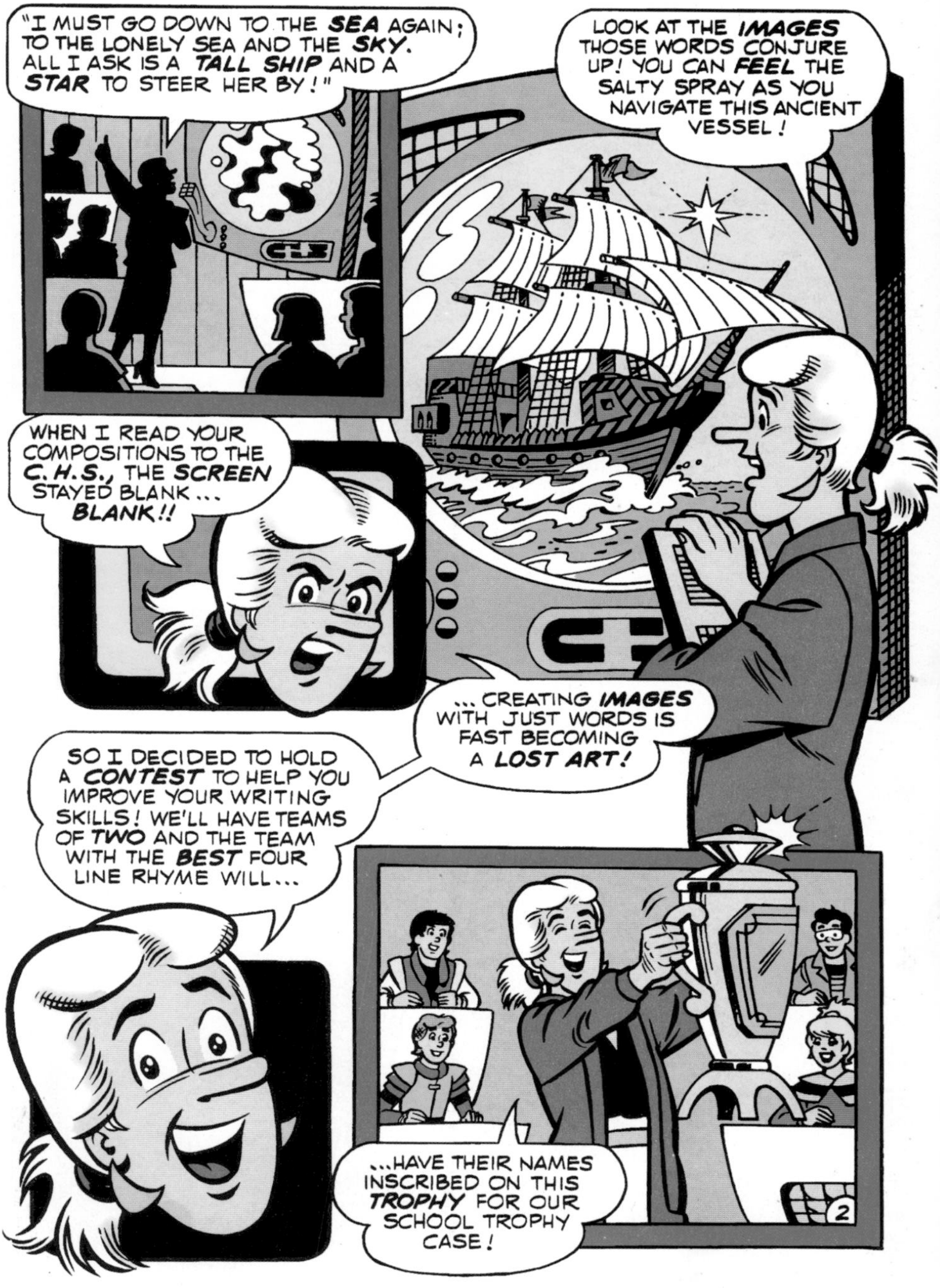
"I MUST GO DOWN TO THE SEA AGAIN; TO THE LONELY SEA AND THE SKY. ALL I ASK IS A TALL SHIP AND A STAR TO STEER HER BY!"
LOOK AT THE IMAGES THOSE WORDS CONJURE UP! YOU CAN FEEL THE SALTY SPRAY AS YOU NAVIGATE THIS ANCIENT VESSEL!
WHEN I READ YOUR COMPOSITIONS TO THE C.H.S., THE SCREEN STAYED BLANK... BLANK!!
...CREATING IMAGES WITH JUST WORDS IS FAST BECOMING A LOST ART!
SO I DECIDED TO HOLD A CONTEST TO HELP YOU IMPROVE YOUR WRITING SKILLS! WE'LL HAVE TEAMS OF TWO AND THE TEAM WITH THE BEST FOUR LINE RHYME WILL...
...HAVE THEIR NAMES INSCRIBED ON THIS TROPHY FOR OUR SCHOOL TROPHY CASE!
2

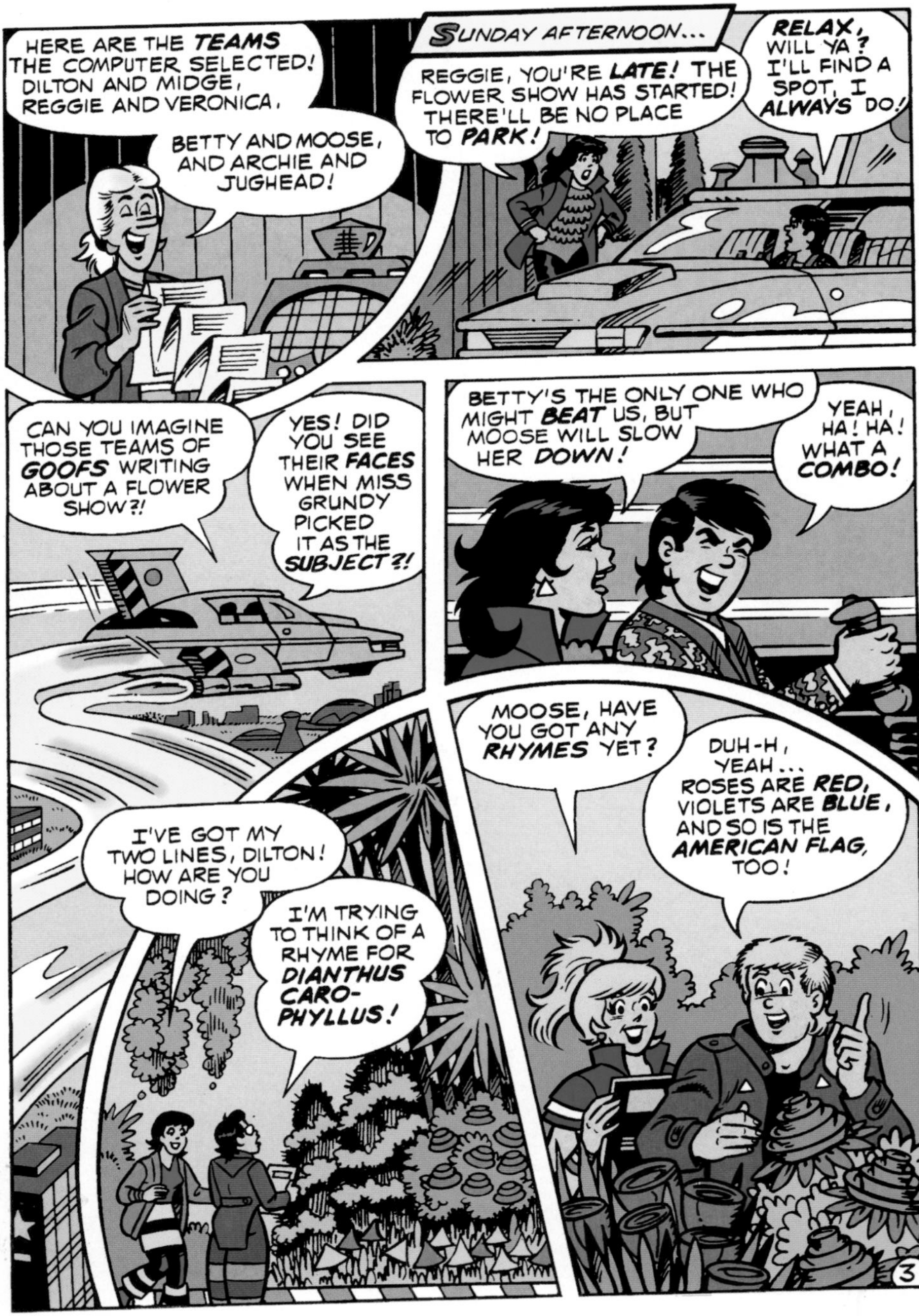
HERE ARE THE TEAMS THE COMPUTER SELECTED! DILTON AND MIDGE, REGGIE AND VERONICA,
BETTY AND MOOSE, AND ARCHIE AND JUGHEAD!
SUNDAY AFTERNOON...
REGGIE, YOU'RE LATE! THE FLOWER SHOW HAS STARTED! THERE'LL BE NO PLACE TO PARK!
RELAX, WILL YA? I'LL FIND A SPOT, I ALWAYS DO!
CAN YOU IMAGINE THOSE TEAMS OF GOOFS WRITING ABOUT A FLOWER SHOW?!
YES! DID YOU SEE THEIR FACES WHEN MISS GRUNDY PICKED IT AS THE SUBJECT?!
BETTY'S THE ONLY ONE WHO MIGHT BEAT US, BUT MOOSE WILL SLOW HER DOWN!
YEAH, HA! HA! WHAT A COMBO!
I'VE GOT MY TWO LINES, DILTON! HOW ARE YOU DOING?
I'M TRYING TO THINK OF A RHYME FOR DIANTHUS CARO-PHYLLUS!
MOOSE, HAVE YOU GOT ANY RHYMES YET?
DUH-H, YEAH... ROSES ARE RED, VIOLETS ARE BLUE, AND SO IS THE AMERICAN FLAG, TOO!
3

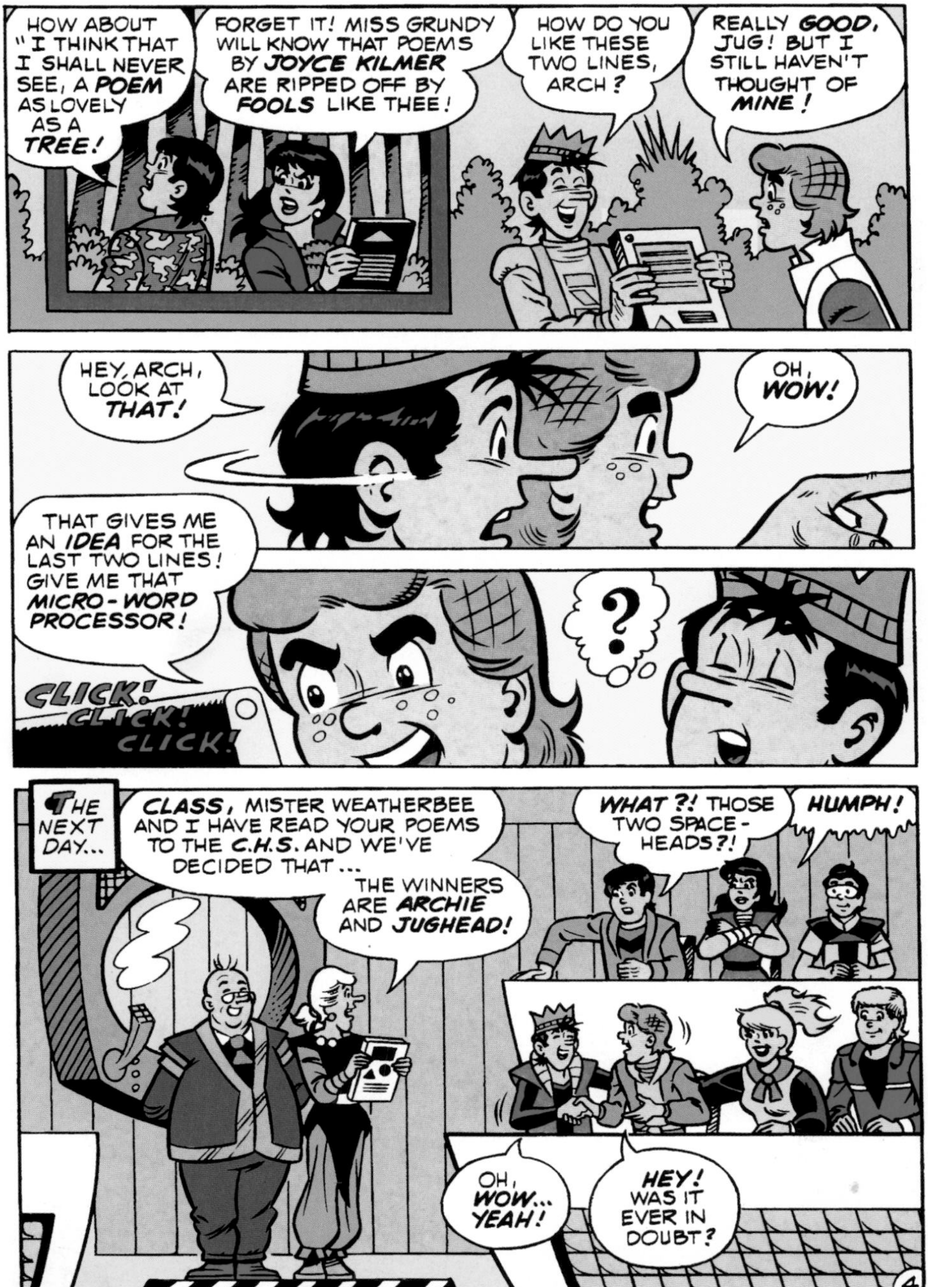
HOW ABOUT "I THINK THAT I SHALL NEVER SEE, A POEM AS LOVELY AS A TREE!
FORGET IT! MISS GRUNDY WILL KNOW THAT POEMS BY JOYCE KILMER ARE RIPPED OFF BY FOOLS LIKE THEE!
HOW DO YOU LIKE THESE TWO LINES, ARCH?
REALLY GOOD, JUG! BUT I STILL HAVEN'T THOUGHT OF MINE!
HEY, ARCH, LOOK AT THAT!
OH, WOW!
THAT GIVES ME AN IDEA FOR THE LAST TWO LINES! GIVE ME THAT MICRO-WORD PROCESSOR!
CLICK! CLICK! CLICK!
?
THE NEXT DAY...
CLASS, MISTER WEATHERBEE AND I HAVE READ YOUR POEMS TO THE C.H.S. AND WE'VE DECIDED THAT...
THE WINNERS ARE ARCHIE AND JUGHEAD!
WHAT?! THOSE TWO SPACE-HEADS?!
HUMPH!
OH, WOW... YEAH!
HEY! WAS IT EVER IN DOUBT?
4

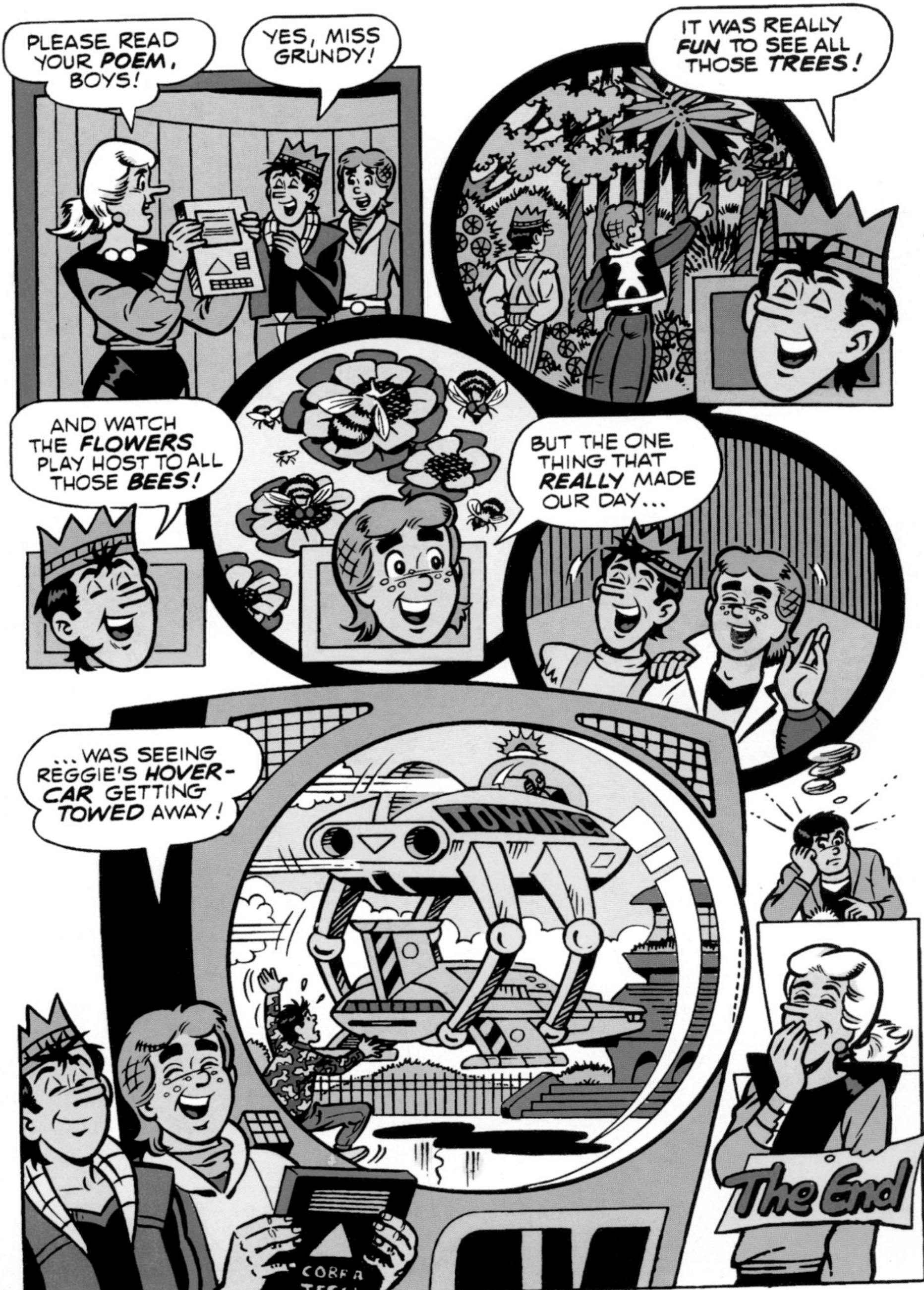
PLEASE READ YOUR POEM, BOYS!
YES, MISS GRUNDY!
IT WAS REALLY FUN TO SEE ALL THOSE TREES!
AND WATCH THE FLOWERS PLAY HOST TO ALL THOSE BEES!
BUT THE ONE THING THAT REALLY MADE OUR DAY...
...WAS SEEING REGGIE'S HOVER-CAR GETTING TOWED AWAY!
TOWING
The End

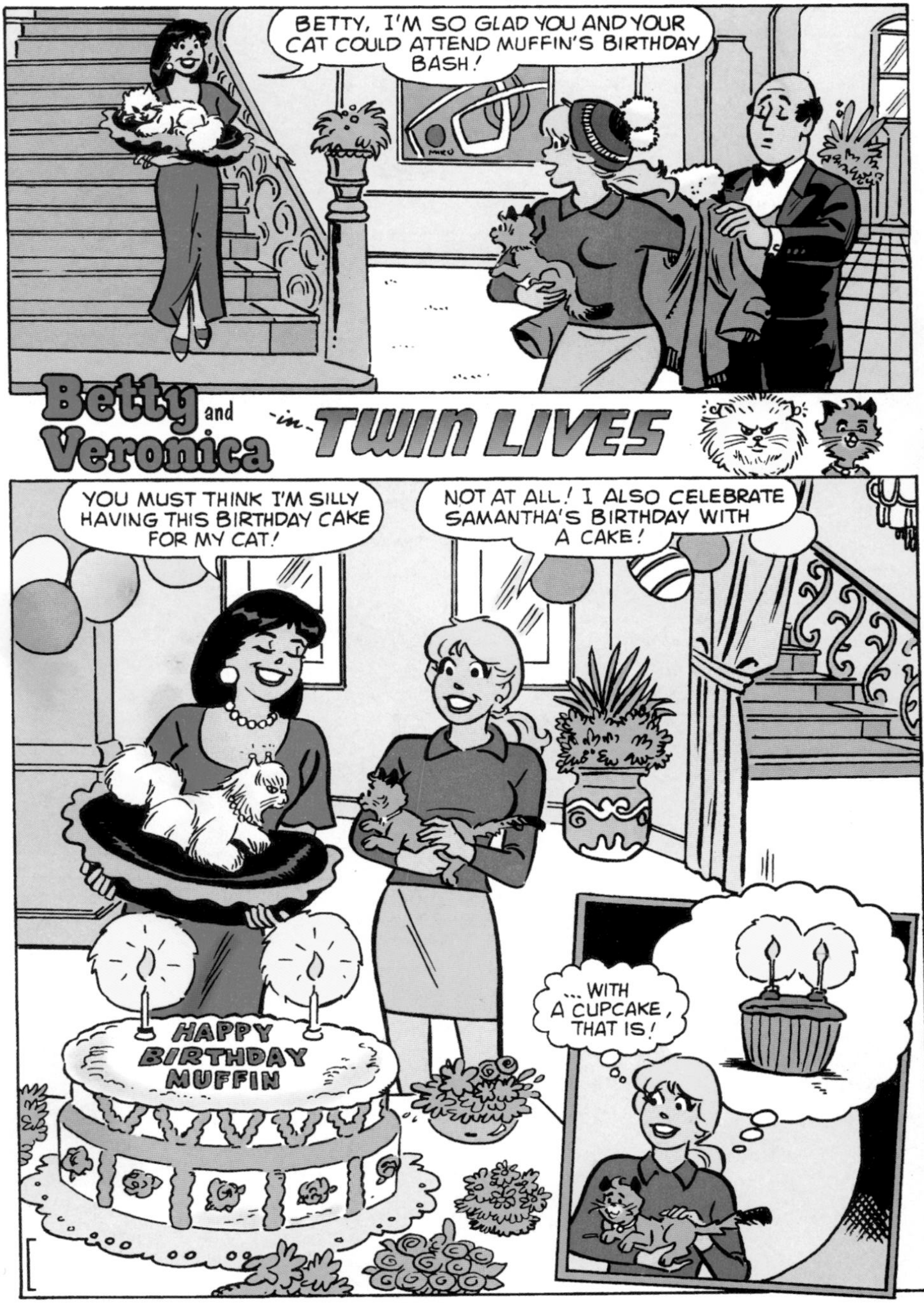
BETTY, I'M SO GLAD YOU AND YOUR CAT COULD ATTEND MUFFIN'S BIRTHDAY BASH!
Betty and Veronica in TWIN LIVES
YOU MUST THINK I'M SILLY HAVING THIS BIRTHDAY CAKE FOR MY CAT!
NOT AT ALL! I ALSO CELEBRATE SAMANTHA'S BIRTHDAY WITH A CAKE!
HAPPY BIRTHDAY MUFFIN
...WITH A CUPCAKE, THAT IS!

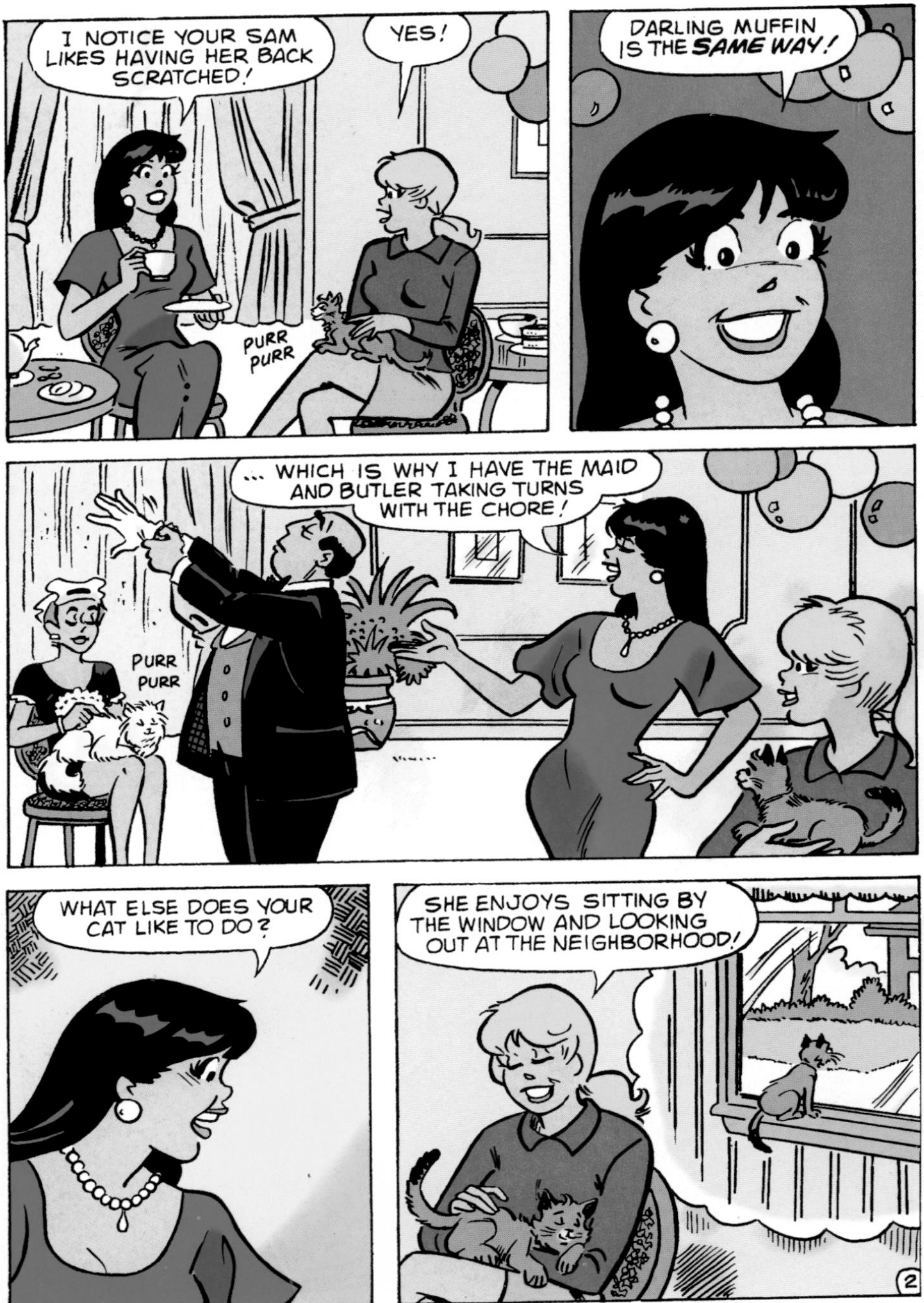
I NOTICE YOUR SAM LIKES HAVING HER BACK SCRATCHED!
YES!
PURR PURR
DARLING MUFFIN IS THE *SAME WAY*!
... WHICH IS WHY I HAVE THE MAID AND BUTLER TAKING TURNS WITH THE CHORE!
PURR PURR
WHAT ELSE DOES YOUR CAT LIKE TO DO?
SHE ENJOYS SITTING BY THE WINDOW AND LOOKING OUT AT THE NEIGHBORHOOD!
2

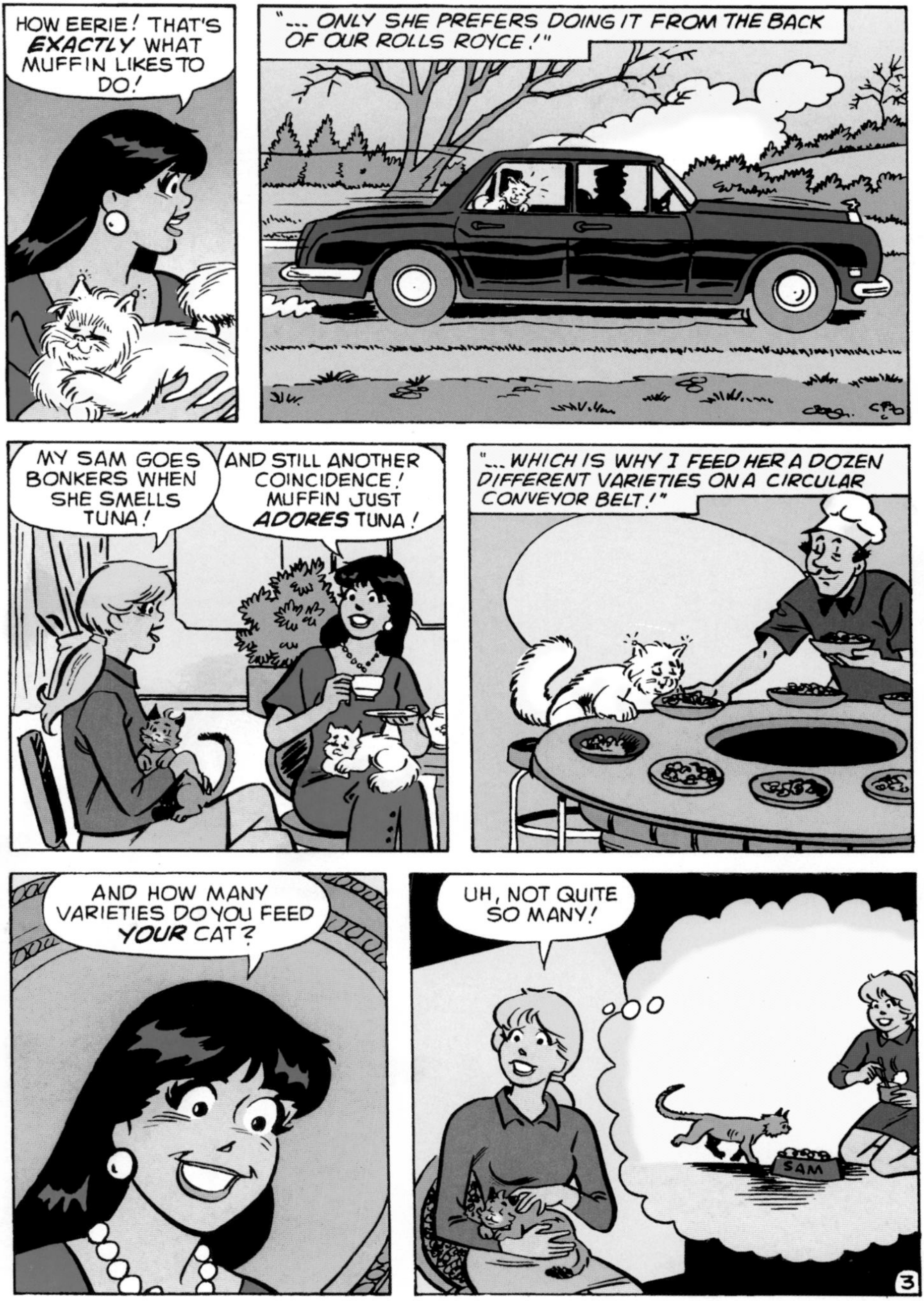
HOW EERIE! THAT'S EXACTLY WHAT MUFFIN LIKES TO DO!
"... ONLY SHE PREFERS DOING IT FROM THE BACK OF OUR ROLLS ROYCE!"
MY SAM GOES BONKERS WHEN SHE SMELLS TUNA!
AND STILL ANOTHER COINCIDENCE! MUFFIN JUST ADORES TUNA!
"... WHICH IS WHY I FEED HER A DOZEN DIFFERENT VARIETIES ON A CIRCULAR CONVEYOR BELT!"
AND HOW MANY VARIETIES DO YOU FEED YOUR CAT?
UH, NOT QUITE SO MANY!
SAM
3

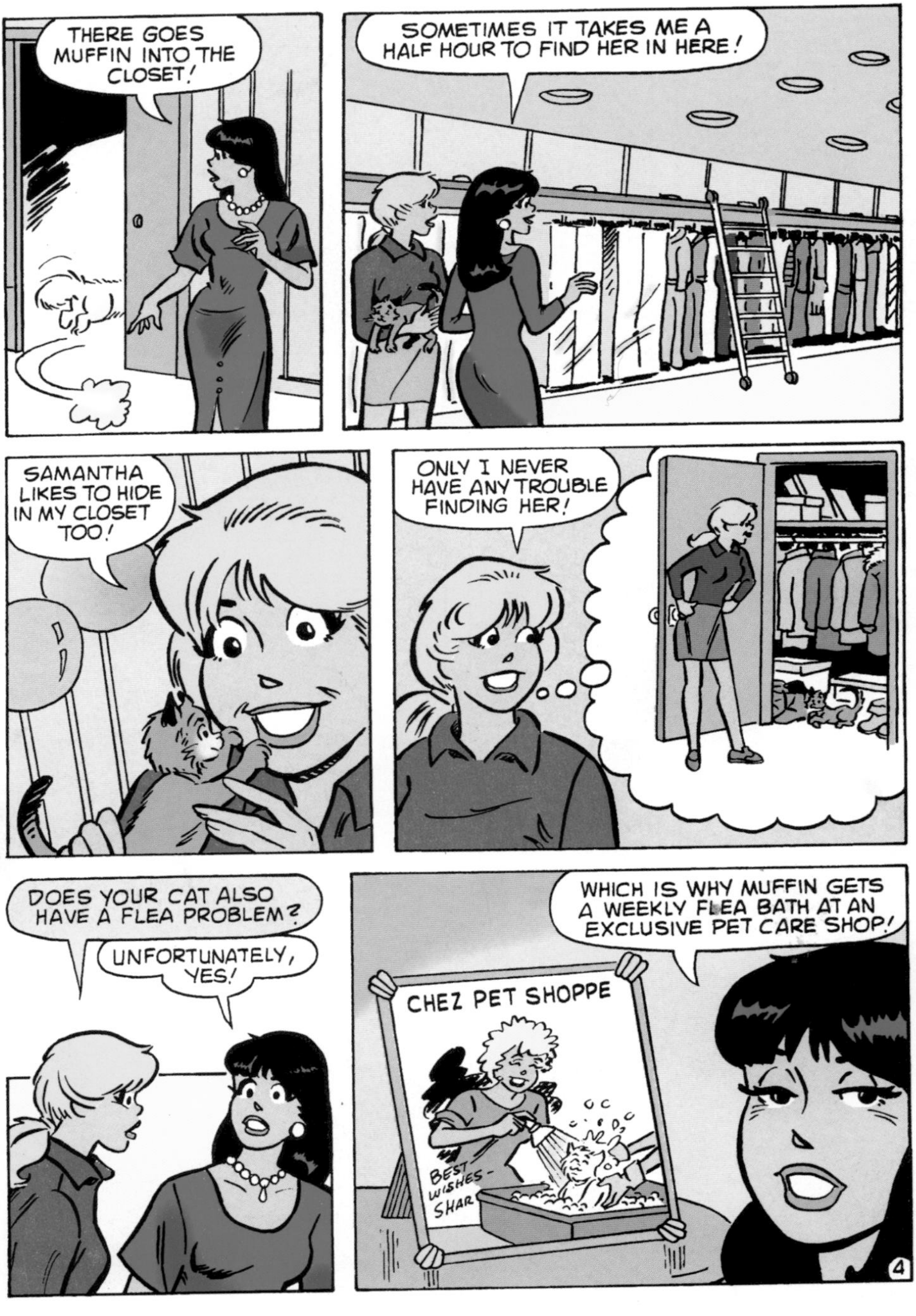
THERE GOES MUFFIN INTO THE CLOSET!
SOMETIMES IT TAKES ME A HALF HOUR TO FIND HER IN HERE!
SAMANTHA LIKES TO HIDE IN MY CLOSET TOO!
ONLY I NEVER HAVE ANY TROUBLE FINDING HER!
DOES YOUR CAT ALSO HAVE A FLEA PROBLEM?
UNFORTUNATELY, YES!
WHICH IS WHY MUFFIN GETS A WEEKLY FLEA BATH AT AN EXCLUSIVE PET CARE SHOP!
CHEZ PET SHOPPE
BEST WISHES - SHAR
4

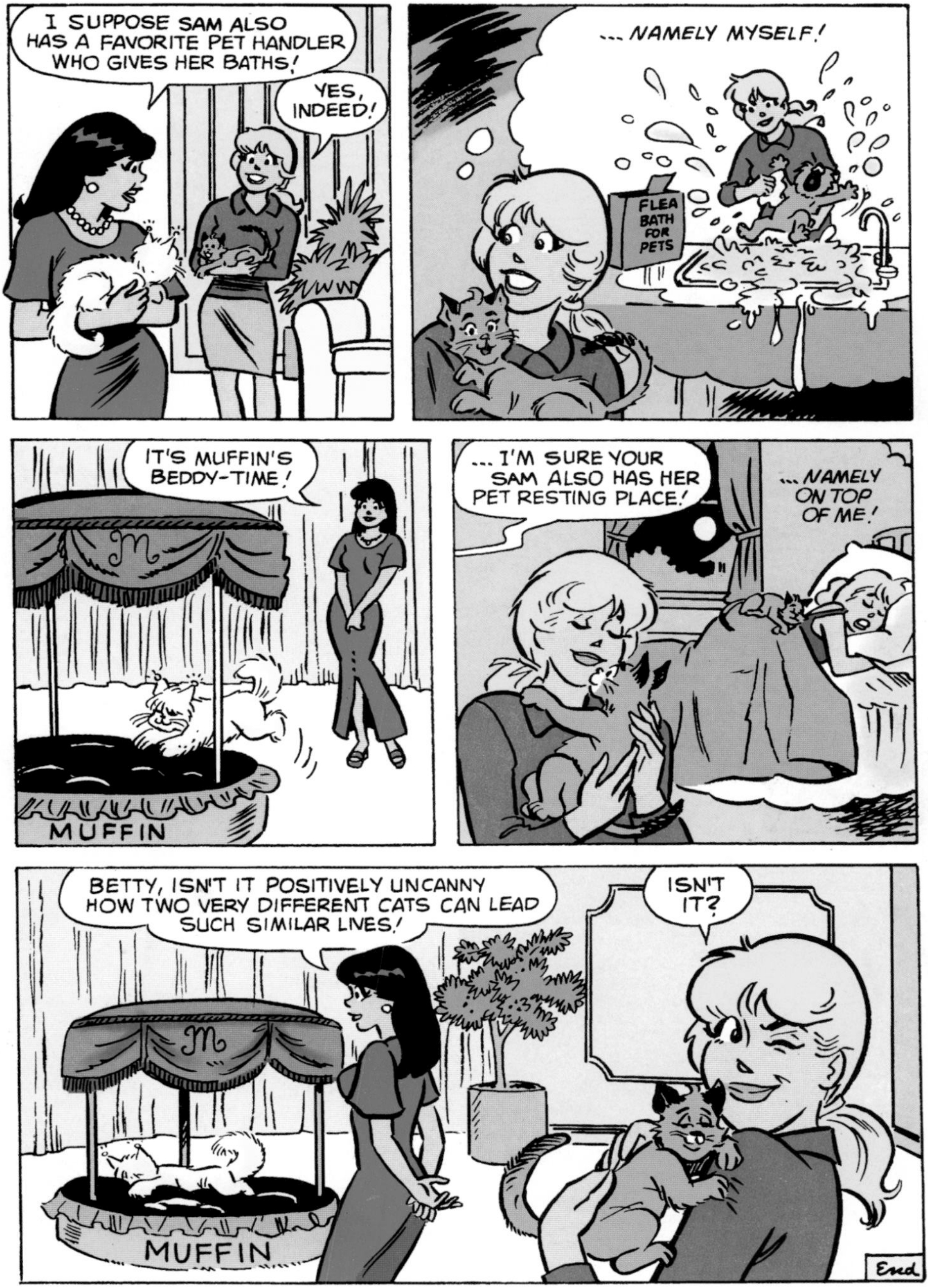
I SUPPOSE SAM ALSO HAS A FAVORITE PET HANDLER WHO GIVES HER BATHS!
YES, INDEED!
...NAMELY MYSELF!
FLEA BATH FOR PETS
IT'S MUFFIN'S BEDDY-TIME!
MUFFIN
...I'M SURE YOUR SAM ALSO HAS HER PET RESTING PLACE!
...NAMELY ON TOP OF ME!
BETTY, ISN'T IT POSITIVELY UNCANNY HOW TWO VERY DIFFERENT CATS CAN LEAD SUCH SIMILAR LIVES!
ISN'T IT?
MUFFIN
End

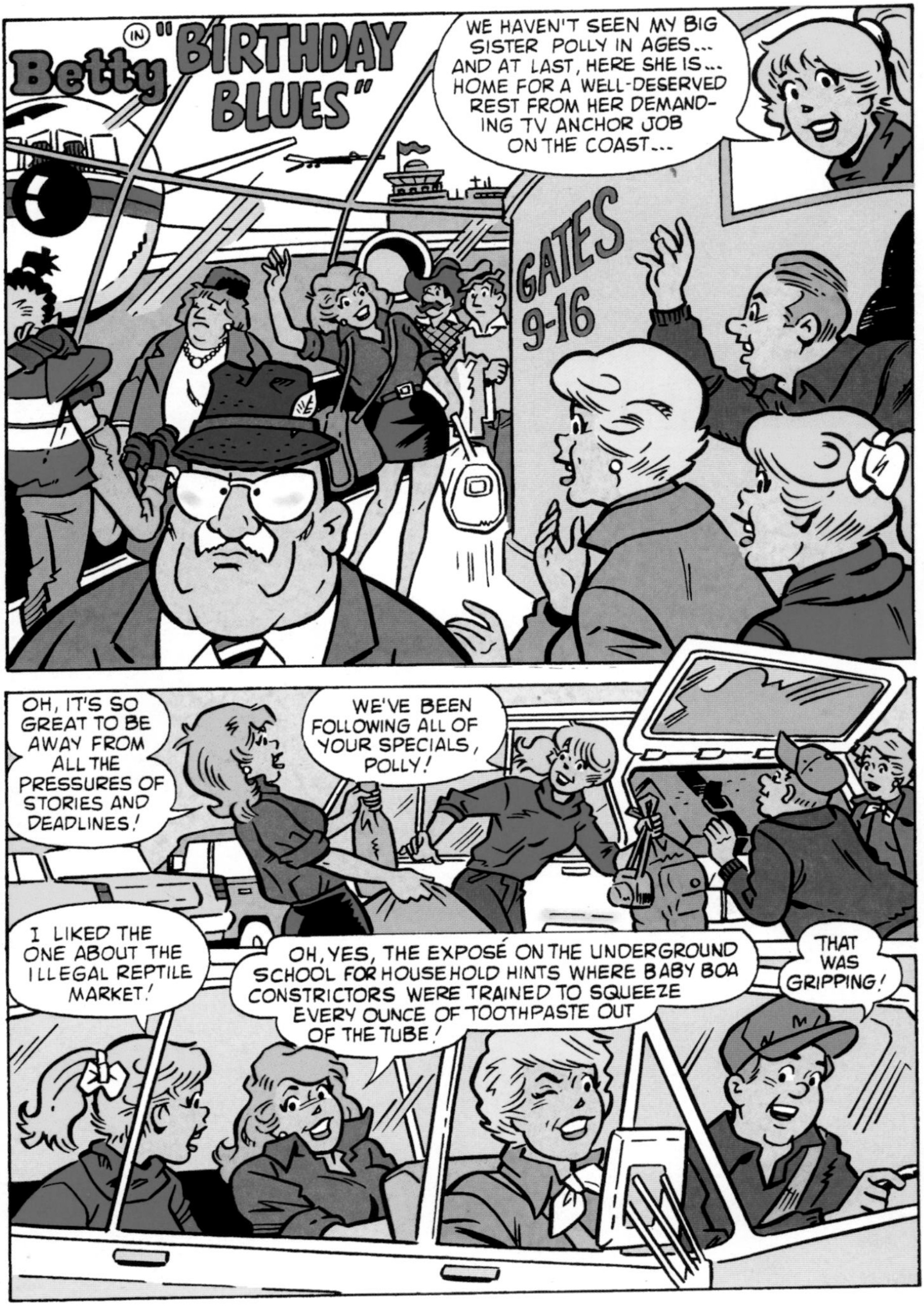
Betty (IN) "BIRTHDAY BLUES"
WE HAVEN'T SEEN MY BIG SISTER POLLY IN AGES... AND AT LAST, HERE SHE IS... HOME FOR A WELL-DESERVED REST FROM HER DEMANDING TV ANCHOR JOB ON THE COAST...
GATES 9-16
OH, IT'S SO GREAT TO BE AWAY FROM ALL THE PRESSURES OF STORIES AND DEADLINES!
WE'VE BEEN FOLLOWING ALL OF YOUR SPECIALS, POLLY!
I LIKED THE ONE ABOUT THE ILLEGAL REPTILE MARKET!
OH, YES, THE EXPOSÉ ON THE UNDERGROUND SCHOOL FOR HOUSEHOLD HINTS WHERE BABY BOA CONSTRICTORS WERE TRAINED TO SQUEEZE EVERY OUNCE OF TOOTHPASTE OUT OF THE TUBE!
THAT WAS GRIPPING!

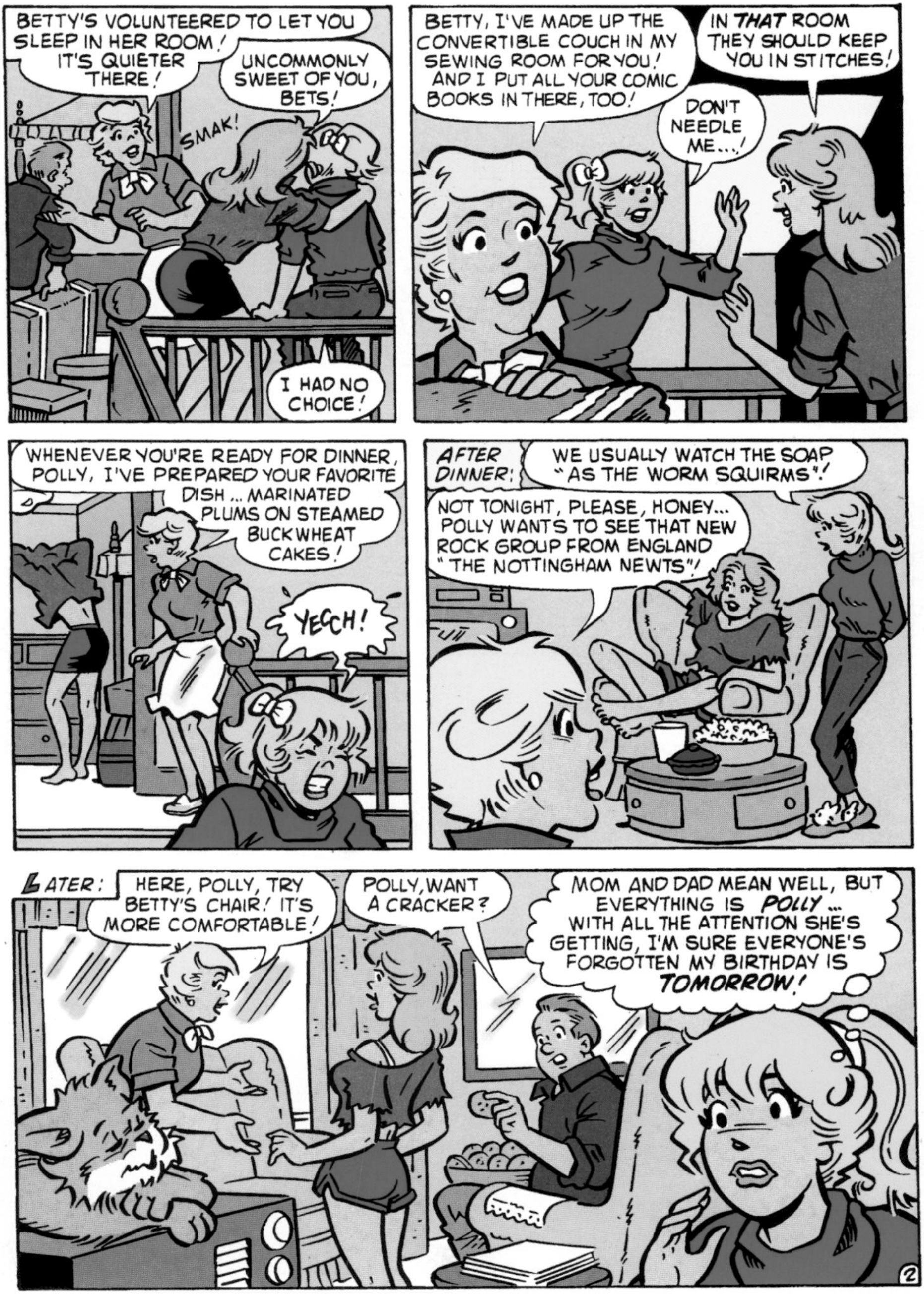
BETTY'S VOLUNTEERED TO LET YOU SLEEP IN HER ROOM! IT'S QUIETER THERE!
UNCOMMONLY SWEET OF YOU, BETS!
SMAK!
I HAD NO CHOICE!
BETTY, I'VE MADE UP THE CONVERTIBLE COUCH IN MY SEWING ROOM FOR YOU! AND I PUT ALL YOUR COMIC BOOKS IN THERE, TOO!
IN THAT ROOM THEY SHOULD KEEP YOU IN STITCHES!
DON'T NEEDLE ME...!
WHENEVER YOU'RE READY FOR DINNER, POLLY, I'VE PREPARED YOUR FAVORITE DISH ... MARINATED PLUMS ON STEAMED BUCKWHEAT CAKES!
YECCH!
AFTER DINNER:
WE USUALLY WATCH THE SOAP "AS THE WORM SQUIRMS"!
NOT TONIGHT, PLEASE, HONEY... POLLY WANTS TO SEE THAT NEW ROCK GROUP FROM ENGLAND "THE NOTTINGHAM NEWTS"!
LATER:
HERE, POLLY, TRY BETTY'S CHAIR! IT'S MORE COMFORTABLE!
POLLY, WANT A CRACKER?
MOM AND DAD MEAN WELL, BUT EVERYTHING IS POLLY ... WITH ALL THE ATTENTION SHE'S GETTING, I'M SURE EVERYONE'S FORGOTTEN MY BIRTHDAY IS TOMORROW!
2

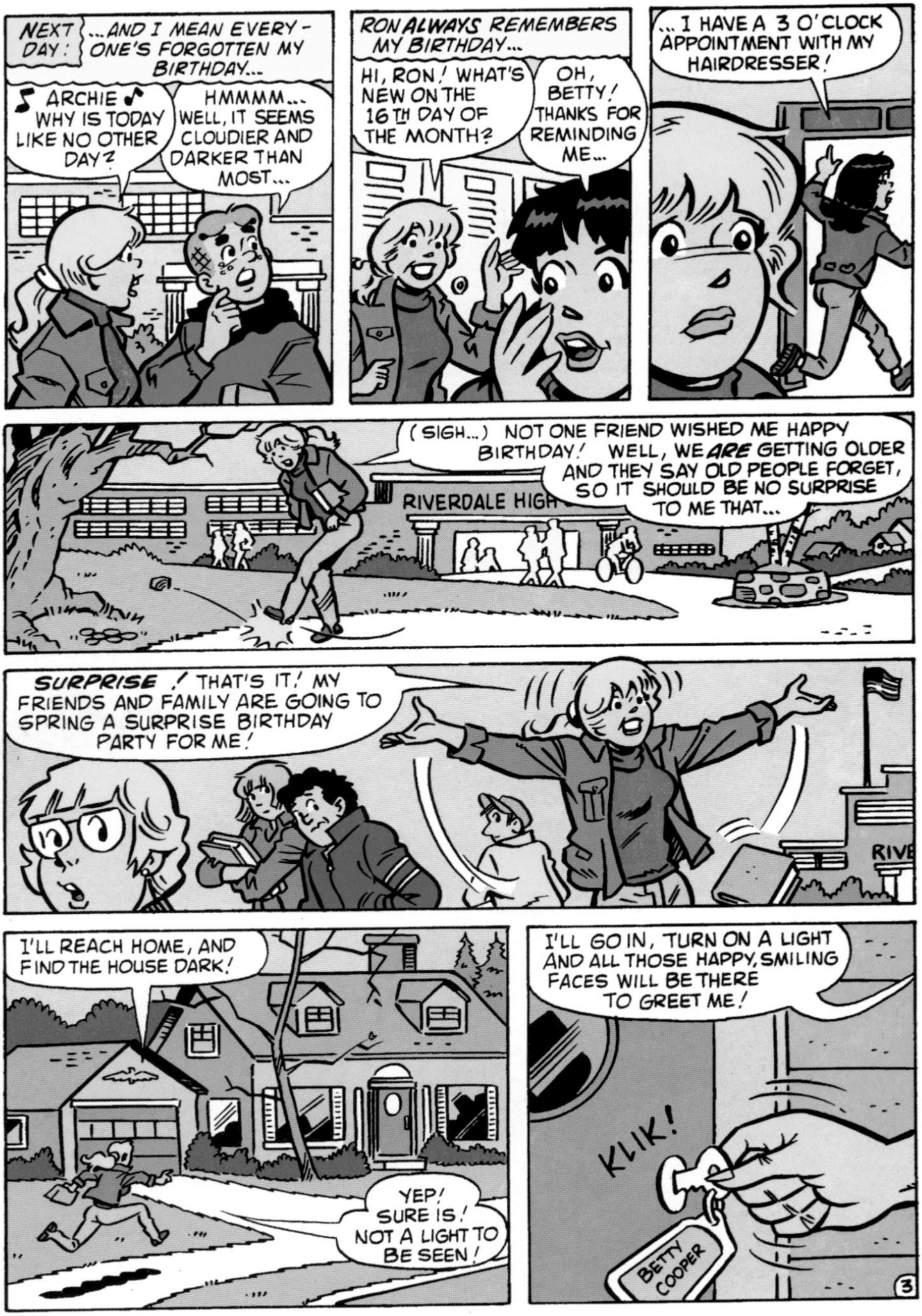
NEXT DAY: ...AND I MEAN EVERY-ONE'S FORGOTTEN MY BIRTHDAY...
ARCHIE WHY IS TODAY LIKE NO OTHER DAY?
HMMMM... WELL, IT SEEMS CLOUDIER AND DARKER THAN MOST...
RON ALWAYS REMEMBERS MY BIRTHDAY...
HI, RON! WHAT'S NEW ON THE 16TH DAY OF THE MONTH?
OH, BETTY! THANKS FOR REMINDING ME...
...I HAVE A 3 O'CLOCK APPOINTMENT WITH MY HAIRDRESSER!
(SIGH...) NOT ONE FRIEND WISHED ME HAPPY BIRTHDAY! WELL, WE ARE GETTING OLDER AND THEY SAY OLD PEOPLE FORGET, SO IT SHOULD BE NO SURPRISE TO ME THAT...
RIVERDALE HIGH
SURPRISE! THAT'S IT! MY FRIENDS AND FAMILY ARE GOING TO SPRING A SURPRISE BIRTHDAY PARTY FOR ME!
RIVE
I'LL REACH HOME, AND FIND THE HOUSE DARK!
YEP! SURE IS! NOT A LIGHT TO BE SEEN!
I'LL GO IN, TURN ON A LIGHT AND ALL THOSE HAPPY, SMILING FACES WILL BE THERE TO GREET ME!
KLIK!
BETTY COOPER
3

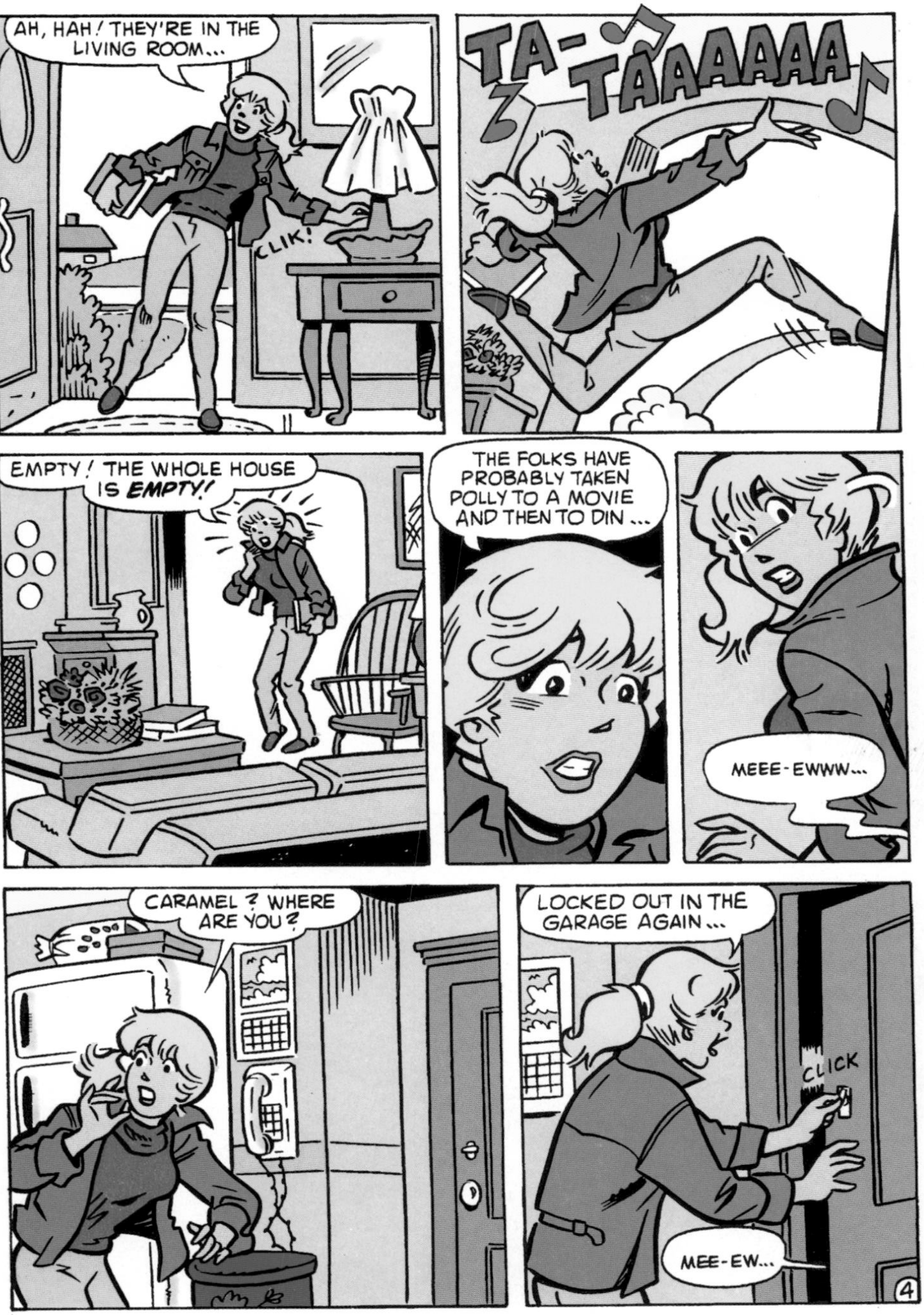
AH, HAH! THEY'RE IN THE LIVING ROOM...
CLIK!
TA-TAAAAAA
EMPTY! THE WHOLE HOUSE IS EMPTY!
THE FOLKS HAVE PROBABLY TAKEN POLLY TO A MOVIE AND THEN TO DIN ...
MEEE-EWWW...
CARAMEL? WHERE ARE YOU?
LOCKED OUT IN THE GARAGE AGAIN...
CLICK
MEE-EW...
4

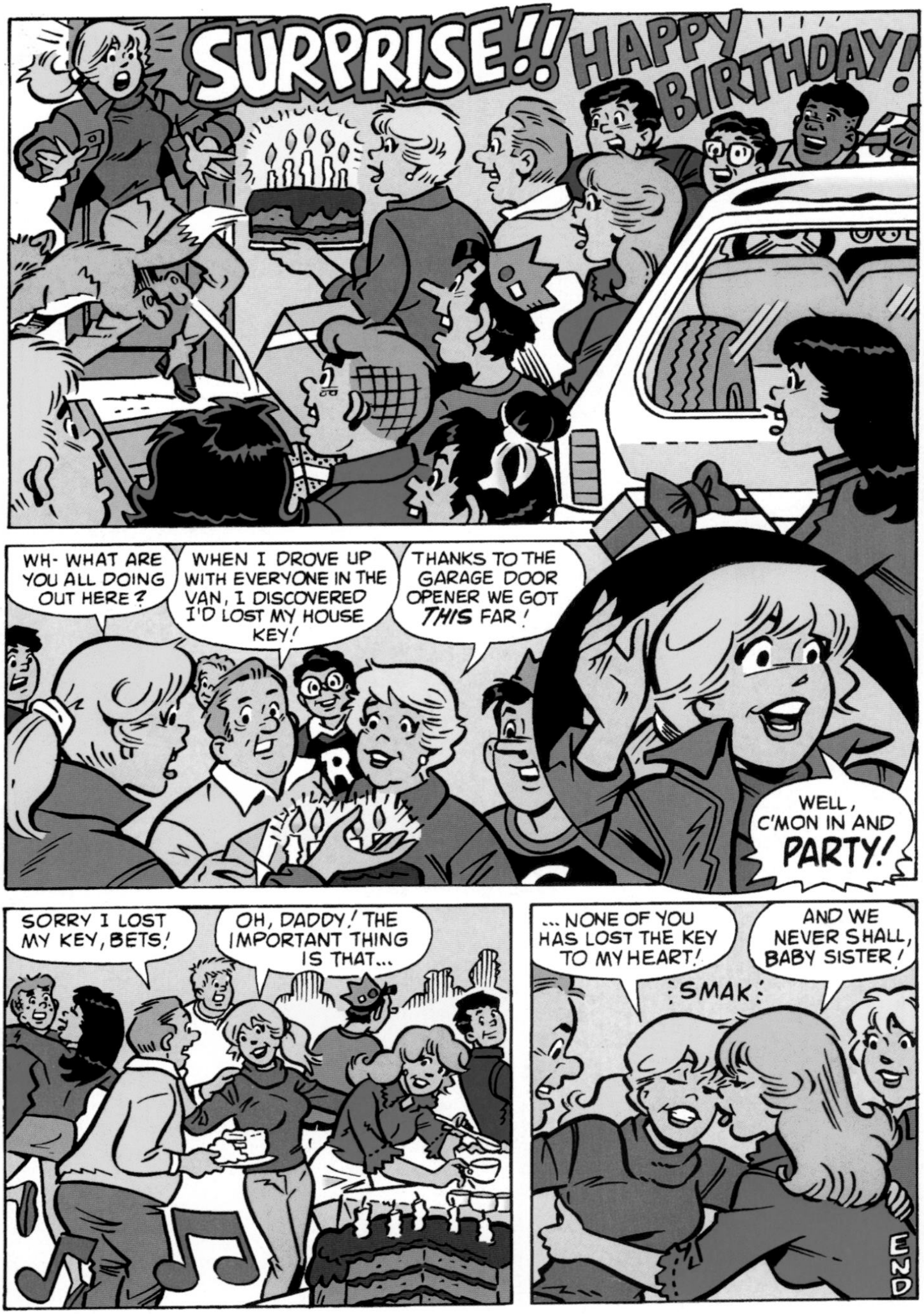
SURPRISE!!
HAPPY BIRTHDAY!
WH- WHAT ARE YOU ALL DOING OUT HERE?
WHEN I DROVE UP WITH EVERYONE IN THE VAN, I DISCOVERED I'D LOST MY HOUSE KEY!
THANKS TO THE GARAGE DOOR OPENER WE GOT THIS FAR!
WELL, C'MON IN AND PARTY!
SORRY I LOST MY KEY, BETS!
OH, DADDY! THE IMPORTANT THING IS THAT...
...NONE OF YOU HAS LOST THE KEY TO MY HEART!
SMAK
AND WE NEVER SHALL, BABY SISTER!
END

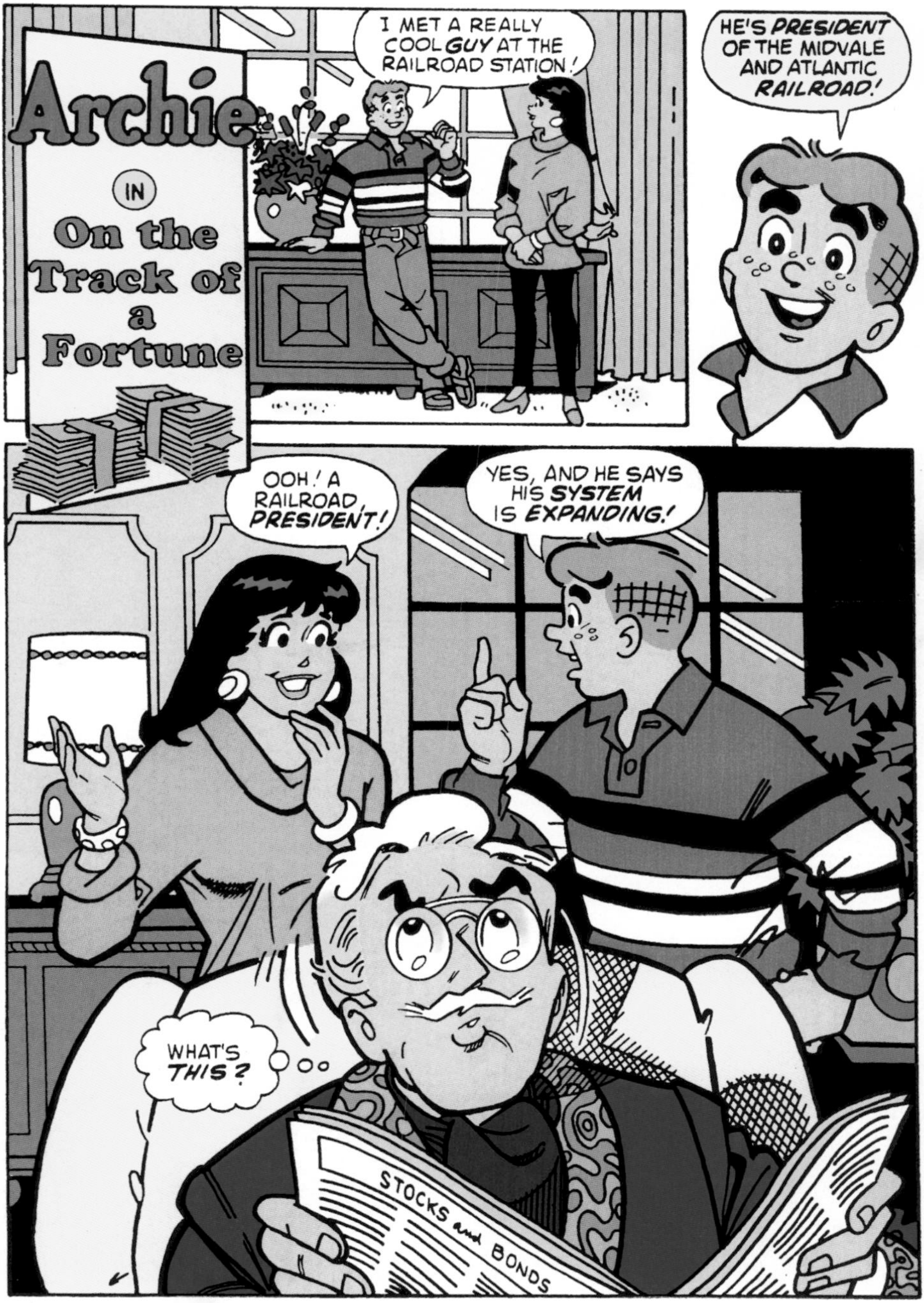
Archie
IN
On the Track of a Fortune
I MET A REALLY COOL GUY AT THE RAILROAD STATION!
HE'S PRESIDENT OF THE MIDVALE AND ATLANTIC RAILROAD!
OOH! A RAILROAD, PRESIDENT!
YES, AND HE SAYS HIS SYSTEM IS EXPANDING!
WHAT'S THIS?
STOCKS and BONDS

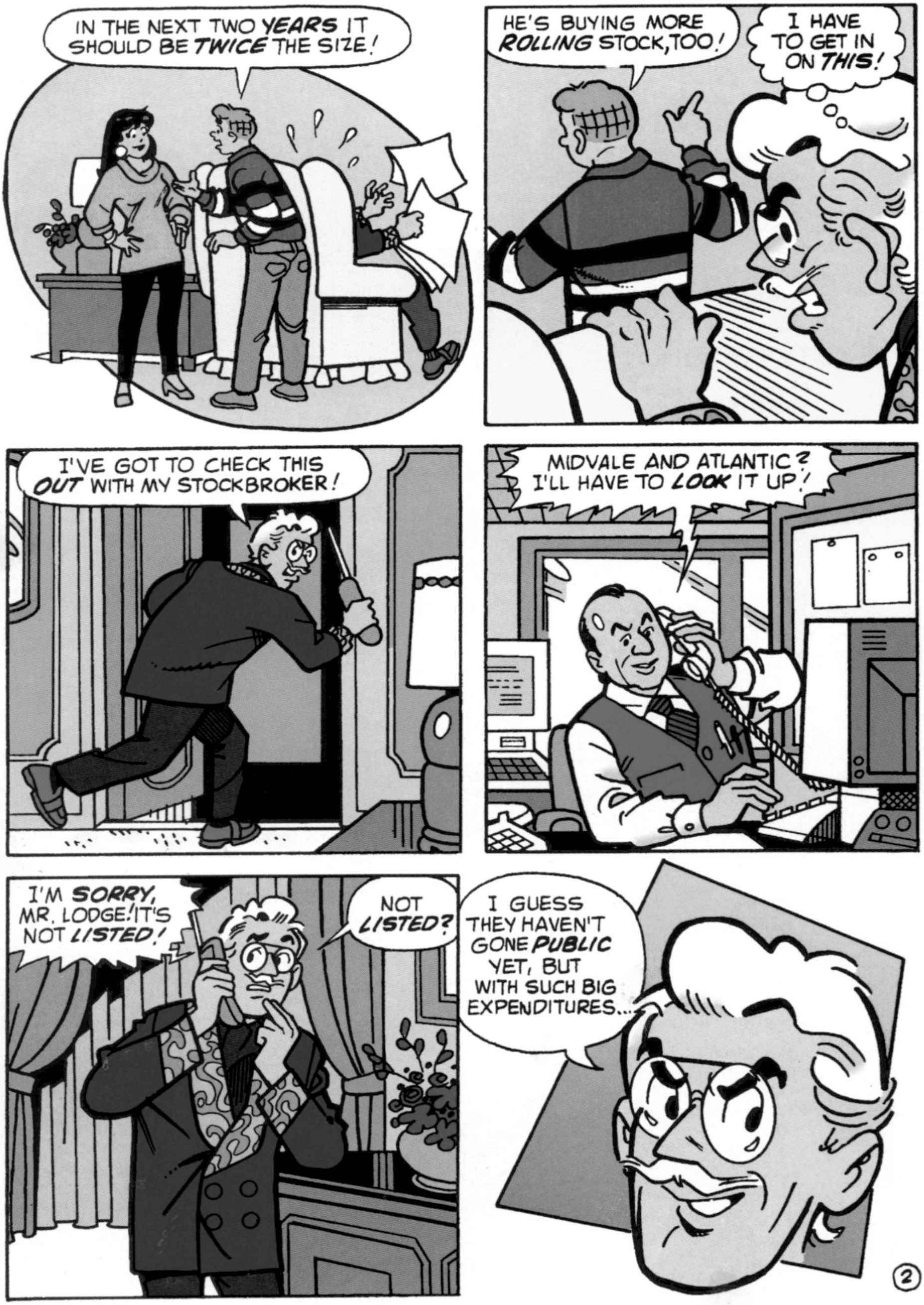
IN THE NEXT TWO YEARS IT SHOULD BE TWICE THE SIZE!
HE'S BUYING MORE ROLLING STOCK, TOO!
I HAVE TO GET IN ON THIS!
I'VE GOT TO CHECK THIS OUT WITH MY STOCKBROKER!
MIDVALE AND ATLANTIC? I'LL HAVE TO LOOK IT UP!
I'M SORRY, MR. LODGE! IT'S NOT LISTED!
NOT LISTED?
I GUESS THEY HAVEN'T GONE PUBLIC YET, BUT WITH SUCH BIG EXPENDITURES...
2

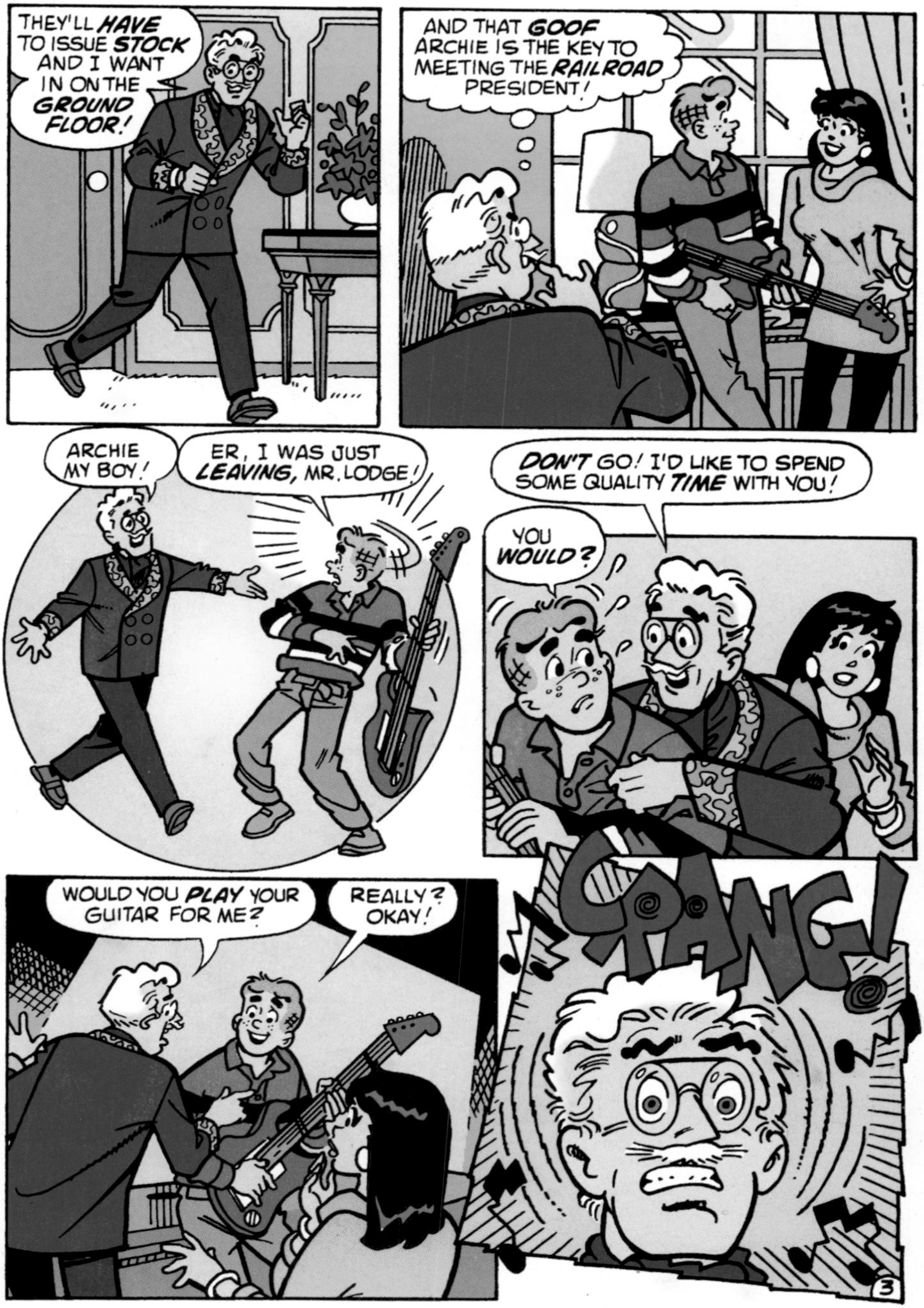
THEY'LL HAVE TO ISSUE STOCK AND I WANT IN ON THE GROUND FLOOR!
AND THAT GOOF ARCHIE IS THE KEY TO MEETING THE RAILROAD PRESIDENT!
ARCHIE MY BOY!
ER, I WAS JUST LEAVING, MR. LODGE!
DON'T GO! I'D LIKE TO SPEND SOME QUALITY TIME WITH YOU!
YOU WOULD?
WOULD YOU PLAY YOUR GUITAR FOR ME?
REALLY? OKAY!
CRANG!
3

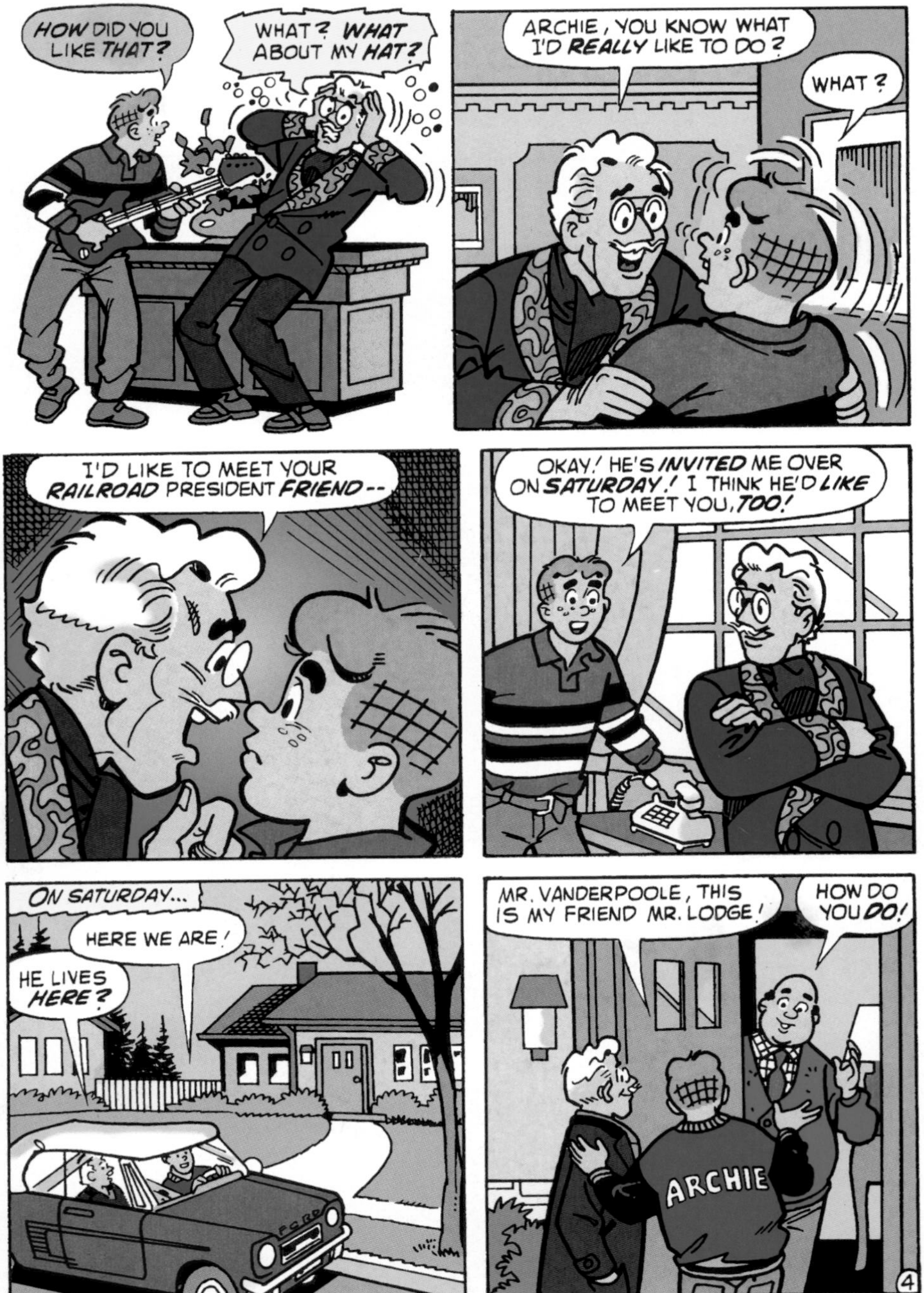
HOW DID YOU LIKE THAT?
WHAT? WHAT ABOUT MY HAT?
ARCHIE, YOU KNOW WHAT I'D REALLY LIKE TO DO?
WHAT?
I'D LIKE TO MEET YOUR RAILROAD PRESIDENT FRIEND--
OKAY! HE'S INVITED ME OVER ON SATURDAY! I THINK HE'D LIKE TO MEET YOU, TOO!
ON SATURDAY...
HERE WE ARE!
HE LIVES HERE?
MR. VANDERPOOLE, THIS IS MY FRIEND MR. LODGE!
HOW DO YOU DO!
ARCHIE
4

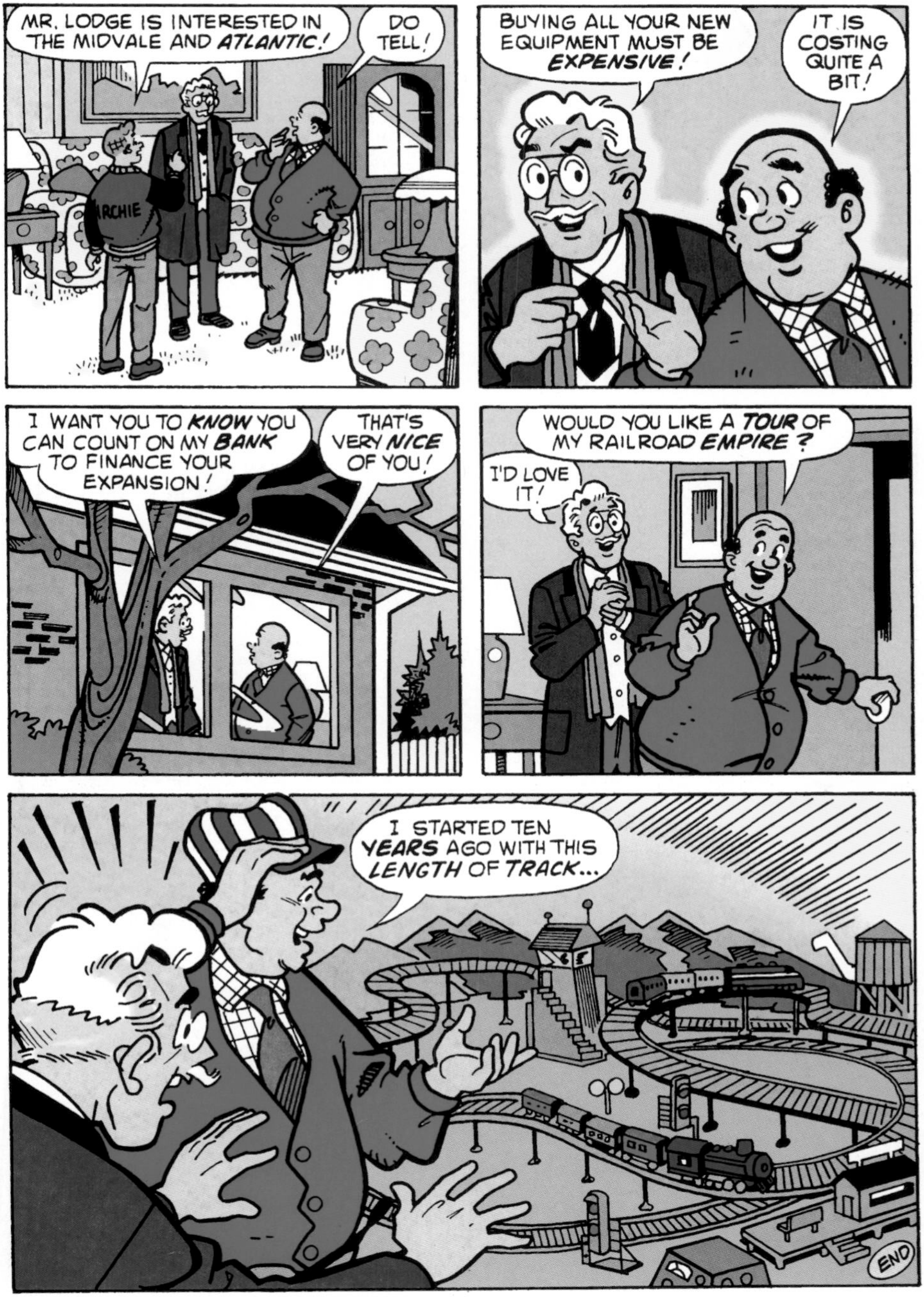
MR. LODGE IS INTERESTED IN THE MIDVALE AND ATLANTIC!
DO TELL!
ARCHIE
BUYING ALL YOUR NEW EQUIPMENT MUST BE EXPENSIVE!
IT IS COSTING QUITE A BIT!
I WANT YOU TO KNOW YOU CAN COUNT ON MY BANK TO FINANCE YOUR EXPANSION!
THAT'S VERY NICE OF YOU!
WOULD YOU LIKE A TOUR OF MY RAILROAD EMPIRE?
I'D LOVE IT!
I STARTED TEN YEARS AGO WITH THIS LENGTH OF TRACK...
END

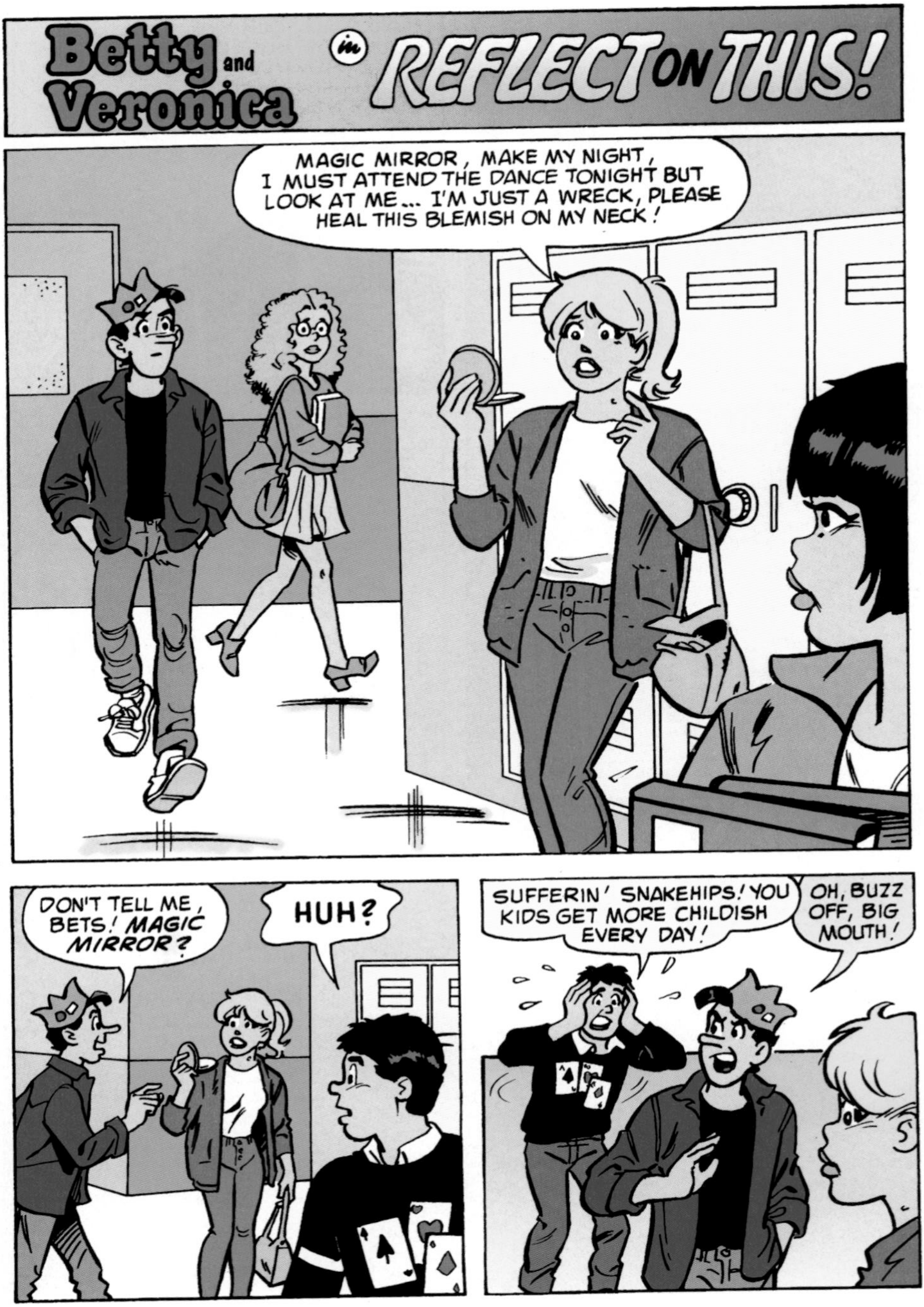
Betty and Veronica in REFLECT ON THIS!
MAGIC MIRROR, MAKE MY NIGHT, I MUST ATTEND THE DANCE TONIGHT BUT LOOK AT ME... I'M JUST A WRECK, PLEASE HEAL THIS BLEMISH ON MY NECK!
DON'T TELL ME, BETS! MAGIC MIRROR?
HUH?
SUFFERIN' SNAKEHIPS! YOU KIDS GET MORE CHILDISH EVERY DAY!
OH, BUZZ OFF, BIG MOUTH!

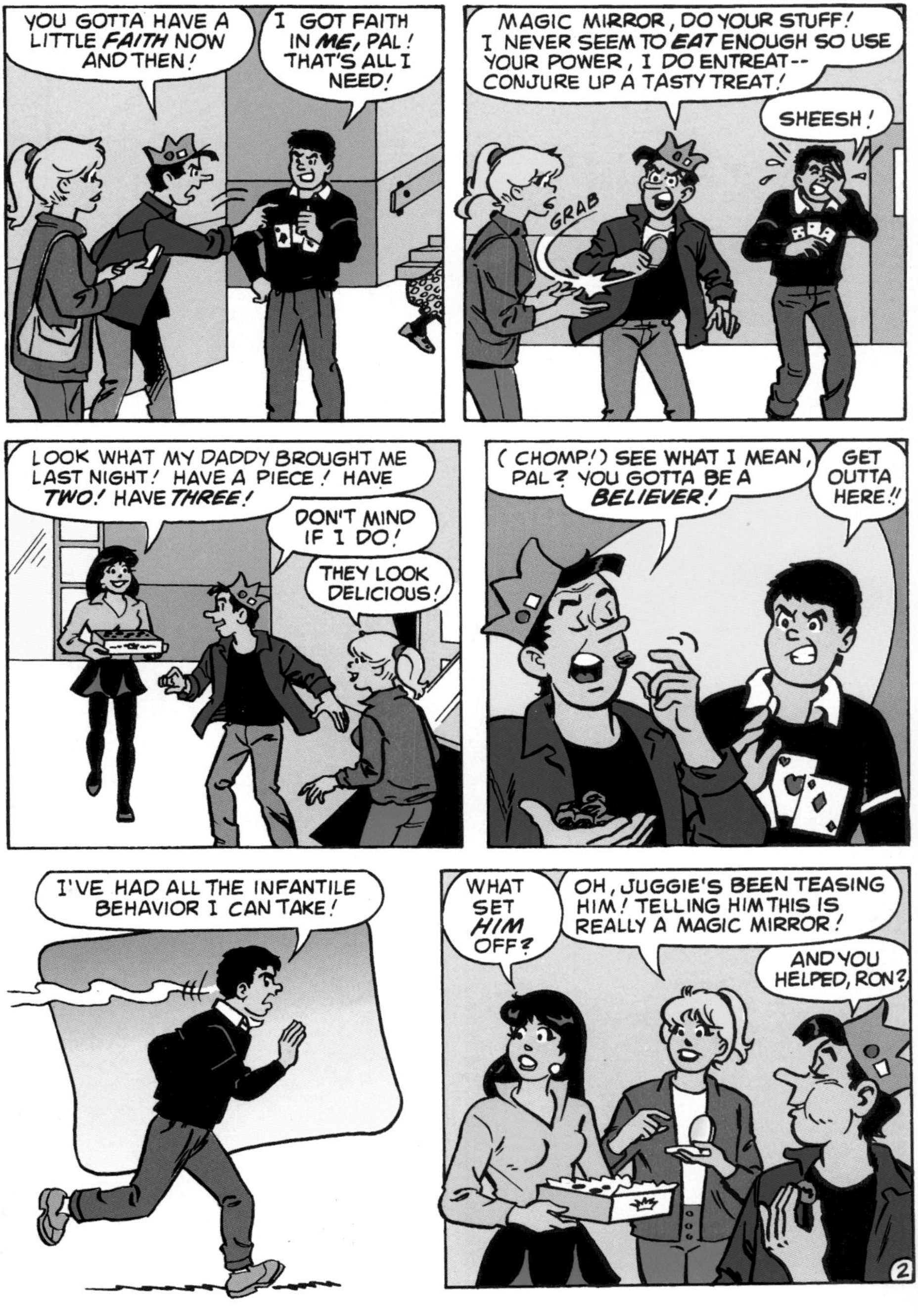
YOU GOTTA HAVE A LITTLE FAITH NOW AND THEN!
I GOT FAITH IN ME, PAL! THAT'S ALL I NEED!
MAGIC MIRROR, DO YOUR STUFF! I NEVER SEEM TO EAT ENOUGH SO USE YOUR POWER, I DO ENTREAT-- CONJURE UP A TASTY TREAT!
SHEESH!
GRAB
LOOK WHAT MY DADDY BROUGHT ME LAST NIGHT! HAVE A PIECE! HAVE TWO! HAVE THREE!
DON'T MIND IF I DO!
THEY LOOK DELICIOUS!
(CHOMP!) SEE WHAT I MEAN, PAL? YOU GOTTA BE A BELIEVER!
GET OUTTA HERE!!
I'VE HAD ALL THE INFANTILE BEHAVIOR I CAN TAKE!
WHAT SET HIM OFF?
OH, JUGGIE'S BEEN TEASING HIM! TELLING HIM THIS IS REALLY A MAGIC MIRROR!
AND YOU HELPED, RON?
2

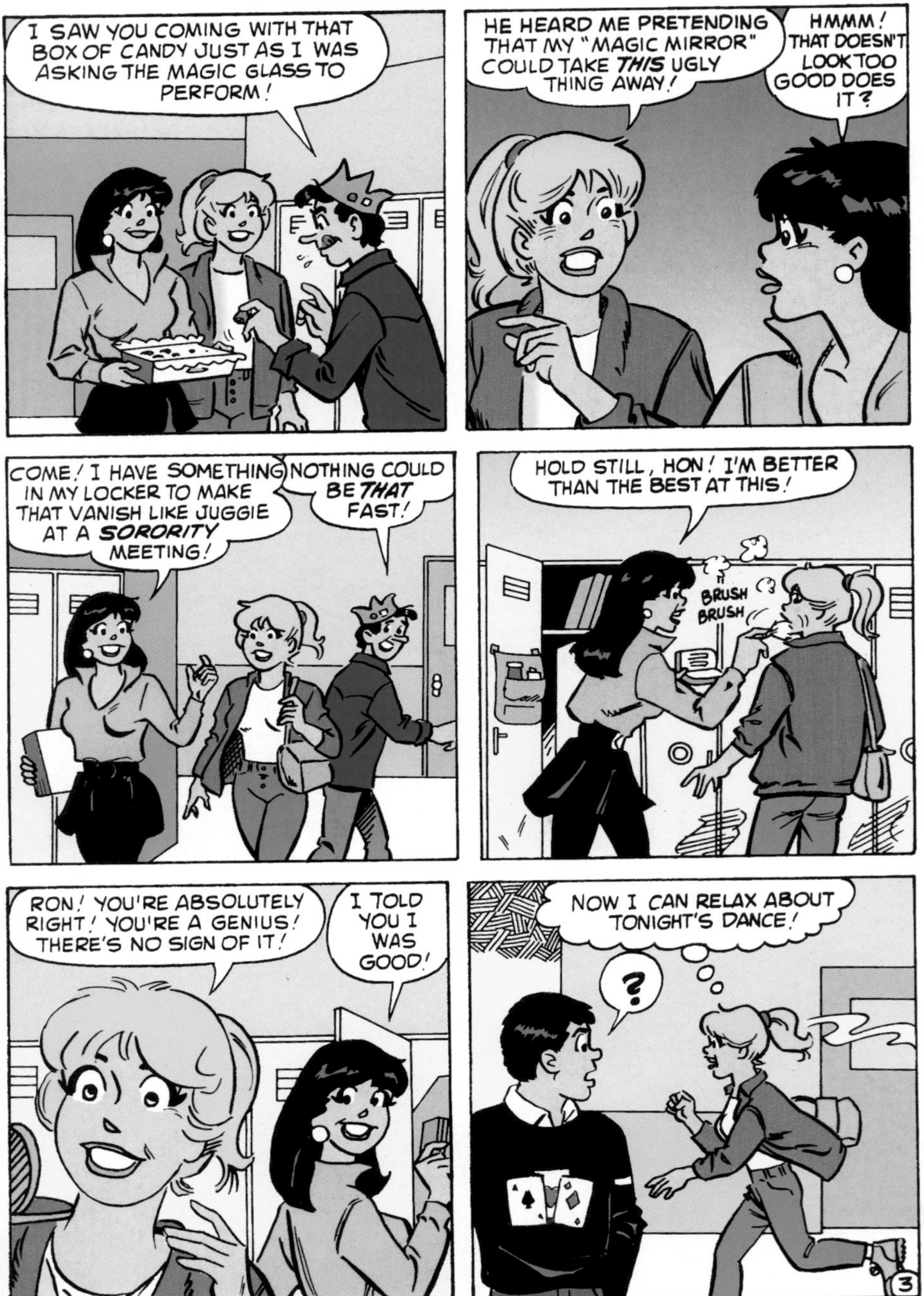
I SAW YOU COMING WITH THAT BOX OF CANDY JUST AS I WAS ASKING THE MAGIC GLASS TO PERFORM!
HE HEARD ME PRETENDING THAT MY "MAGIC MIRROR" COULD TAKE THIS UGLY THING AWAY!
HMMM! THAT DOESN'T LOOK TOO GOOD DOES IT?
COME! I HAVE SOMETHING IN MY LOCKER TO MAKE THAT VANISH LIKE JUGGIE AT A SORORITY MEETING!
NOTHING COULD BE THAT FAST!
HOLD STILL, HON! I'M BETTER THAN THE BEST AT THIS!
BRUSH BRUSH
RON! YOU'RE ABSOLUTELY RIGHT! YOU'RE A GENIUS! THERE'S NO SIGN OF IT!
I TOLD YOU I WAS GOOD!
NOW I CAN RELAX ABOUT TONIGHT'S DANCE!
?
3

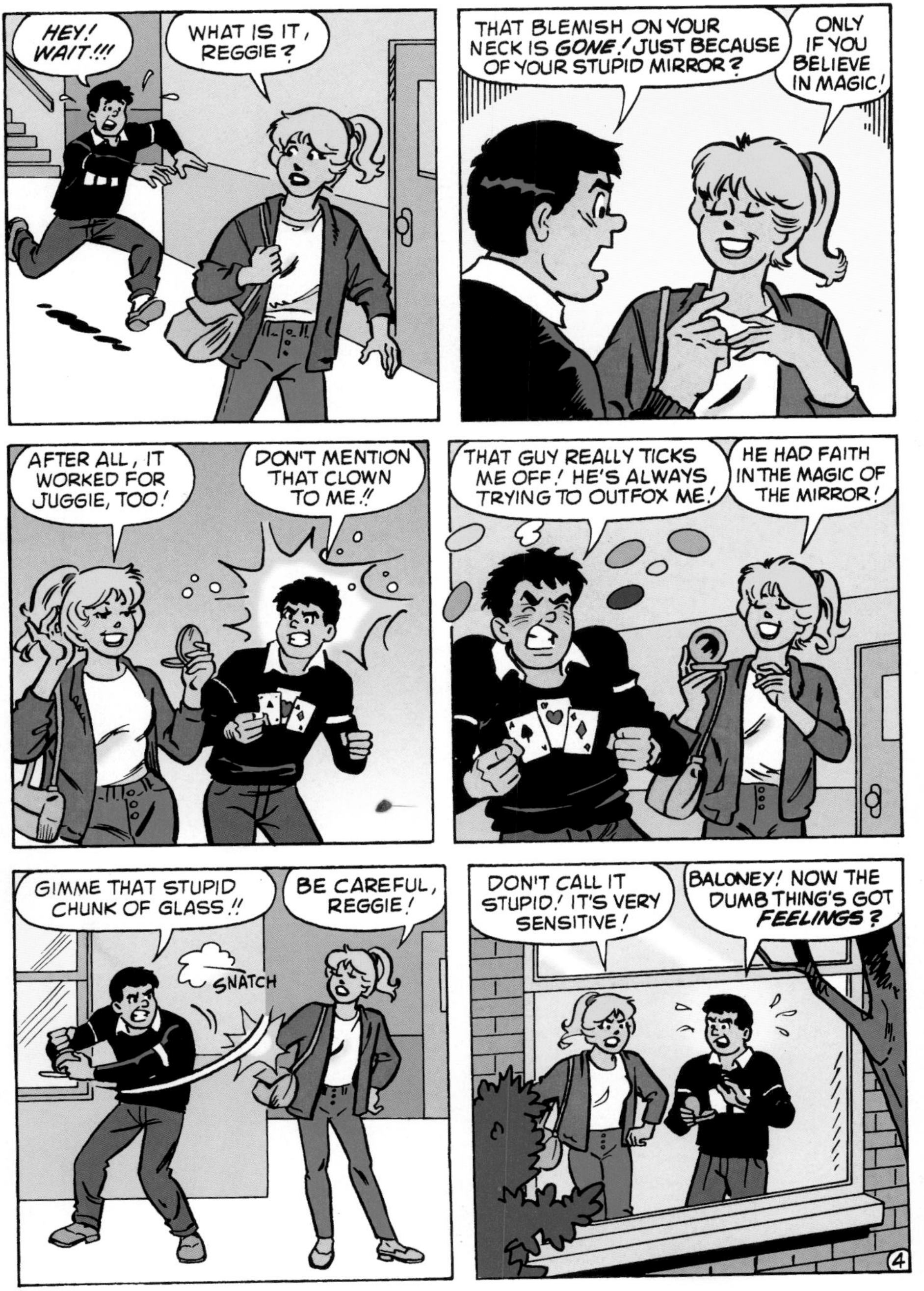
HEY! WAIT!!!
WHAT IS IT, REGGIE?
THAT BLEMISH ON YOUR NECK IS GONE! JUST BECAUSE OF YOUR STUPID MIRROR?
ONLY IF YOU BELIEVE IN MAGIC!
AFTER ALL, IT WORKED FOR JUGGIE, TOO!
DON'T MENTION THAT CLOWN TO ME!!
THAT GUY REALLY TICKS ME OFF! HE'S ALWAYS TRYING TO OUTFOX ME!
HE HAD FAITH IN THE MAGIC OF THE MIRROR!
GIMME THAT STUPID CHUNK OF GLASS!!
SNATCH
BE CAREFUL, REGGIE!
DON'T CALL IT STUPID! IT'S VERY SENSITIVE!
BALONEY! NOW THE DUMB THING'S GOT FEELINGS?
4

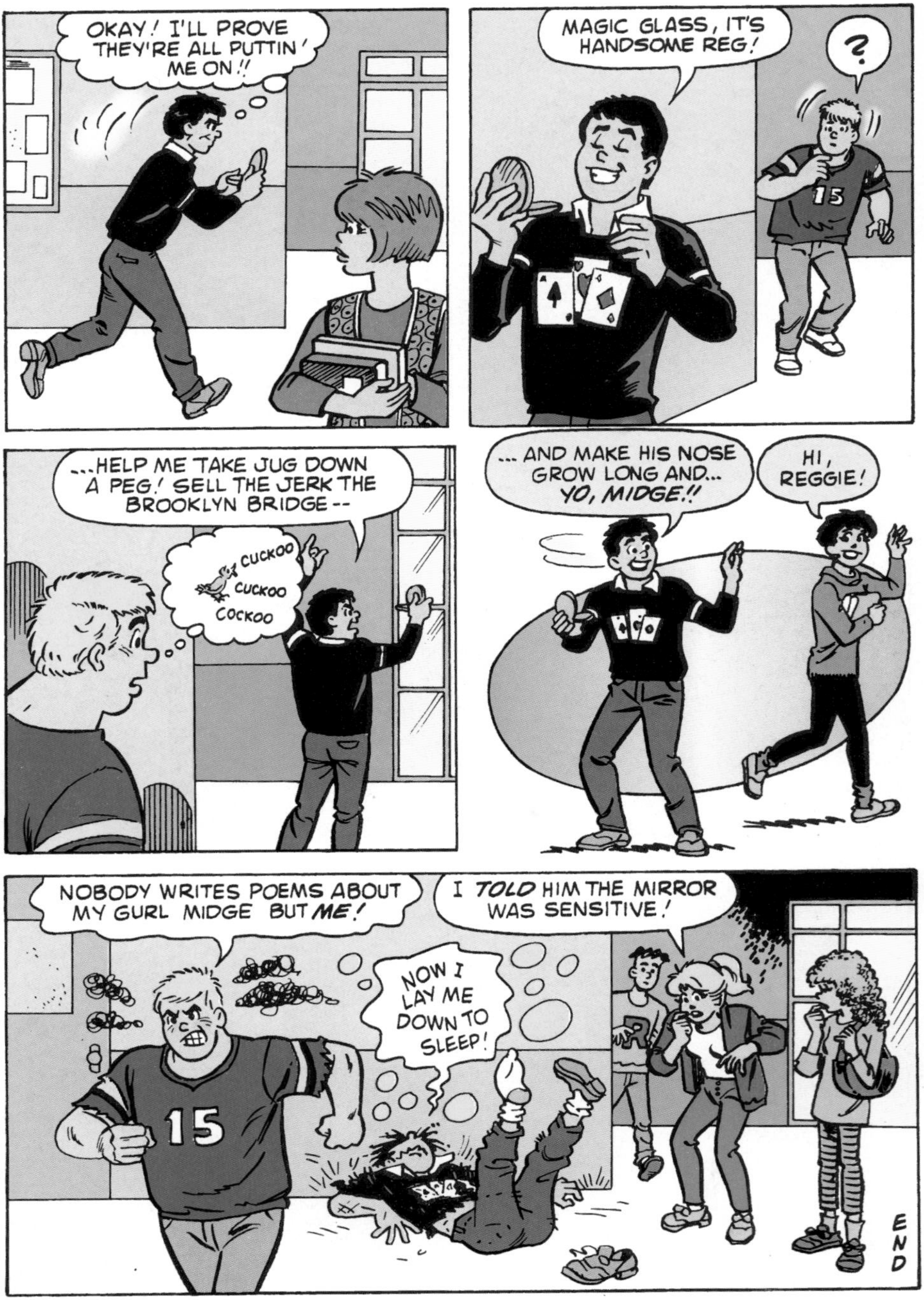
OKAY! I'LL PROVE THEY'RE ALL PUTTIN' ME ON!!
MAGIC GLASS, IT'S HANDSOME REG!
?
...HELP ME TAKE JUG DOWN A PEG! SELL THE JERK THE BROOKLYN BRIDGE--
CUCKOO
CUCKOO
COCKOO
... AND MAKE HIS NOSE GROW LONG AND... YO, MIDGE!!
HI, REGGIE!
NOBODY WRITES POEMS ABOUT MY GURL MIDGE BUT ME!
I TOLD HIM THE MIRROR WAS SENSITIVE!
NOW I LAY ME DOWN TO SLEEP!
15
END

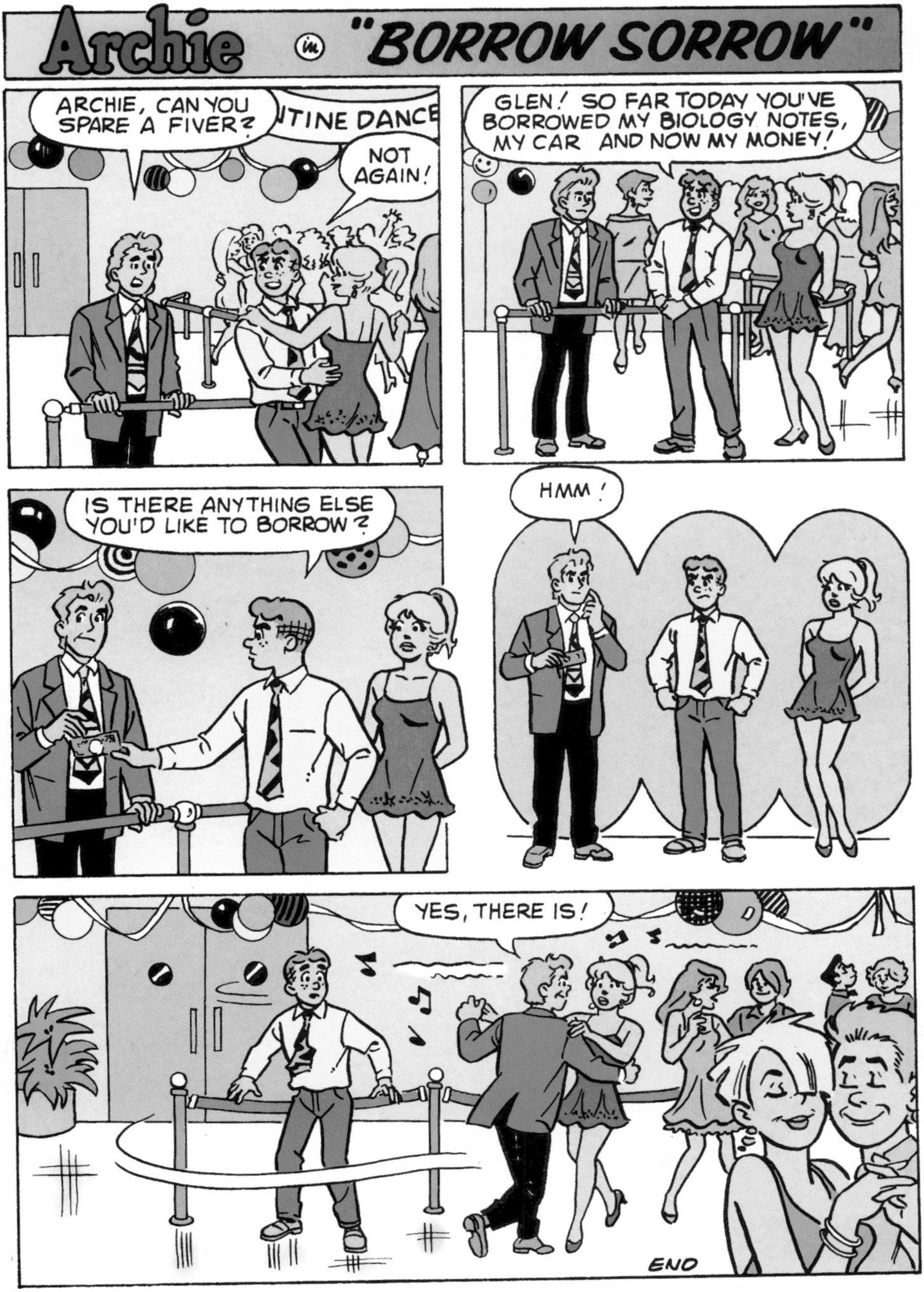
Archie in "BORROW SORROW"
ARCHIE, CAN YOU SPARE A FIVER?
NOT AGAIN!
GLEN! SO FAR TODAY YOU'VE BORROWED MY BIOLOGY NOTES, MY CAR AND NOW MY MONEY!
IS THERE ANYTHING ELSE YOU'D LIKE TO BORROW?
HMM!
YES, THERE IS!
END

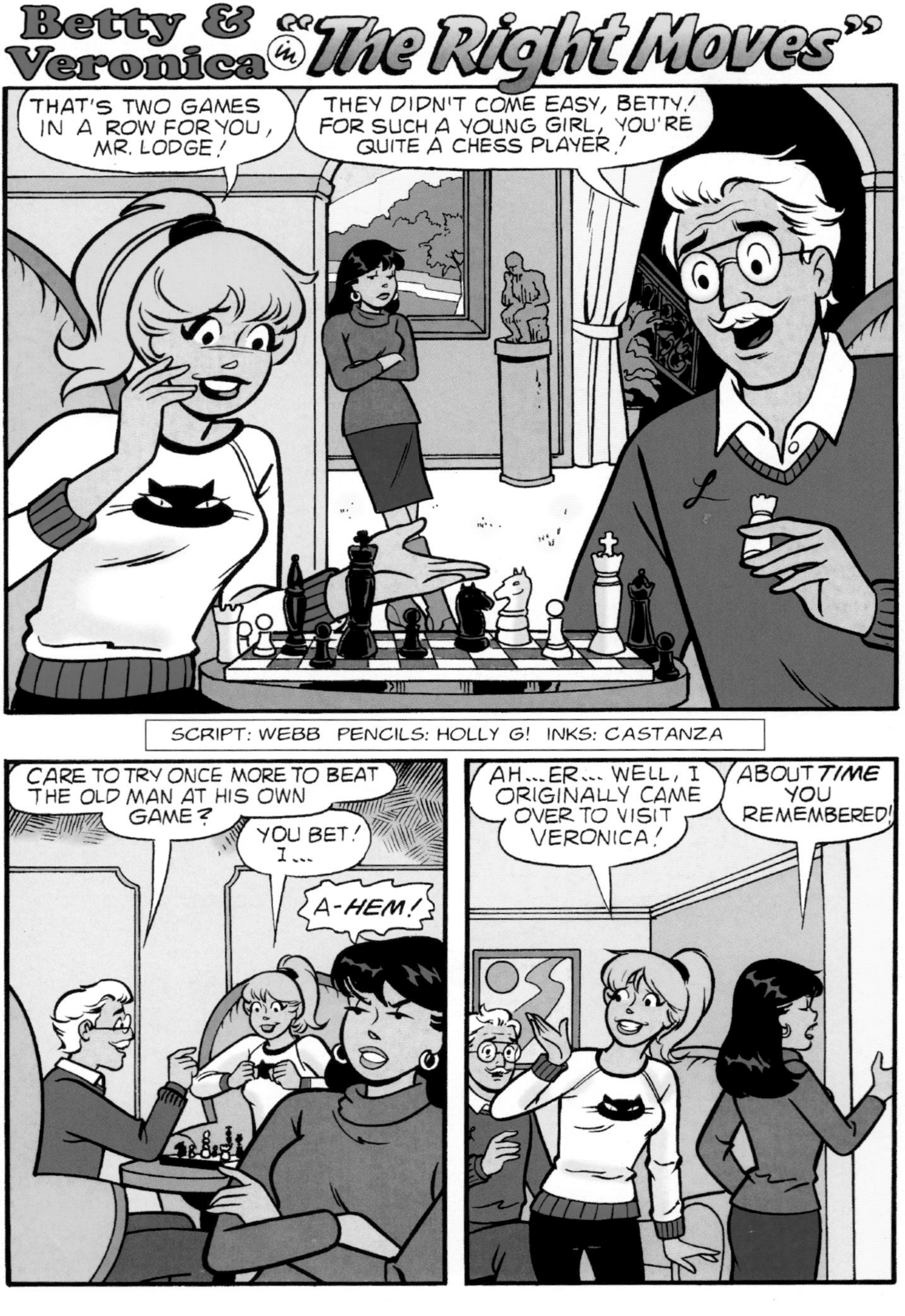
Betty & Veronica in "The Right Moves"
THAT'S TWO GAMES IN A ROW FOR YOU, MR. LODGE!
THEY DIDN'T COME EASY, BETTY! FOR SUCH A YOUNG GIRL, YOU'RE QUITE A CHESS PLAYER!
SCRIPT: WEBB PENCILS: HOLLY G! INKS: CASTANZA
CARE TO TRY ONCE MORE TO BEAT THE OLD MAN AT HIS OWN GAME?
YOU BET! I...
A-HEM!
AH...ER... WELL, I ORIGINALLY CAME OVER TO VISIT VERONICA!
ABOUT TIME YOU REMEMBERED!

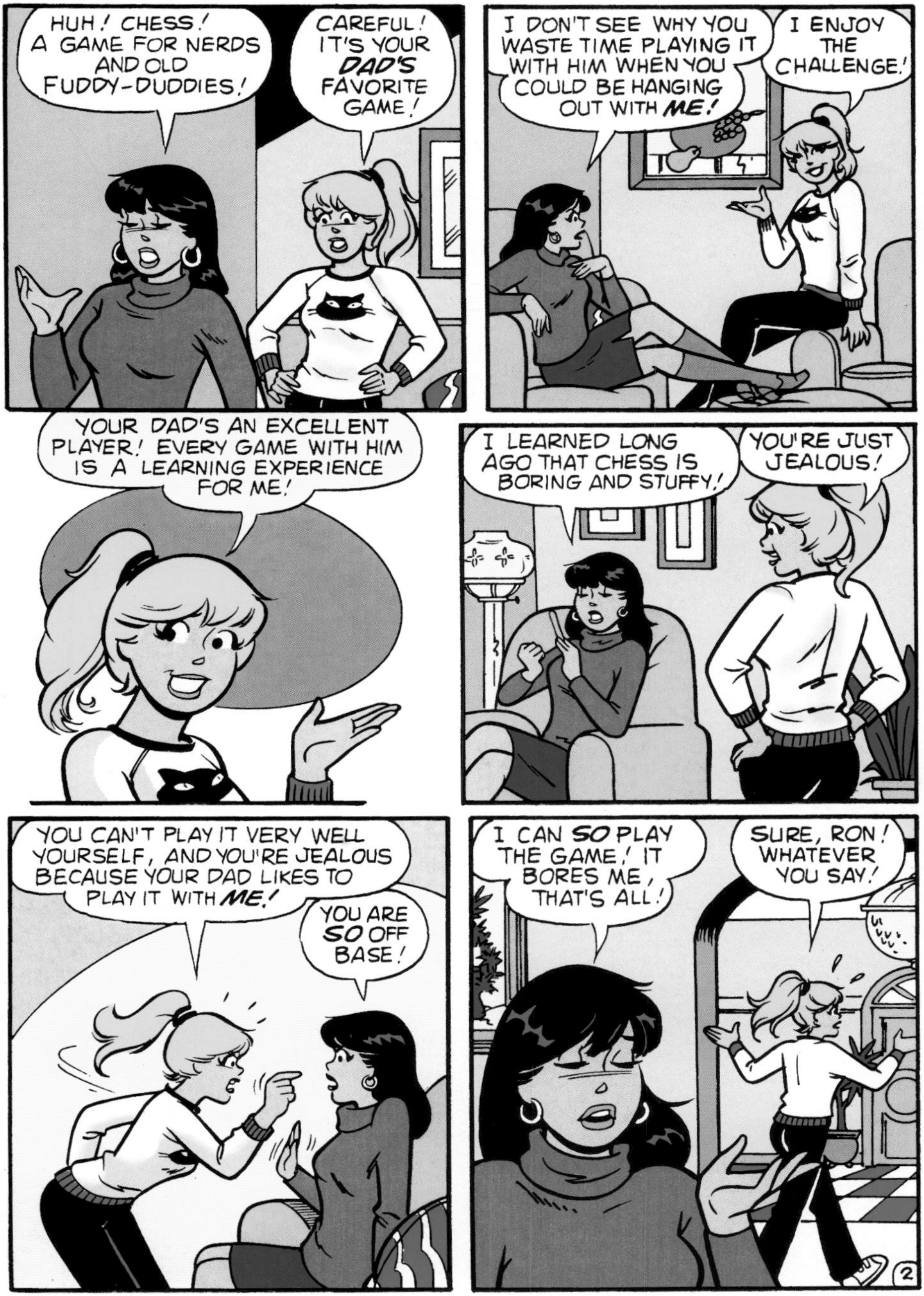
HUH! CHESS! A GAME FOR NERDS AND OLD FUDDY-DUDDIES!
CAREFUL! IT'S YOUR DAD'S FAVORITE GAME!
I DON'T SEE WHY YOU WASTE TIME PLAYING IT WITH HIM WHEN YOU COULD BE HANGING OUT WITH ME!
I ENJOY THE CHALLENGE!
YOUR DAD'S AN EXCELLENT PLAYER! EVERY GAME WITH HIM IS A LEARNING EXPERIENCE FOR ME!
I LEARNED LONG AGO THAT CHESS IS BORING AND STUFFY!
YOU'RE JUST JEALOUS!
YOU CAN'T PLAY IT VERY WELL YOURSELF, AND YOU'RE JEALOUS BECAUSE YOUR DAD LIKES TO PLAY IT WITH ME!
YOU ARE SO OFF BASE!
I CAN SO PLAY THE GAME! IT BORES ME, THAT'S ALL!
SURE, RON! WHATEVER YOU SAY!
2

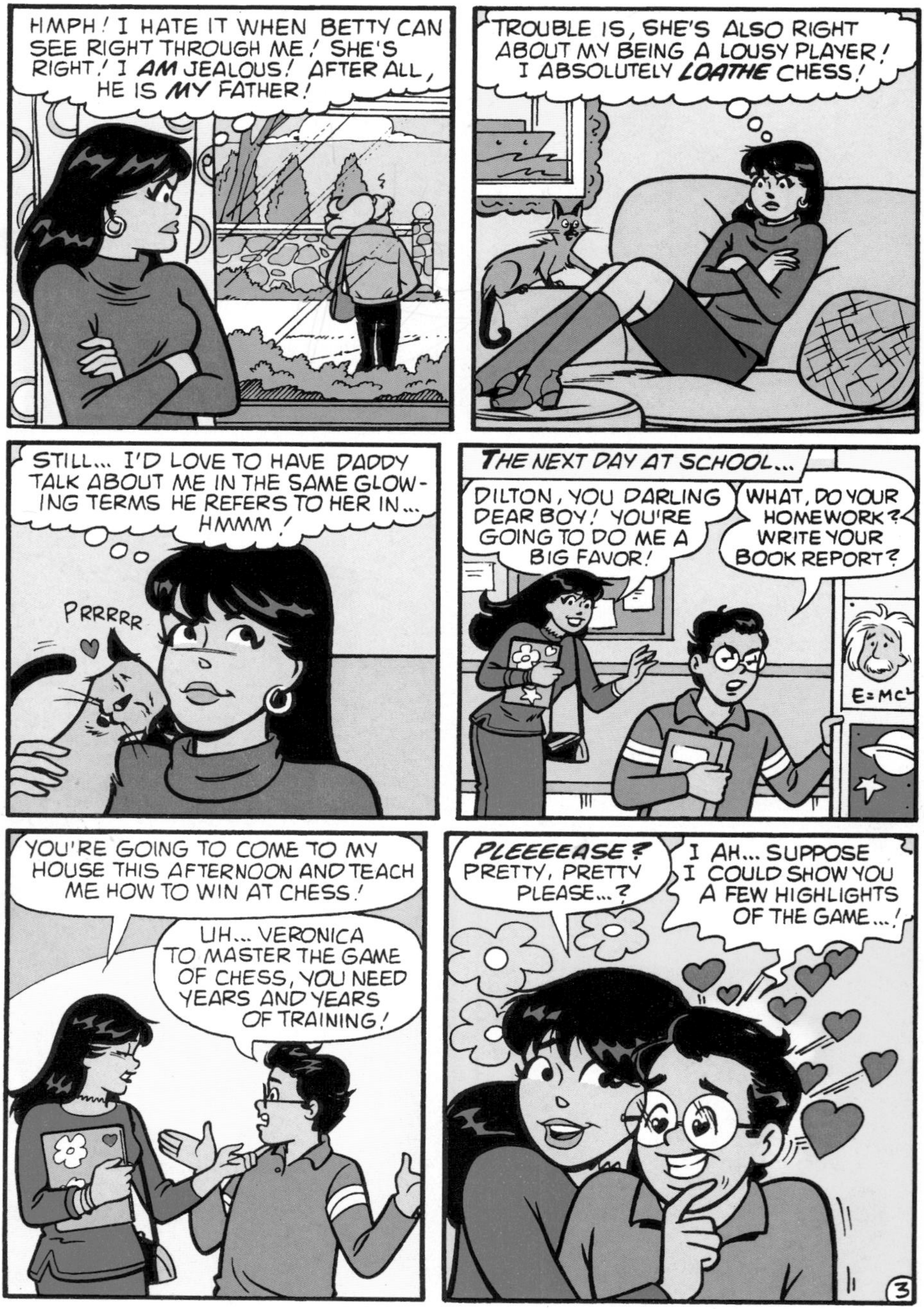
HMPH! I HATE IT WHEN BETTY CAN SEE RIGHT THROUGH ME! SHE'S RIGHT! I AM JEALOUS! AFTER ALL, HE IS MY FATHER!
TROUBLE IS, SHE'S ALSO RIGHT ABOUT MY BEING A LOUSY PLAYER! I ABSOLUTELY LOATHE CHESS!
STILL... I'D LOVE TO HAVE DADDY TALK ABOUT ME IN THE SAME GLOWING TERMS HE REFERS TO HER IN... HMMM!
PRRRRR
THE NEXT DAY AT SCHOOL...
DILTON, YOU DARLING DEAR BOY! YOU'RE GOING TO DO ME A BIG FAVOR!
WHAT, DO YOUR HOMEWORK? WRITE YOUR BOOK REPORT?
E=MC²
YOU'RE GOING TO COME TO MY HOUSE THIS AFTERNOON AND TEACH ME HOW TO WIN AT CHESS!
UH... VERONICA TO MASTER THE GAME OF CHESS, YOU NEED YEARS AND YEARS OF TRAINING!
PLEEEEASE? PRETTY, PRETTY PLEASE...?
I AH... SUPPOSE I COULD SHOW YOU A FEW HIGHLIGHTS OF THE GAME...!
3

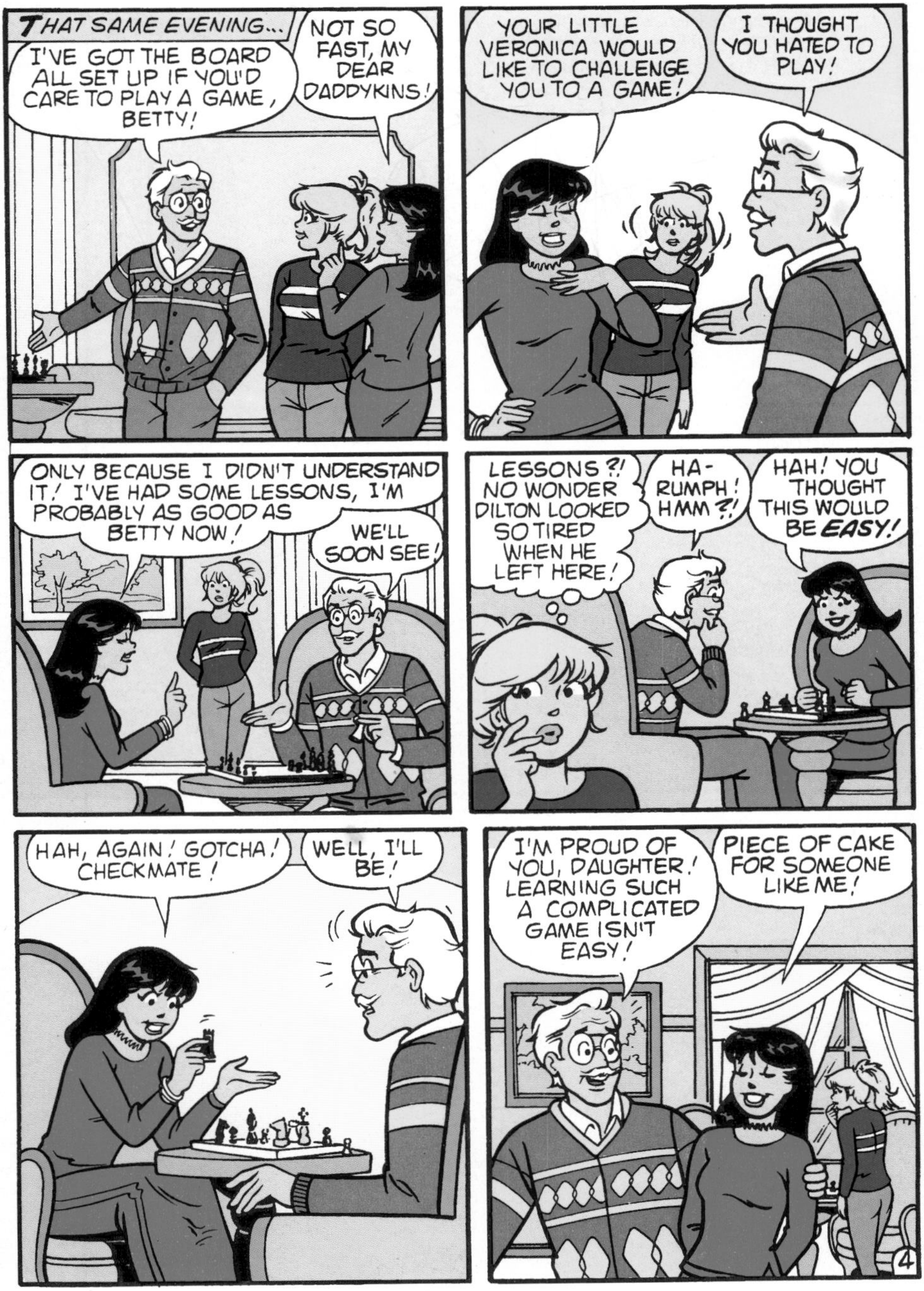
THAT SAME EVENING...
I'VE GOT THE BOARD ALL SET UP IF YOU'D CARE TO PLAY A GAME, BETTY!
NOT SO FAST, MY DEAR DADDYKINS!
YOUR LITTLE VERONICA WOULD LIKE TO CHALLENGE YOU TO A GAME!
I THOUGHT YOU HATED TO PLAY!
ONLY BECAUSE I DIDN'T UNDERSTAND IT! I'VE HAD SOME LESSONS, I'M PROBABLY AS GOOD AS BETTY NOW!
WE'LL SOON SEE!
LESSONS ?! NO WONDER DILTON LOOKED SO TIRED WHEN HE LEFT HERE!
HA-RUMPH! HMM ?!
HAH! YOU THOUGHT THIS WOULD BE EASY!
HAH, AGAIN! GOTCHA! CHECKMATE!
WELL, I'LL BE!
I'M PROUD OF YOU, DAUGHTER! LEARNING SUCH A COMPLICATED GAME ISN'T EASY!
PIECE OF CAKE FOR SOMEONE LIKE ME!
4

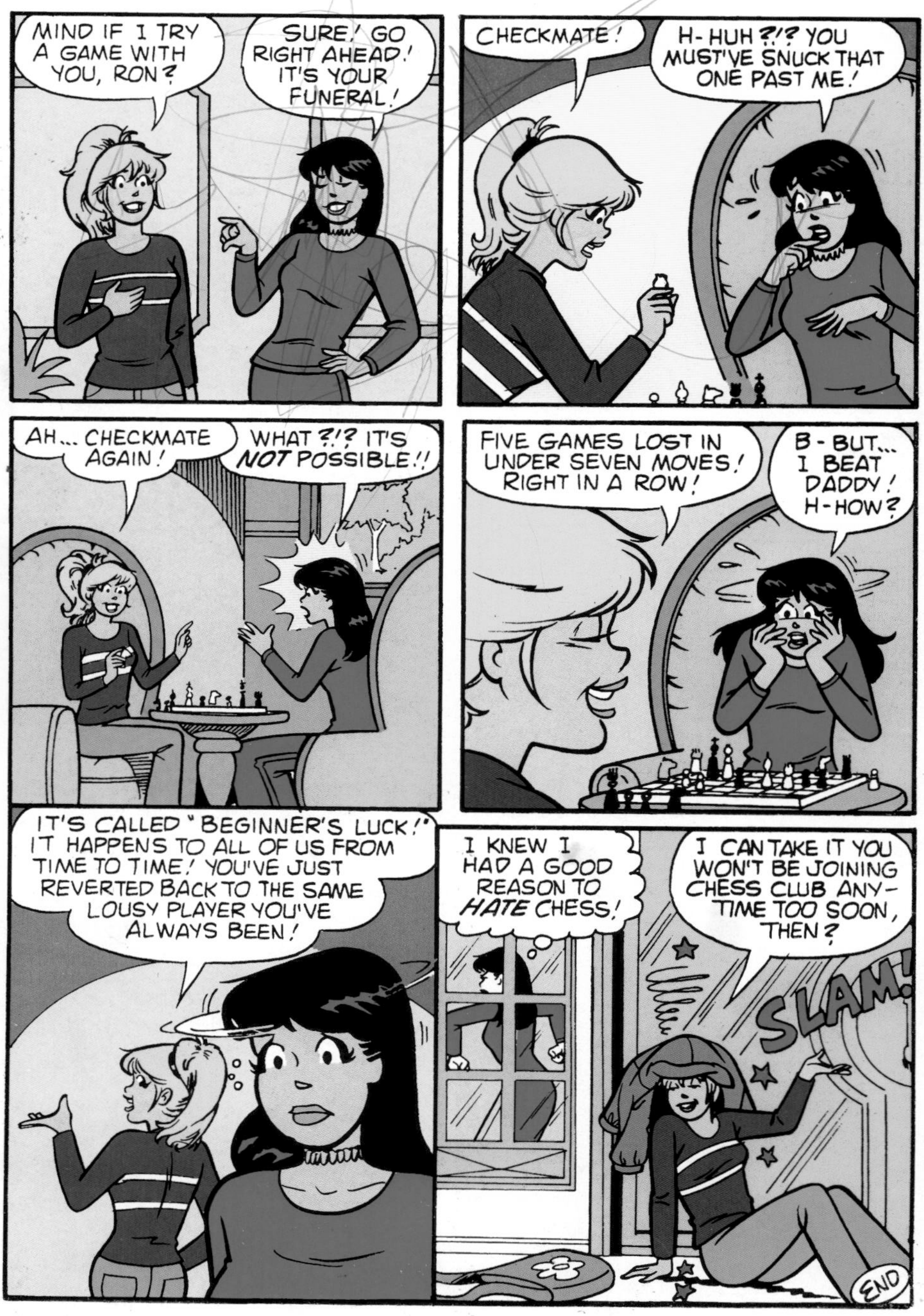
MIND IF I TRY A GAME WITH YOU, RON?
SURE! GO RIGHT AHEAD! IT'S YOUR FUNERAL!
CHECKMATE!
H-HUH ?!? YOU MUST'VE SNUCK THAT ONE PAST ME!
AH... CHECKMATE AGAIN!
WHAT ?!? IT'S NOT POSSIBLE!!
FIVE GAMES LOST IN UNDER SEVEN MOVES! RIGHT IN A ROW!
B-BUT... I BEAT DADDY! H-HOW?
IT'S CALLED "BEGINNER'S LUCK!" IT HAPPENS TO ALL OF US FROM TIME TO TIME! YOU'VE JUST REVERTED BACK TO THE SAME LOUSY PLAYER YOU'VE ALWAYS BEEN!
I KNEW I HAD A GOOD REASON TO HATE CHESS!
I CAN TAKE IT YOU WON'T BE JOINING CHESS CLUB ANY-TIME TOO SOON, THEN?
SLAM!
END

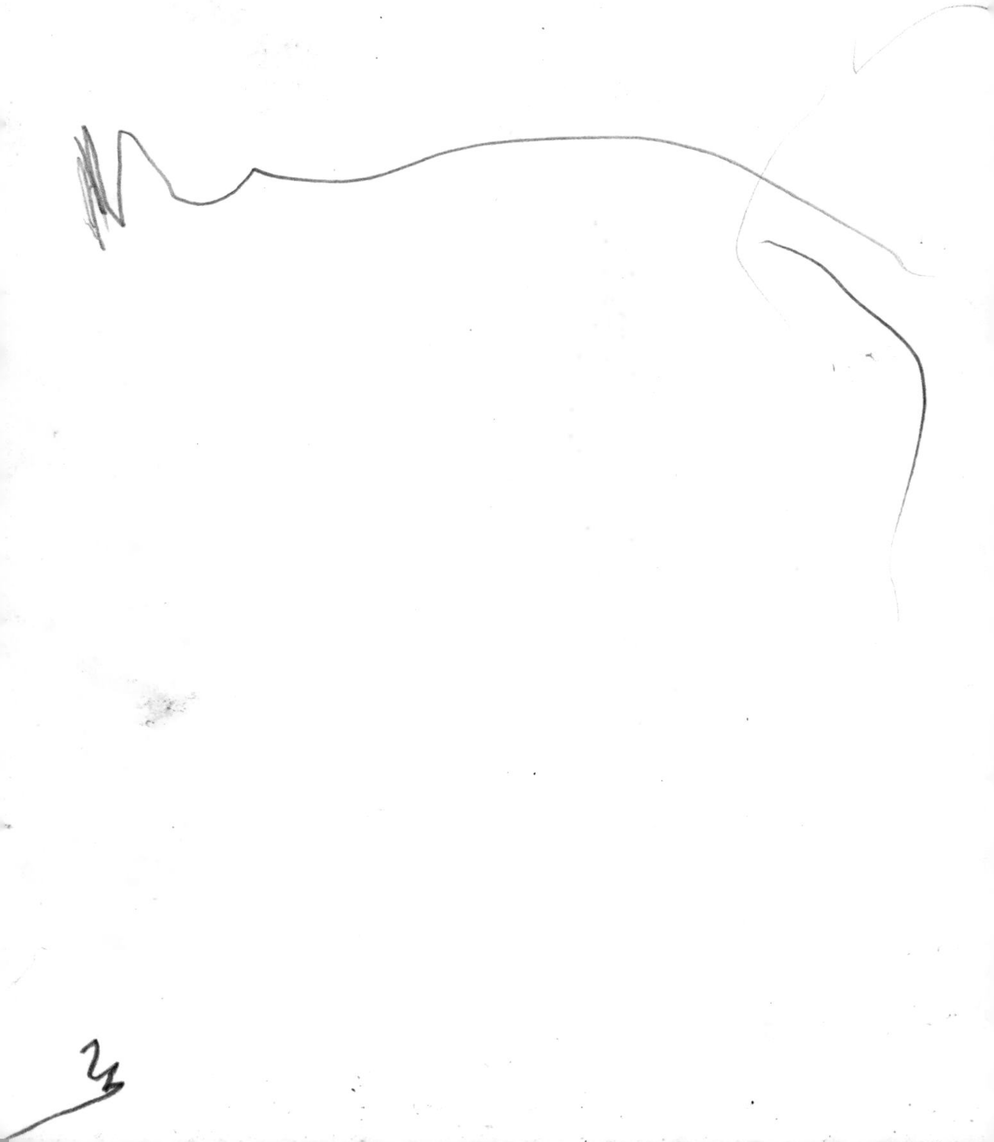